Easton at the PASS

Book Four of the *Easton* Series

PRAISE FOR THE *Easton* SERIES

A heartwarming read full of memorable characters. If you loved the Mitford series, you'll love this.
—**Bill Myers**, bestselling author of *Eli*

What fun! A fantastic representation of the fascinating stories one can uncover when they dive into their genealogy while also capturing the energy and adventure of the search. I wish everyone took the time to tell their story this way.
—**D. Joshua Taylor**, nationally known and recognized genealogical author, lecturer, and researcher

A fascinating story about a modern-day Easton historian whose discovery of centuries-old family secrets helps her confront a complicated mix of family, professional and romantic challenges.
—**Scott L. Reda**, managing director/executive producer, Lou Reda Productions

A fitting continuation of Ms. Price Janey's charming story lines, that weave together modern and Revolutionary War Easton. Brings to life the issues of both times—complete with a battle scene not-to-be-missed!
—**Richard F. Hope**, historian, author of *Easton, PA: A History*

Janney's love for American and Pennsylvania history shines through every page of *Easton at the Crossroads* to enrich this story of intrigue and overcoming false accusations on the journey to true freedom. This gentle read interweaves past and present to craft a story that makes you feel as if you've come home to Easton, even if you've never been there before.

—**Marlo Schalesky**, award-winning author of *Reaching for Wonder*

Rebecca Price Janney's *Easton at the Crossroads* grabs you with wonderful detail, transporting you from her heroine's new home to a fledgling country seeking its independence. Janney has told a story of lives that parallel and is sure to satisfy both the contemporary and historical reader.

—**Debbie Lynne Costello**, author of the #1 Amazon bestseller, *Sword of Forgiveness*, a medieval romance, and two other series

Rebecca's delightful book paints the landscape for a living, breathing Easton of the 1760s. Names we have only read in dry history books come to life. *Easton at the Forks* is a treat!

—**Christopher Black**, artistic director of the Bachmann Players

Rebecca Price Janney captures a story that is both historical and entertaining as her main character, Erin, strives to learn everything about her ancestral family lineage. Rebecca takes you from the present quest to search the family tree back to the 18th century with actual happenings of Erin's ancestor's role in the establishment of this great country we call America. The book is thoroughly enjoyable reading and presents an interesting format between then and now.

—**Salvatore J. Panto Jr.**, mayor, City of Easton, PA

Easton at the PASS

Book Four of the *Easton* Series

REBECCA PRICE JANNEY

ELK LAKE PUBLISHING INC
PUBLISHING THE POSITIVE
Plymouth, Massachusetts

Cover and Interior Design: Derinda Babcock

Editor(s): Deb Haggerty

Author Represented By: WordWise Literary Services

PUBLISHED BY: Elk Lake Publishing, Inc., 35 Dogwood Drive, Plymouth, MA 02360, 2020

Library Cataloging Data

Names: Janney, Rebecca Price (Rebecca Price Janney)

Easton at the Pass—Book Four of the Easton Series / Rebecca Price Janney

350 p. 23cm × 15cm (9in × 6 in.)

Identifiers: ISBN-13: 978-1-64949-058-2 (paperback) | 978-1-64949-059-9 (trade paperback) | 978-1-6494-060-5 (e-book)

Key Words: Colonial Times, Revolutionary War, Dual Time Periods, Easton, Pennsylvania, Family, Relationships

LCCN: 2020944498 Fiction

"For I know the plans I have for you,"
declares the LORD,
"plans to prosper you and not to harm you,
plans to give you hope and a future."
—Jeremiah 29:11 (NIV)

Map *of*
Downtown
Easton
PENNSYLVANIA
TODAY

Easton Area
Public Library

Church St.

Bank St.

Sixth St.

Fifth St.

Fourth St.

Artists in the Alley

State Theater

Hotel
Lafayette

Easton Public
Market

Northampton St.

Sigal
Museum

C
Exp

Pine St.

Parsons-Taylor
House

Ferry St.

Jacob
Nicholas
House

Washington St.

Lehigh River

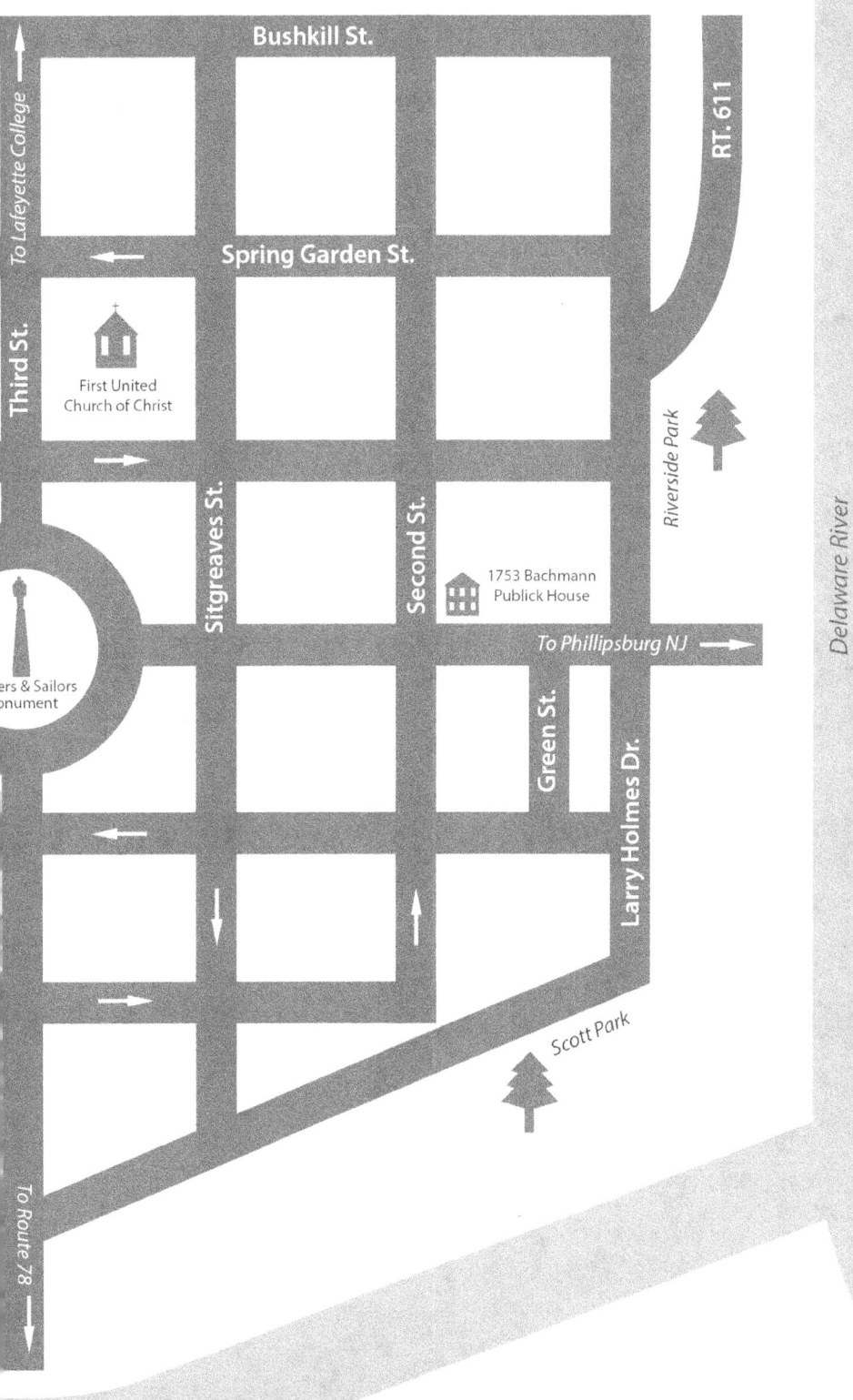

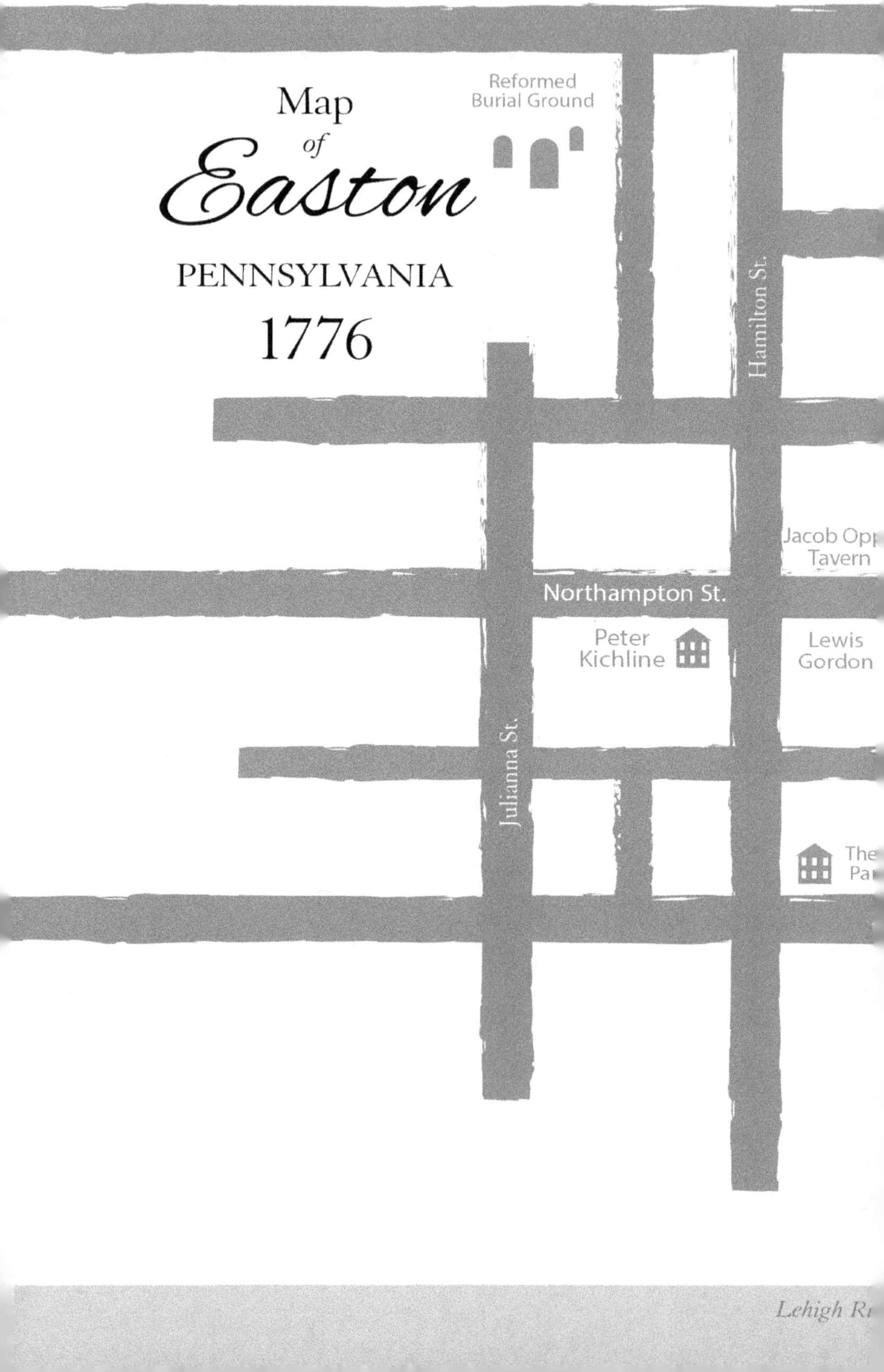

Map
of
Easton
PENNSYLVANIA
1776

Reformed
Burial Ground

Hamilton St.

Jacob Op
Tavern

Northampton St.

Peter
Kichline

Lewis
Gordon

Julianna St.

The
Pa

Lehigh R

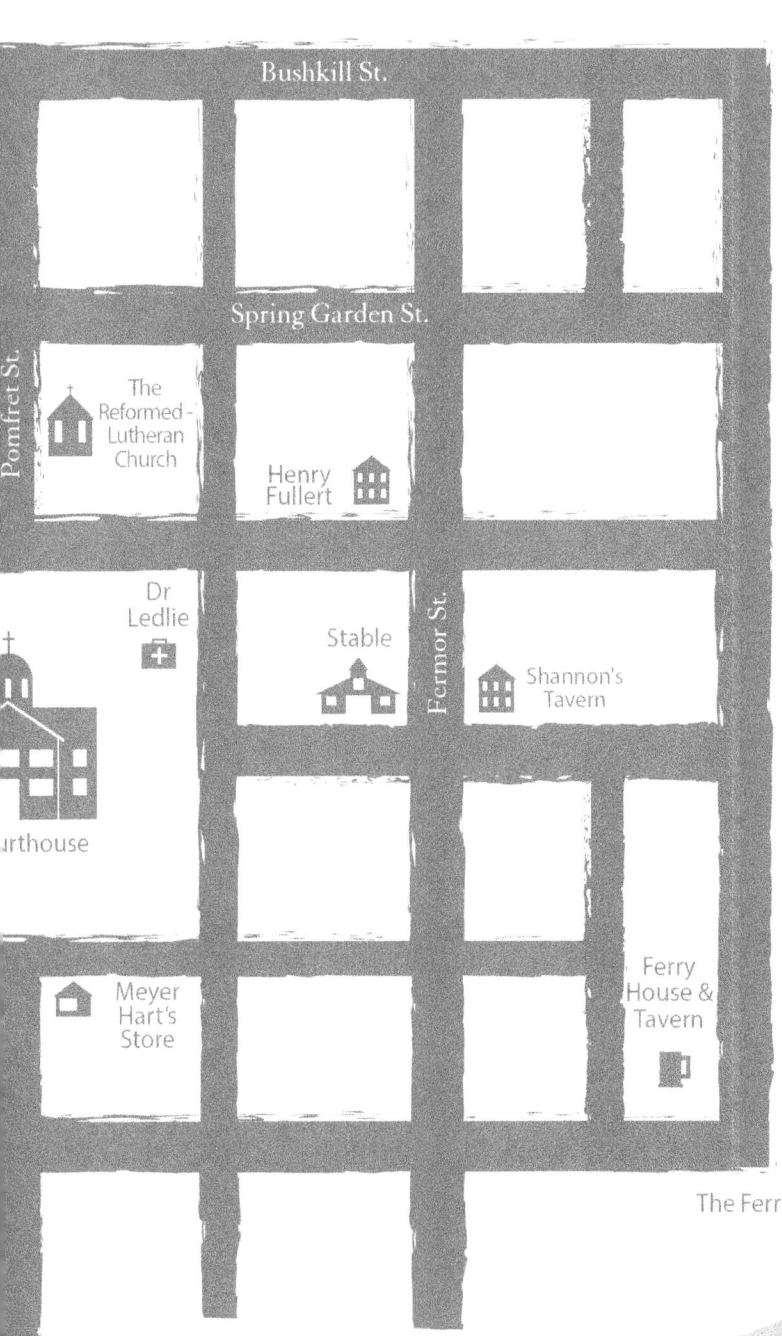

Bushkill St.

Spring Garden St.

Pomfret St.

The Reformed Lutheran Church

Henry Fullert

Dr Ledlie

Stable

Fermor St.

Shannon's Tavern

urthouse

Meyer Hart's Store

Ferry House & Tavern

The Ferry

Delaware River

When the ground shifts, where do you stand?

DEDICATION

In honor of the Daughters of the American Revolution
who continue the legacy of their patriot ancestors
for God, Home, and Country.

CHAPTER ONE

"I have you scheduled for ten o'clock on April 5th to meet with the electrician."

Erin held back a full-bore groan, the consultation with a codes inspector a few days earlier seared into her memory. She could still see herself trailing him around the old building, mindlessly nodding her head as if she were following a single word he was saying. She might have understood him better if he'd been speaking in ancient Cuneiform. The dazzle of heading up the restoration of her ancestor's 1750s tavern had begun to tarnish, rubbing against the woeful reality of technical aspects far above her pay grade as a history professor. She was an Icelander in Fiji.

Her focus came to rest on the lime green streak in her new administrative assistant's blondish-white hair. What was the occasion? St. Patrick's Day? Easter? The first day of spring? She glanced out her office window toward the lush greening of the Quad then back to her wall calendar featuring a silk gown once worn by Dolly Madison. *March 20th*. The past few weeks had passed at warp speed. She willed herself to focus on Caroline Sweet, wondering when the energetic senior would stop handing Erin balls she couldn't juggle.

"Do you know if Mr. Bassett has the specs yet for the tavern?"

"Um, I believe he's still researching."

She smooshed her pink lips together. "The sooner the better."

Caroline's comment felt like a pebble between Erin's toes. She bit back her first reaction—*You don't find eighteenth century documents at Walmart.*

"Dr. Weinreich wants to see you tomorrow after your first class to discuss the fall semester. Oh, wait!" She peered closer at her iPad. "We'll have to schedule that for after your ten o'clock conference call with Derek McCutcheon." She looked up, blue eyes shining. "I think it's great you're collaborating on a book with him. I'm a big fan—I've seen every documentary he's ever made and read all his books."

Erin sincerely hoped she wouldn't be required to teach in addition to overseeing the renovation of the old tavern's 20th century storefront to its original 1750s appearance and function. She'd have to discuss her book deadline with Derek. She still couldn't believe she was in a working relationship with the popular historian. In addition, there were shepherding her fifth grader, caring for her aging parents, and planning a wedding. Erin's plate was full enough to satisfy any glutton. Sometimes she imagined her activities all rolled together and cascading over the falls at the forks of the Lehigh and Delaware Rivers at flood stage. She squinted at a notation she'd made in her datebook for today: "Ortho, 3:30, Pastor Stan, Seven." All at once, she let loose with a personal rendition of *The Scream.*

Caroline pressed her hand against her chest. "My goodness, Dr. Miles! What is wrong?"

"I just realized today is today and not yesterday."

"Come again?"

"Somehow, I thought today was Thursday, but it's

actually Wednesday, and I have two appointments left." At least she didn't have any more classes. She looked at her watch. "I have two hours before I have to pick up Ethan at school. Maybe I could talk with Dr. Weinreich now. Do you know if he's available?"

"I'll …"

Erin's cell phone interrupted the exchange. "Hello, Mom, how are you?"

"I'm feeling impatient, that's how I am."

Audrey's sour voice pickled Erin's spirit. "Why? What's happening?"

"I'm waiting for you to take me to the eye doctor. Have you forgotten?"

She shot straight out of her chair. "Yikes! I'll be right over."

"You better be."

"I'm sorry, Caroline, but I have to scoot." She began collecting her coat, scarf, messenger bag, and keys. "I forgot my mother has an eye doctor's appointment."

"Oh, and she has macular degeneration, too, poor thing. My husband's second-oldest brother's ex-wife has that and …"

"Yes, you were telling me. Would you mind closing up?"

"Not at all, Dr. Miles." She watched as Erin stumbled through the doorway.

At two-forty-five, Erin felt a tingle of panic. She and her mother had waited for nearly an hour before a woman finally had taken Audrey to an examining room. She ran two tests, administered eye drops, and sent them back to the teeming waiting room.

"Was that your doctor?" Erin asked.

"No, I'm not sure who she was."

A different woman came for Audrey, and Erin followed them back to another room for a battery of questions as she entered the answers on a computer with her back turned to them. "The doctor will be with you shortly," the woman finally said as she rose. "Have a seat in the waiting room."

Erin was not to be put off. "Excuse me, but we've been waiting quite long enough to see the doctor, and I have to leave in fifteen minutes to pick my son up at school in Easton."

The nurse, or whoever she was, peered at Erin. "I'll tell Doctor. Just stay here."

When the man arrived, Erin thought he looked a bit familiar, maybe someone she'd known in high school, but she wasn't in any frame of mind for chit-chat. Besides, Audrey was telling him how difficult she was finding life since she'd stopped driving.

"And I can barely read anymore. I need a magnifying glass to see my mail."

Erin felt for her mother, who had to sit directly in front of her TV to watch her shows. Doing puzzles in the recreation room and playing cards no longer carried the same amount of pleasure they once had.

The doctor squeezed Audrey's slender hand. "All my patients with your condition say the same thing."

"Isn't there anything you can do?"

He shook his head. "I wish I could offer a cure. At this point, you need to preserve your remaining eyesight."

Erin started twisting a lock of hair. "Is macular degeneration inherited?"

"No. It's usually caused by sun exposure or smoking."

"I wear sunglasses a lot."

"Wear them all the time when you're outdoors, even on cloudy days." He turned to Audrey. "I can put in for assistance from an organization for the blind. They can help you find ways and strategies to cope with your condition."

Audrey flung a stinging scowl at the physician. "I am not blind!"

He just looked at Erin, who shrugged.

"Mom, you're late."

"Well, hello to you too," she said, pulling out of the car line at school. Only one child lingered, tethered to earbuds.

"I know, and I'm sorry. Grammy Audrey had an eye doctor's appointment that took forever and a day, and then I had to drop her off and get back here in ten minutes. Of course, I needed twenty because of the traffic."

Ethan smiled. "That's okay, Mom. I understand."

"You do?"

"Sure. I'm never in a hurry to see the orthodontist."

She wished she could have rescheduled the meeting with Pastor Stan for next week, but would those days be any less cluttered? She and Paul needed to settle on a wedding date before they could proceed with pre-marital sessions and venue planning, something they were eager to get in place. If only the burger drive-through had offered dessert … Erin hadn't had time to make refreshments. She opened the freezer door hoping to find leftover pieces of cake or pie only to discover a half-eaten Klondike Bar and a blackberry tart with serious freezer burn. "Bummer." She hated blackberries, but hadn't wanted to hurt her new neighbor's feelings when she'd offered the housewarming gift back in September. Now the pie was way past all possible expiration dates. She pitched the contents into the waste basket while her basset hound regarded her accusingly.

"Trust me, Toby, you did not want to eat that pie."

She cased the pantry. Hidden behind the popcorn and Cheez-its, she might find biscotti or ginger snaps. Maybe the Nutter Butters would do in a pinch. When she tasted one, however, she winced at the soggy texture. "I really must get to the store, or better yet, try one of those online grocery deliveries. That would be just the ticket!" Before Erin closed the door, she noticed an opened dark chocolate bar and snapped off a piece, letting the bitter sweetness enliven her grateful taste buds. She could run down the Hill for cupcakes, but she didn't feel like leaving the house. The sight of two over-ripe bananas in her fruit basket provided a sudden inspiration. "I'll make banana bread. My recipe doesn't even require a mixer, and the bread bakes in under an hour."

She turned on the oven to 325° and began gathering bowls, measuring cups and spoons, milk, eggs, oil, sugar, baking soda, and vanilla. Lining them up on the counter, she regretted not having enough time to bring the eggs to room temperature. Instead, she carefully put them into the microwave and set the dial to 45 seconds at power level three. *Same as room temperature.*

While waiting, the memory of the dark chocolate lured her back to the pantry. She reached into the candy box just as Hell and Toby suddenly broke loose. A loud explosion blew open the microwave door and detonated tiny fragments of white and yellow shrapnel into the kitchen. Her heart thumping, Erin gaped at the chaos raining down on every surface from floor to upper cabinets. Toby bayed. If she hadn't been sneaking another piece of chocolate, she would have been standing directly in the line of fire. She might have sustained a nasty eye injury. Once she regained a modicum of composure, she understood she had punched in four-and-a-half minutes at power level ten. *How could I possibly be that distracted?*

She heard the thumping of Ethan's footsteps in the upstairs hallway, and he called over the banister, "Hey, Mom! What was that noise? Toby, quit yowling. Eww! What is that smell?"

Toby started putting his mouth to a different use, methodically licking pieces of cooked eggs and shells as Paul wandered through the door to the garage.

"What in the world?" His jaw dropped.

She grabbed the dog's collar and dragged him into his crate. Looking at Paul through slitted eyes, she demanded, "Are you smirking?"

"Well, I uh …"

"Yes, you are." She too was beginning to see the humor in the situation.

"What were you trying to do?" He stepped carefully toward her as she pointed to the oven, completely encrusted in detonated eggs.

Erin explained about bringing eggs to room temperature. "I'm so glad I went to the pantry for chocolate. Otherwise …"

He kissed her cheek and said, "How can I help?"

"Well, this needs to be cleaned up before Pastor Stan gets here, and I still don't have anything to serve him."

"I'll help you get a start on clean-up, and once the room is mostly under control, I'll run out and buy pastries or something."

I guess I'll make banana bread tomorrow, if I have time. Lately she always seemed to come up short on that particular commodity.

"Where's the vacuum cleaner?"

Ethan had entered the kitchen, his shoulders shaking. "How did you manage this?"

"You could try to make yourself useful here." She threw a wet dishcloth in his direction, which he caught.

"I think you have too many windows open, Mom."

She frowned, lifting a roll of paper towels from their holder. "Too many windows open?"

"Yeah, like on a computer. If too many are open, the program starts getting wonky."

That's me all right—completely, totally wonky.

No one would have known by his slender frame about Pastor Stan's sweet tooth. He closed his eyes with enjoyment, clueless about the coffee cake's humble convenience store origins. "This is very good. Did you make this, Erin?"

She avoided looking at Paul. "No, I confess I haven't had time to bake." She didn't add, "Or cook, or clean." She hoped he didn't notice the cobweb swinging along the crown molding above his head. Her mother would have a fit.

He sipped his Darjeeling then put the mug back onto a

coaster. "So, how are you two coming along?"

Paul slipped his hand into Erin's. "I'm on cloud nine."

The men looked in her direction. "Oh, me too!" Erin looked at her engagement ring sparking in the lamplight and decided to be completely honest. "Frankly, I want to be as excited as Paul and our marriage warrant." Seeing Paul's lips part, she quickly covered her tracks. "I am so busy with work I haven't even had time to go grocery shopping, except when I take one of my parents and grab a few things for myself. Today is a case in point." She recounted the afternoon's events, concluding with the detonated eggs. Erin forgave the minister's grin. "I'm doing two jobs at Lafayette, plus the new book with Derek McCutcheon, plus being a mom and a very-much needed daughter." She raised her palms. "I don't mean to whine. My life is so very good, but I just don't know how to handle the everyday things, let alone plan a wedding."

A toilet flushed overhead, and they heard Ethan pad across the upstairs hall to his room. Paul blanched. "Are you saying you want to call it off?"

"Not at all. I want to have a special celebration and build this home with you." She teared up. "I just don't know how to find the time."

Her fiancé closed his eyes and expelled a deep breath. Pastor Stan looked from him back to her. "I've been wanting to bring this up but wasn't sure how," Paul said. "I've been deeply concerned about your schedule."

"Let me understand this." Stan Grube leaned forward. "Erin, you are teaching full time and directing the renovation of the Kichline building project?" She nodded. "Well, that doesn't seem right to me, doing the work of two people."

"And collaborating on a book," she added.

Paul faced her. "Herman should have cut back on your teaching or postponed starting the center until after the spring semester."

"He did get me a part-time administrative assistant," she said.

"Which is essential."

"But not enough." Erin sighed. "Something's gotta give."

"Yes, and I don't want that something to be you." Firmness threaded through his words. Erin squeezed his hand, grateful. Jim had always been in her court too.

"Suppose you are able to cut back on, say, your teaching," Stan said. "How much would that help you?"

"I would be less burdened."

A long moment passed. "Would you like to try to set a date tonight for the wedding, then schedule the pre-marital counseling sessions after you get your work situation in order?"

Paul smiled. "That works for me. Erin?"

She said what she thought he wanted to hear. "Sure."

Erin knocked on the side of Herman Weinreich's door and poked her head inside. "You wanted to see me?"

The history department head looked up from his tablet and smiled. "Come in and have a seat." He looked back at his device. "Just ... let ... me ... close this out." He tapped a few keys, then snapped the lid shut.

As usual, the only chair in the room harbored the professor's detritus—books, magazines, papers, a partially eaten Payday. She scooped up and laid the pile on the floor next to another heap. Some of the contents spilled over, but he waved her away from fixing the mess.

"How is Paul, and how are your plans coming along?"

"He's doing well, and we've decided on a date—Saturday, July 15th."

His gray eyes twinkled. "Should I mark my calendar?"

"You bet." Her enthusiasm had the feeling of a day-old helium balloon. Once her schedule eased up, she'd be fine, except one thought nagged. *I've never supervised anything besides a bake sale before. I don't know the first thing about managing masons, plumbers, or electricians.* Her worries encircled her.

"Well, then, something has come to my attention, and I consider myself quite the dolt for not recognizing this before." He folded his hands on his desk. "Caroline tells me you're overbooked and overwhelmed by teaching full time, heading up the Kichline Center, collaborating on that McCutcheon book, taking care of your son and your parents and, well, the beat goes on. She's wondering how you'll ever find time to plan your wedding."

Erin couldn't find words—he'd taken them right out of her mouth. *Bless that Caroline.*

"No one can keep up with that kind of grind, and I owe you an apology for not seeing this sooner." He tilted his head to the side. "Forgive me?"

"Of course." *Should I mention anything about how clueless I am about the technical aspects of this renovation?*

He leaned far back in his chair, hands behind his head. "How about I bring an adjunct on board to finish the semester and cut back your Kichline Center hours to around thirty? You could start full time in August."

The weight hadn't exactly lifted, but this was an improvement. "I'm grateful, Herman."

"I always told my kids when they were growing up, 'Whenever there's a problem, we solve the problem.'"

She wasn't sure about problems on steroids.

CHAPTER TWO

Late March, 1777

He was itching to be out of the house, itching to be exchanged so he could further aid the Cause, itching to put his hand in running his mills, and itching to be active in Easton's affairs. He felt like a colossal wound beginning to heal. His doctor and wife-enforced rest had gone a long way in helping Peter recover from multiple setbacks including a bayonet wound, malnutrition, and the effects of walking from New York to Easton on foot, inadequately shod, in the bitter cold and snow. All told, he had mended quite well despite persistent twinges in his arm and gnawing headaches, which mercifully were becoming less frequent. The cure, however, had resulted in a severe case of cabin fever.

He would prevail upon Catherine to allow him some fresh air today, or at least relatively fresh. These days Easton's population had swelled to include wounded soldiers and prisoners of war. Before the conflict, the sheep and pigs wallowing in the pond near the courthouse caused more than one resident with a sensitive nose to flee in the opposite direction. Now a steady stench rose from the German Reformed Church, the gaol, and a makeshift barracks near the top of Julianna Street, all overflowing with war's casualties.

Susannah swished into the parlor, her intent gaze

signifying she was a young woman on a mission. "Good day, Papa. You're looking almost hale." She kissed his cheek.

"If not hearty, Daughter."

"Just keep feeding on *Frau* Hamster's good cooking, and you'll be filling out your clothes in no time."

Philip Chatterfield served Easton as its only tailor after the death of his counterpart at Brooklyn, and Peter didn't want to bother him with resizing his clothes. His wife and *Frau* Hamster were doing an adequate job of keeping him from overexposing himself during the lengthy convalescence. They also induced him to eat until he might explode, which he manfully did to please them.

"Where are you off to?"

She spoke while pulling on a red woolen cape and gloves. "I'm going to the prison up the street with provisions for the men."

Peter noticed a large covered basket in the entryway and figured he wasn't the only person *Frau* Hamster was trying to fatten, or at least keep basically nourished. He appreciated his beautiful young daughter's heart for the less fortunate.

"Do they have adequate supplies ?" he asked.

Susannah frowned. "Not nearly. There just aren't enough clothes and food for all the sick and prisoners. The first of the rations go to our wounded, then the prisoners get the rest."

"Have you run into any difficulty?"

She pursed her lips. "Nothing to worry about, Papa."

"But?" He gazed into her eyes.

"Once in a while someone will chide me for helping 'them.'"

"That's to be expected I suppose, but then, our Lord

made no distinctions when calling upon us to care for prisoners."

"I feel the same way." She moved toward the hallway and her basket.

"Do, uh, the prisoners treat you with respect?"

She grinned, apparently getting his meaning. "They have no choice. I take Mr. Schneider with me just in case."

As if to underscore her point, a knock sounded at the front door. Peter watched Susannah move quickly, and the sound of men's voices filled the anteroom.

"Come in, Mr. Schneider, hello, Mr. Traill." She called into the parlor. "Papa, you have company."

Peter rose from his wing chair and walked stiffly toward the men, the familiar though now slower steps of *Frau* Hamster moving toward them with faithful Joe following just behind. No longer a little boy, the slave Peter had rescued from the auction block before the war sported broader shoulders and was now taller than the diminutive housekeeper by several inches. To his surprise, Peter sighted his little Elizabeth toddling after the two, her smile winsome under a layer of elderberry jam.

He reached out and shook Traill's thick hand and nodded toward Schneider, an indentured servant who, by Catherine's accounts, had been invaluable to the family during Peter's captivity. While he was naturally grateful, he wondered why the young man wasn't at the mill, though he did prefer Schneider's protective presence with Susannah on her gritty errands of mercy. After all, a comely, seventeen-year-old woman could most certainly set a prisoner's heart aflutter, if not aflame.

The servant seemed to read his mind. "Sir, if I may, do I have your permission to accompany *Fräulein* Kichline this morning? *Herr* Andrew said he could spare me for an hour."

Peter liked this young man in whom there appeared to be no guile.

"Yes, of course. I'm grateful for your protection."

"Let's go then!" Susannah said. "*Bis später,* Papa!"

"*Ich werde Erfrischungen bekommen.*" *Frau* Hamster called over her shoulder as she and Joe hustled toward the kitchen to get refreshments. Two-year-old Elizabeth stumbled to keep up.

"You are looking well, this morning, Peter." Traill's smile revealed his pleasure. "Are you putting on a little weight?"

"Perhaps. I am feeling better daily." He lowered his voice and tightly gripped the arms of his chair after they sat. "I'm also abundantly happy to see you. My family tiptoes around me as if I will break while exerting myself even a little. I simply must know the news." He leaned closer. "I know I can count on you to fill me in."

The sound of a baby crying on the second floor signaled to Peter his over-protective wife would be preoccupied with Abraham for at least a quarter of an hour, perhaps more. He'd have enough time to get some earnestly-desired information.

Traill emitted a low rumble from his barreled chest. "That you may. Let's sit down before your good lady has a chance to censor our conversation, and before I am called away to tend to my own, very expectant wife."

Peter bent forward. "So, what have you been up to, my friend?"

"Tending to the affairs of state and awaiting our next child."

He grinned, knowing the joys and perils of childbirth. "Catherine is on the alert, ready to help at a moment's notice."

"She is like your Flying Camp, except with a different purpose."

Peter raised his tankard of cider in a salute.

"As for the non-domestic part of my life, I have been a whirling dervish. Let's see … " He looked up at the ceiling, spattered with candle light. "I'm in charge of procuring supplies for the Continental Army, as well as raising funds."

"And how are they coming along?"

"Like finding hen's teeth. The Continental dollar is worth about as much as spent tobacco these days, but the patriotic folk of Easton always find ways to contribute. Many go without a new pair of shoes or sugar in their tea in order to help. Oh, and I have been named to serve as major of the Fifth Pennsylvania Battalion."

Peter fought a surge of envy, an emotion he generally avoided. If only he could be out there, giving his all in the fight for independence. *You nearly did give your all,"* he could almost hear Catherine saying, but he knew he had so much left to offer. He wondered how his mother would weigh in, the woman who'd raised him on the conviction, "To whom much is given, much is required."

He frowned, pressing his lips together, then changed the subject. "I have heard a rumor Lewis Gordon is unwell. Is this true?"

Traill shook his head slowly from side to side. "Not exactly unwell, although he isn't in the most robust health."

"Oh, perhaps I misunderstood."

His pinched expression forewarned Peter of unpleasant news. "There is no easy way to put this, my friend. Mr. Gordon resigned from the Committee last December and withdrew his support of all patriotic services."

Peter gave a low whistle. "He's always been such a stalwart defender of our Cause."

"Defender, yes, stalwart? Perhaps not as much as we once thought. He's under house arrest for now, since taking the Oath is required by the Test Act."

"Was he charged with treason?" He knew what such a verdict could mean.

"Not treason, but having been an officer in the King's court."

Peter understood how this bit of verbal wrangling worked. He was relieved his old friend wouldn't be facing execution, though grieved and angry at Lewis's turn.

"Naturally, the ferry has been seized from his control due to its strategic importance." Traill stared into the low-burning fire. "I haven't seen him in many weeks."

"Why did he turn away?" he asked so quietly he almost couldn't hear his own voice.

"No one really knows for certain; Lewis wouldn't give an explanation." He looked out the window to people passing along the street. "I have an idea, though."

"Which is?"

"Have you heard any military intelligence or news since your return?"

Peter closed his eyes. "I have been woefully ignorant."

"I regret to say General Washington has met with a good deal of hardship and more than a few setbacks since the New York campaign. Except for his victory over the Hessians at Trenton on Christmas night, he's suffered many losses."

"What happened in Trenton?" He felt as if he were emerging from a miasma, the likes of which he'd known following the death of his wife Margaretta eleven years earlier.

Traill filled in the gaps of his friend's knowledge concluding, "If not for that victory, I fear the united colonies might have collectively despaired of our quest for independence." He took another sip, brushing foam from his upper lip with the back of his hand. "I suspect Mr. Gordon may no longer be able to swing his support behind our troops, believing ours is a lost cause." He shrugged his shoulders. "Then again, he remained hopeful right up until July Fourth that our grievances could be settled apart from war."

Peter felt the pulsing of his heart in his ears. He remembered the scenes of scarcity and despair from his imprisonment, including Andrew Fartenius's vacant stare in his nearly mortal illness. For a fleeting moment, he wondered whether all that anguish might have been in vain. "How many share Mr. Gordon's opinion?"

"Not too many in Easton I'm happy to say, but elsewhere … You know we've never enjoyed unanimity."

"Who has control of the Committee?"

Traill's mouth curved to the side. "Levers."

"Well, then, he's a good and faithful servant."

"Faithful at least."

Peter wanted to pursue the subject, but the front door opened, and his oldest son's wife appeared. She nearly skidded to a halt when she saw Robert Traill with her father-in-law. "Oh, do pardon me. I didn't realize you had company, Father Peter."

"I'm so very glad you've come. Please join us." He was hungry for news of Peter Jr.'s whereabouts, having heard he'd managed to escape from Brooklyn, but very little after that.

"No, thank you." She backed out of the room, her features as if she were being stretched on a loom. "I'm here to see Mother Catherine."

"But ..."

"Good day." Sarah curtsied and walked briskly down the hall.

Peter turned to Traill. "She seems distracted these days. I suppose my good wife was in a similar state during my imprisonment."

His friend sighed. "There's so much uncertainty."

He reached for his walking stick, something he'd never used before the Brooklyn Campaign, and looked over his shoulder. He just wanted to be outside for once, not all cooped up like some trapper's catch of the day, but if Catherine saw him ... The coast being clear, he started toward the front door just as his wife sidled into the room, cushioning Abraham against her breast. Her slight limp seemed less pronounced these days.

"Baby asleep," Elizabeth announced in a whisper as she tottered to her red-faced father's side.

That Catherine didn't try to stop him smoothed over his irritation at being discovered. He very much disliked the battles he'd been waging lately with impatience and annoyance, a fight he all too often lost.

His wife stood by him, rocking the child. "Did Mr. Traill

bring news of Elizabeth?"

"She seems to be doing well. I believe the babe will come any day now."

Something niggled his spirit, a stubborn seed caught between his teeth. "My dear, what is happening with Peter's Sarah? Something has been on her mind, yet I remain ignorant of my son and any difficulty he might be having."

She looked down at the baby, quiet.

His blue eyes narrowed. "Has he been wounded, or in some kind of trouble?"

"Not now."

He took a deep breath, hoping to fend off a rush of sarcasm. "And when do you suppose I might find out?"

"I think it's time you spoke to Sarah." She leaned over and kissed his cheek. "Peter, darling, don't worry. Everyone has their dramas, and they have been through one. It's over now. We are hopeful for his safe return in the near future."

He despised ignorance and being overprotected. He imagined himself under the weight of one of his millstones.

CHAPTER THREE

She took Wednesday off and drove to her friend Melissa's house with a five pocket notebook and a bridal magazine. There had never been any doubt as to who her matron of honor would be, but all certainty ended there. How big should a second wedding be, and at her age? As her father had so bluntly stated two days earlier when he thought she was too busy, "You're no spring chicken anymore." At the first traffic light after getting off the Northeast Extension's Lansdale exit, she glanced into the rearview mirror. Except for a smattering of laugh lines around her eyes and a few gray hairs sprouting around her ears, Erin's taut skin would never betray her age, which was forty-seven in August. She'd kept her figure well enough, but whereas she'd worn a size four when she married Jim, she'd be happy if she could fit into an eight now. Although her mother was still basically slender at eighty-two, extra pounds had nestled around her thighs. *Am I becoming my mother?* She perished the thought, but to be honest with herself, she didn't know exactly what she was becoming. Life had been so uncomplicated before Jim's death. Now she was a single mother, caregiving daughter, widow, and another man's fiancé. She had been a history professor, but her work was in transition. The ground had shifted, and she didn't know exactly where to stand. Fear prickled her scalp, and she willed her mind in a different direction, the wedding.

What about the bridal party? Did she want more than one attendant? Would Paul desire to have more than a best man? When she'd broached the subject the night before, he'd smiled. "I'll have what you're having."

"But you've never had a wedding before, so I want this to be the fulfillment of your dreams too."

He'd kissed her hand. "My sweet Erin, men don't dream about their weddings. They dream about their honeymoons."

This morning she could still feel the rush of warmth accompanying those words, so why was she feeling so uncertain? She didn't know what she wanted either. She was counting on Melissa to navigate this strange new world.

She drove slowly by her former house in Lansdale before stopping at Melissa's, grateful none of the neighbors were outside on this overcast April morning. Her throat tightened when she saw tiny buds appearing on the blood red maple tree her husband had planted to celebrate Ethan's birth. Tulips and daffodils rimmed the front border, a flashy display of yellow and red, the theme she'd chosen for the main rooms of the house. Her renters had kept the lawn trimmed neatly, and there wasn't a trace of green mold clinging to the side of the house.

Erin missed living here with Jim, Ethan, and Toby, missed the sound of the garage door opening and closing when he came home at night, the chatty neighbors, and kids calling out "Hi, Mrs. Miles!" Tears puddled in the corners of her eyes, then spilled onto her cheeks when she blinked. She pulled a tissue from a box in the console and wiped them away. This was one of those times when she just didn't feel ready for a new life, but ready or not, here it came.

"So I told Ryan to pick up five pounds of potatoes for a salad I was going to make for the church potluck, and what do you think he came home with?" Melissa poured hot water into mugs as she spoke.

"Uh …"

"Ten pounds of sweet potatoes! Honestly, Erin, my son may be getting A's in his college classes, but he is so obtuse about life in general."

She was on a roll.

"Speaking of which … he got an A in his physics class, and I was so proud because the subject is so difficult for him. I hated physics in college. We had this professor who used to come to class and forget to take off his coat. There he'd be, starting to teach, sometimes even still wearing gloves for Pete's sake, and we'd be sniggering behind our hands. I had another teacher who forgot to remove the hanger when she wore her dress to school."

Erin telegraphed "tangent alert," and Melissa closed her eyes. "There I go again! So, let's forget about sweet potatoes—although I have no idea what to do with them— oh, maybe I could make some pies or bread. You know, zucchini makes good bread. Maybe sweet potatoes do too."

Erin bobbed her tea bag up and down, breathing in the minty scent, waiting for her friend to wind down. She always did, eventually.

"I have cranberry bread from Merrymead. Would you like some with your tea?"

"Sure. And some mustard please, the grainy kind if you have it."

Melissa stared at her, then they both grinned. "I go off on tangents, and you mash up food groups. Aren't we a pair?"

"Yes, we are."

"We're certainly not boring!" Melissa continued speaking as she unwrapped the loaf of dessert bread and cut chunky slices. "And your life isn't boring either. I'm so relieved Herman Weinreich gave you that reprieve. I was really getting worried about how you were going to keep up that grueling schedule." Melissa put the plate before Erin and reached into the refrigerator for a jar of mustard. "I'm happy you set a date for the wedding, and July is beautiful, though hot."

Erin stared at her hands. "Jim and I got married in May."

"I'll bet your wedding photos were beautiful."

"Oh, they were. Do you remember ..." She caught herself and gave a laugh. "I forget sometimes we didn't know each other until a couple of years after I married Jim."

"When you built your house here in Lansdale and started going to my church."

Erin sipped her tea. Then she slathered mustard all over the cranberry bread. "We've been through a lot together."

"Yes, and there's more to come, mostly good stuff I hope. I'm touched you want me to be matron of honor. Of course, you and Paul did have your first date here." She grinned. "I'd like to work with your mother and mother-in-law to put together a bridal shower."

"Oh, that would be nice."

"Do you think Lansdale or Easton would work best since you have friends and family in both places?"

"Wow, I haven't thought about a shower." *How in the world am I going to squeeze in a shower, and shopping for a wedding dress, and flowers, and the cake?* She had the sensation of being on a runaway train, hurtling down train tracks, clinging to the sides for dear life, hoping the passenger cars didn't fly completely out of control like they did in nightmares.

"Uh, do I even need a shower? I mean, I already have a home and kitchen supplies and bedding." She spun her engagement ring around on her finger.

"Every bride needs a shower. You and Paul will want some of your own things. Do you have a registry yet?"

Erin could almost make out the baying of wolves at her friend's front door. *I don't even have time to shop for groceries let alone put together a registry.* And then, she didn't really know Paul's taste in things, not like she had known Jim's, right down to where he kept his collar stays in an empty breath mint container.

"We could do Easton since it's your home base now. I think folks around here would enjoy going up there, you know, seeing where you live. Let's be sure to invite your DAR friends." She tapped a pen to her lips before writing something on a notepad. "Maybe Paul's family would come, too. Of course, for them Easton or Lansdale wouldn't really matter, but then again, Easton is where you live, so I vote for Easton."

"Easton it is." Feeling warm, she rolled up the sleeves of her blouse.

"As for a venue, is there a restaurant you really like?"

Erin started thinking about a place on William Penn

Highway—or was it Freemansburg Highway, she always got those two confused—where her nieces' showers had been. "There is a nice restaurant, but I can't think of the name right now. Of course, if that's too expensive, we might just use the church's fellowship hall."

Melissa made a tsking sound. "Unless this place is the Ritz, no problem." She brought up a different subject. "Have you decided how many to have in your wedding party, or how big or small you want things to be?"

"I'm not sure. I've already had a big wedding, and maybe that's all anyone should really get."

Melissa leaned forward, picking up her mug with both hands. "Why do you think so?"

Erin looked down at the floor and noticed a stray twist tie near the chair. "I'm not really sure." Her emotions were damming up inside her.

"You know what that sounds like?" Erin shook her head. "Like something my grandmother used to say—"Women should wear their hair short after twenty-five.""

"Really? She said that?" Erin was suddenly aware of Melissa's and her shoulder length and longer tresses. "I guess she'd disapprove of us both then."

"Probably. She was a real stickler for stuff like not wearing white before Memorial Day and never leaving the house in curlers."

Erin laughed out loud, enjoying the emotional release. "She sounds like my grandmother."

"These days we get to do pretty much as we please."

"In some ways, though, decisions are harder because we don't have rules or guidelines to help us along."

"True." She paused to take a bite of bread. "What does Paul want?"

"He's having what I'm having." Her hand trembled when she lifted the tea cup. "He wants me to be happy, but he does become a little animated when we discuss a bigger celebration. Mind you, not the entire town, or second and third cousins, but close friends and relatives, some colleagues."

"Would that be about a hundred people? More, less?"

A car horn honked outside.

"Um, I think so."

"Do you want more than one attendant?"

"I had six when I married Jim." She'd lost touch with all but two, her oldest niece and her oldest friend, but anymore the rest just exchanged Christmas cards. "My great-niece could be flower girl, and I'd like Connie to be an attendant."

"Great choices! Then Paul can pick two guys, and maybe some ushers. Do you want Ethan to be an usher? I'll bet he would love to, and maybe a few others could assist." She scribbled away.

"Sure."

"And then, have you thought about what kind of dress you want?"

"I don't really know." She started breaking into a sweat.

"Well, you need to decide soon. You don't have much time, Erin, and they usually need to make alterations, which isn't an overnight thing."

She managed not to growl. "I realize that."

"Oh! And the reception. Have you thought about where?"

Erin's throat went as dry as if she'd swallowed sand. "I, uh, I'm feeling a little overwhelmed, Melissa."

Her friend came up for air. Seeing Erin's blanched color, she exclaimed, "Oh, honey, I'm sorry. I'm going way too fast."

She nodded. "I just feel, well, overwhelmed."

"Too many details?" She covered Erin's hand with hers.

"Yes, and I'm barely treading water as it is. And then sometimes I, well ..." She lowered her voice, her pulse pounding in her ears. "I don't know if I really want to do this." There. She'd put to words what she had refused to even think until now.

Melissa's sharp intake of breath seemed to speak for both of them. After a few moments she asked, "You're having doubts about Paul?"

How could she tell her best friend she was having doubts about Paul *and* her new job? She felt downright ashamed of herself when she had life so good.

"Yes." She closed her eyes and waved her hands. "No! How to explain this? When I married Jim, we were so young, so full of plans. And now ..." Her voice caught. "What do I do with my love for Jim?" Erin twisted her napkin into a tight cylinder. "I haven't stopped loving him, Melissa."

"I don't think you're supposed to. I think you just make room for loving someone else too." She fell silent for a few moments then asked, "So, you're not sure about getting married again?"

"I think that must be what I'm feeling, but I don't want to lose Paul. If I marry again, I'd want someone just like him." She shivered, hearing herself speak of him in the past.

Melissa's eyes filled with tears. "Guys like him are rare, and he adores you."

"I loved Jim so much. I feel like I'm betraying what we had together. I mean, how can I ... you know, be with someone else?"

"Naturally I can't speak from experience, Erin. I just

know people remarry all the time including after a spouse dies. They probably have similar feelings if they had a good marriage. Personally, I don't think you'd betray Jim by being with Paul because Jim wanted you to remarry if you found the right person."

Melissa was talking her down from a cliff.

"I can imagine, though, you'd feel strange driving in a different lane." When Erin frowned, her friend explained. "We start driving in a certain direction when we get married, and we wear a rut into the roadway." She waved her hands. "Oh, I don't exactly mean rut, that's too negative. More like a groove, and it goes deep and becomes part of our lives. Then if the marriage ends, there's still a groove. Oh, is this making any sense?" She threw her hands up.

"I think so."

"Well, you've got this old groove, but now you're riding in a different car, and at first you keep getting caught in the old groove, until you start making a new one in the new car with the new person."

She sighed. "My poor Grandfather Peter. He ended up with three grooves. I imagine he had similar feelings as I do."

"Perhaps, at least in terms of creating a new path when the old was so familiar. But back then, people depended on each other even more than today just to survive, although I know he was wealthy. Still, he needed a mother for his children, and a companion for himself." She laughed. "I'm lecturing a history professor."

Erin felt a comfortable warmth as she sensed once again her strong connection with her beloved ancestor. Peter Kichline had lived over two hundred and fifty years ago, but he had traveled a similar journey, in the same place.

"I'll support you whatever you decide, Erin, but I will tell you this—Paul is one in a million. If you think you do want to get married again, he has my seal of approval."

He had everyone's seal of approval, including hers. But did she want to remarry? If she did, she still had a sense they might just be moving entirely too fast.

♛

He had listened to her without offering comments or asking questions, just let her speak her heart. Erin set her face toward spilling the contents of her doubts, knowing this simply had to be said no matter how uncomfortable for both of them. When she finished, he gazed at her for a long moment, then half-smiled.

"I suspected you might be going through this."

She put her hand to her chest. "How did you know?"

"I know you." He emphasized the word "you."

"Are you upset?"

He shook his head. "Your feelings make perfect sense to me."

"They do?"

Toby came over and rested his head on Erin's lap. She was glad Ethan was at a new friend's house so she and Paul could speak freely.

"If I had been happily married for twenty years and my wife died suddenly, I assure you I wouldn't heal from the pain any time soon. I'd want to hold on to what we'd had for as long as I could, and I would never stop loving her. I'd also be concerned about the effect of marrying again on my child."

She wiped her eyes with a tissue. He really did know her.

"I can't ever be what Jim was to you—or to Ethan. I can only be myself and offer the best I have in me. I promise to do everything I can to bring you joy and contentment, a peaceful and loving home for you and Ethan. If you choose." He paused. "Do you feel strange about, well, the physical part?"

He had exposed her depths. Blushing, she said, "Sometimes. In other ways, I'm very much anticipating that."

"Well, that's good to know." He grinned. "I won't push you. Personally, I think the engagement period is for preparation, not fulfillment. Do you understand?"

"Yes," she whispered, relieved.

"I know the majority of people disagree, but then, I'm not the majority of people."

Erin smiled. "That you are not."

"Good." He took a deep breath. "If you need more time, if you need to pull back, if …" His voice cracked. "If you want me to stay away while you work this out, I'll do whatever you need."

If only she knew what she needed. She didn't know where to step on this uneven ground.

CHAPTER FOUR

Familiar scenes comforted Peter's wounded spirit—the homes of his dear friends and family, the businesses clustering Northampton Street, the sound of cowbells and hum of people passing by. Greed overtook him, so eager was he to ingest the sounds and smells all at once, that he came flat up against his diminished capacity. He'd been confined to his home for most of the past month being coddled and fed custards like an invalid.

Robert Bell of all people was the first to encounter him, surprising Peter when he stopped and gave a nearly imperceptible bow of his head. "Welcome home, Colonel."

"Thank you, Mr. Bell. I am pleased to be here." For a moment, he felt happy to have seen Easton's notorious detester of Germans, who continued on his way. There were so many people Peter wanted to see, wishing he could gather them about himself and just look upon their faces for a long time, then catch up on their news. The thought dizzied him. He felt the pressure of Joe's hand on his right arm.

"Are you okay, sir?"

Peter smiled at the boy. "Yes, son, I'm okay. Thank you."

"Mrs. *Frau* Kichline says I need to watch out in case you get the wobbles."

"She did, did she?"

"Yes, sir."

"Well, I am in good hands, then."

The truth was, his legs did feel wobbly. *Walk slowly.* He might have been in a hurry to see his home town and everyone in it, but he wasn't on a schedule. The thought disoriented him, left him pondering almost constantly what lay ahead for him. According to his parole, he couldn't take up arms against the King or his agents. According to his body, broken in the field of battle followed by months of imprisonment, he needed to proceed into the future at roughly the pace of a wooly bear. He understood the need to mend, but he didn't know how to *be* in the meantime.

He stood before the courthouse feeling late March's signature blast against his face, the wind threatening to fling his hat toward one of Easton's two rivers. Joe clapped his free hand to his own head and mashed the black felt hat further down so only the tops of his coffee-colored eyes showed. Was that a broken window pane on the east side of the building? Peter had difficulty ascertaining if what he was seeing was a crack or a smudge. Every window on the lower level of the Northampton County Courthouse basked in grime. Rather than reflect the nearby pond in which sheep and pigs lolled, the otherwise beautiful edifice seemed to have become an extension of the muck.

Anger boiled in his chest and spilled from his lips. "This is disgraceful! Where is Ziba Wiggins?" He looked around for the familiar keeper of the courthouse, the man who had helped build this temple of justice ten years earlier and stayed on to guard and cosset the place. Peter felt the whiplash of a conflicting emotion. He closed his eyes and pressed his lips together. The courthouse was a mess because Ziba Wiggins had died in battle before Peter's eyes. Something had to be done to bring the edifice back to its former glory, and he was just the person to commission such a project as a memorial to Ziba, and a way for him to feel useful again.

For today, he decided to visit Easton's stabler, Conrad Fartenius, who had barely survived imprisonment in a New York sugar house. All the way across New Jersey in the deeps of winter, Peter had done his utmost to keep him alive, making sure he rode in the wagon and always received a portion of their scant supplies. By the time the ferry conveyed the remnants of Northampton County's Flying Camp across the Delaware River, Fartenius's grip on life was slipping. The presence of his wife and daughter, the ministrations of Easton's women, and the benevolence of the Almighty had ushered the young man back to the land of the living. Peter needed to know how he was faring now, a month later.

Maria met them at the door to the log cabin with its commanding view of the forks. "Colonel Kichline! How very good to see you, sir." The little girl greeted them in her native German as if she were eighteen instead of eight.

"*Ist deine Mutter hier?*"

Maria tilted her head. "Mother is at the stables. She's been doing Papa's work, and I've been helping Papa get well again." She grinned, apparently pleased with herself.

"How nice for your father. How is he today?"

"He is getting stronger, sir. How are you?"

"Much better, *danke. Fraulein* Maria, I'd like to present Joe."

"I am happy to meet you." She curtsied.

"Uh, *ja,* I am happy too."

"*Bitte kommt, sir.*" Maria opened the door all the way so they could enter the house, cozy with firelight and a clove-laced fragrance. Peter made sure to crouch through the door which, if he went head-on, would have banged straight into his eyes. Across the room, sitting near the hearth, Fartenius broke into a smile as he pushed down with his right hand to get up.

"Colonel Kichline, how very good to see you!"

Peter covered the distance between them in one stride, reaching his hand out and finding his soldier's bird-like. He could have fit two of himself in Fartenius's shirt and breeches. The man was a shadow of his pre-battle self, yet a brilliant light compared to his near-death version.

Maria busied herself at a coarsely-fashioned table, then brought them each a small glass of cider and a plate of molasses cookies.

"*Vielen dank, Liebes.*"

"*Gern geschehen, Papa.*" The girl returned to the table where she busied herself.

"You are looking much improved, Fartenius."

"I feel much improved, sir. My wife and daughter are daily working to fatten me, so that at times I worry they are preparing to take me to market."

Peter chuckled, grateful the private hadn't lost his sense of humor.

"Sir, what do you hear of the others?"

He had taken a large bite of the cookie and chewed quickly to address the question. "Nothing yet, I'm afraid.

This is the first time my wife has let me out since our return."

Fartenius's eyes glimmered. "And you came to see me?"

"Of course. I have been very concerned for your well-being."

"And I for yours." His voice had thickened.

The room was quiet except for the movement of Maria's knife against a cutting board.

Fartenius spoke the next words as if he were driving a stubborn mule. "Are you, uh, sorry you went through all you did, sir?"

Peter inhaled, the words Robert Levers had spoken on July 8 of the previous year marching through his mind—*with a firm reliance on the Protection of divine Providence, we mutually pledge to each other our Lives, our Fortunes, and our sacred Honor.* "Not for a minute," he answered. "And you?"

"Not one minute."

He yearned to cut loose the restraints of the past weeks of confinement, but while his spirit was willing, his body was ready for a lengthy nap.

Joe spoke as they walked side-by-side up Northampton Street. "My hair, I think you might want to be getting on home."

Peter smiled down at the boy. "Perhaps you have forgotten, you either say '*mein herr*' or 'sir,' not 'my hair.'"

Joe clapped the palm of his right hand to his forehead. "I get the words tangled, sir."

He placed his arm about the boy's shoulders. "Not to worry, son. We all have to learn to think before we speak."

"So, sir, should we best be going home?"

"Yes, but not just yet. There is one more person I very much want to see."

Inside the tavern, an army of memories marched across his mind's eye, beginning with his earliest days in Easton when he and Margaretta built the place. The early courts had met in the large room upstairs, and they'd hosted Assemblyman Benjamin Franklin during the fear-filled Christmas of 1755 when the village trembled under the threat of an Indian attack. Just to the north and west, the peaceful Moravians of Gnadenheutten had been brutally massacred, and Northampton County's sparse settlements had appealed to the Pennsylvania Assembly for help. The crisis had been averted, thanks be to God, and Mr. Franklin had gone on to make a big noise in the quest for independence from Great Britain. Peter had moved on as well, selling the tavern to *Frau* Eckert and her first husband after Peter's appointment as sheriff of Northampton County. His post forbade him to sell spirits, and he was not unhappy to turn instead to his milling operations on the Bushkill Creek to earn a livelihood.

When Ziba Wiggins became a widower, he had married *Frau* Eckert and had two children with her. Now she was alone again.

"Would you like to take a seat, sir?"

A man in the vicinity of thirty, someone Peter had never seen before, greeted them. Peter was nonplused not to have encountered *Frau* Eckert, in fact, to not be recognized at all as the former owner of this place, along with all his distinguished titles—former assemblyman, judge, commissioner, committeeman among them. Was that who he was now, *the former*?

"Yes, I'd like a seat by the hearth if you please."

"Right this way, sir." The man, Peter saw, dragged one leg across the floor as if it were a child clinging to him. He hadn't meant to stare, but the fellow caught his glance. "Ft. Washington," he said simply. "I bumped into a cannon ball."

"How did you happen to come to Easton?" Peter asked as he and Joe sat. At this early hour, they were the only ones in the tavern.

"I was brought here to recover at the hospital, uh, church down the street."

"I'm pleased to meet you, my good man. I'm Colonel Kichline of the Northampton County Flying Camp."

The man's hazel eyes sparkled as he gave a bow. "I've heard a lot about you, sir. Are you well now?"

"Much better, thank you. And you might be?"

"Thomas Bassett, sir, from southern New York."

"Colonel Kichline!"

He would have recognized her voice, and her breath, anywhere. *Frau* Wiggins, whom everyone in Easton still called "Eckert," swooped into the room and cut through their conversation. She grabbed Peter's hands and held them for a long moment, Bassett scurrying into the background.

"I am so very happy to see you, and looking well again." Her eyes moistened.

He lowered his voice to a near-whisper. "I came to pay my respects. Mr. Wiggins was a good man."

She sat down, something rarely seen in Easton history. Her eyes hungry, she asked, "Did he suffer?"

Peter shook his head, "seeing" what had happened on the battlefield. "He went very quickly." He hoped she didn't press for details, breathing easier when she did not.

"I do wish he'd been laid to rest here. Do you think he had a decent burial?"

He had no idea what had happened to the bodies of his fallen men. What should he tell her? A long moment later he said, "I like to think he did. "

March 28, 1777

My dear Colonel Miles,

You are very much on my mind on this beautiful day when the promise of a new season is driven on the wind. My good wife at last gave her blessing for me to take a ramble through the village, and I saw every budding flower and tree as if for the very first time. I trust you are in good health and able to take your own rambles around the Vink home in which we passed so many days and nights. My one regret in leaving New York was knowing you had not yet been paroled to your own home in Philadelphia. I trust the Almighty to guide and bless you in this meantime, and to allow for your safe return to your family.

Today I visited the young man in my unit who had the most serious injury, Conrad Fartenius. Mercifully he is making a steady, albeit slow, recovery while his wife and daughter run the stable business and home. So many of our women and children have stepped forward to hold down the fort as it were while their husbands, fathers, sons, and brothers fight for our liberty. I am filled with the utmost respect and admiration for them. My own

Catherine and daughter Susannah continue to minister to the sick and imprisoned in Easton, as well as to sew clothing and knit stockings for our troops by night.

As for Fartentius, and another wounded veteran I have just encountered, being in their company is a balm to my spirit. We share a bond no one else can quite understand. At times, I feel I am keeping something from my dear wife, but then I am reminded she has given birth twice, something I cannot fully understand.

I am itchy, my friend, to get back into the fight now that I am mending, but my wife regularly admonishes me not to push. She says I have done my part and must rest. I think there is still much in me to contribute, and I yearn for that day to come, even as I pray for patience to endure this season. One thing I plan to do is oversee a thorough cleanup of our courthouse, its keeper having died in New York.

I am enclosing some money for you to use as you see fit, either for yourself or your men. I also plan to include socks and comestibles.

May the Almighty strengthen and protect you.

Your humble servant,

Peter Kichline

CHAPTER FIVE

Ethan padded into the kitchen, Toby trundling after him. "What are you making Mom? I'm hungry."

When Erin looked up to find her late husband's luminous eyes looking back at her, she squirted mustard onto her white shirt. She let go an audible sigh and headed to the sink. Mustard stains were a bear to get out of clothes. "I don't think you'd be interested," she said.

Her son inclined his head toward the various containers on the island. "Try me."

She dabbed vigorously at the yellow splotch. "I was experimenting with mustard, sriracha, and espresso."

Ethan wrinkled his nose. "On what?"

"Actually in, not on." She cleared her throat. "Greek yogurt." There was no way she'd mention the yogurt was already peach flavored.

"Aw, Mom, just have some chocolate sauce and marshmallows like normal people."

Wasn't he too young to start being embarrassed by her? If Jim were still here, would Ethan be growing ashamed of him, too? She cringed at the thought.

"Don't we have Tasty Kakes or ice cream?"

"Not until you've had some fruit or vegetables, young man."

He opened the refrigerator door. "If I eat an apple, could I have some ice cream?"

"Yes."

Her cell phone started ringing. When she saw the caller ID, her heart pounded. Was something wrong with her mother? "Hello, Aunt Fran."

"Now, how did you know it was me?"

"Caller ID."

"These new-fangled phones never cease to amaze me. In my day you never knew who was on the other end."

"Is everything okay?"

"Everything is just fine. Your mom asked me to call you."

Erin frowned. "Why didn't she call me herself?"

Fran whispered. "Between you, me, and the signpost, she can't see the numbers anymore."

This was bad. There were, however, phones with large displays to accommodate poor vision.

"Does Mom need something?"

"I'll let her tell you. She's right here."

"Erin?"

"Hi, Mom. How are you?" She stopped trying to wipe the stain from her shirt and pitched the paper towel into the trash.

"Pretty good. How are you?"

"Doing well."

"That's good. I just wanted to remind you that you're taking me for groceries tomorrow at eleven." She paused. "You forgot the last time."

"Nearly forgot. And this time I remembered, but thanks for the reminder."

"Now, Erin, I don't like those big cans of vegetables. I

like the little ones with the pop tops. Remember you got me those big ones before, and I couldn't use them."

Audrey had mentioned the incident from several months ago every time they went food shopping. Was she destined to hear this scratchy recording for the rest of her life, or at least her mother's life? And how long would Audrey live? Jim had been a few years shy of fifty, and here was her mother at eighty-two. These days her dead husband seemed to be breaking into her thoughts at every turn.

"Erin?"

"Uh, yes, Mom, I know about the small cans with the pop tops."

"Are these the ones?"

Audrey leaned so close to the shelf she was practically nose-to-nose with a can of collard greens. Erin intervened, pulling the right veggies from the display. "This is what you like."

"Then what are these?"

"Collard greens."

"Collard greens! I never ate a collard green in my life. Who eats those?" Sniffing, she replaced the can, on the wrong shelf, as if she were handling a snake. "I'm telling you, Erin, my vision is getting worse and worse."

"I know, Mom. I'm sorry."

"I just wish something could be done. I'm not used to feeling so helpless."

Neither am I.

"I know you're really busy, but I found some family photos I'd like to show you," Audrey told her daughter, who was finishing unpacking groceries.

Erin glanced up at the clock above the kitchen sink. "Sure, Mom, I have a half hour before I need to leave."

"How about you make some tea while I get the photos?"

Erin knew all about her mother's tea bags, which predated the 1976 Olympics. Every time she'd suggested buying new ones, Audrey's eyes had widened. "I don't need tea. I have plenty of tea." Next time she took her mom shopping, she would just pick up a new package and discreetly replace the old stash. As for the cups? Her mom's motley collection contained sepia-toned stains, like rings on a tree. Audrey had always been a meticulous housekeeper, except for her habit of letting certain foods live way past their expiration dates. Erin discreetly ran hot water in the sink and gave two of the mugs a solid scrubbing while looking over her shoulder so her mom didn't catch her in the act.

Audrey headed toward the table between her kitchenette and living area. "I'm not exactly sure who these pictures are of, but I recognize this box. Grammy Ott used to keep it in her chifforobe."

Erin smiled as she filled the tea kettle halfway and turned on the stove. "Now there's a word you don't hear every day. Chifforobe." She moved to the table and hovered over her mom. Audrey seemed to be shrinking.

Her mom examined the contents for several minutes. "This came from an old department store on Northampton Street."

Erin read the logo. "Laubachs." She smiled, thinking of Paul's proposal at Maxim's, which occupied the site now. *That's a good sign, right? I'm smiling at a memory of him.* Her mind went directly to the subject she'd been obsessing over since she'd seen Melissa. *He is such a wonderful man, and I do love him—differently than I loved Jim, though. Maybe Jim's love was more like April with summer ahead, and Paul's is like September. Maybe we should get married, just not quite so soon. Maybe we should wait until autumn.* She was surprised when an ever-present clenching in her stomach suddenly eased.

She rested in the thought until the whistling tea kettle drew her attention. Her mother was talking, seemingly finishing a sentence Erin hadn't begun to hear. "Do you want sugar, Mom?"

"No sugar. No milk."

Erin would have preferred sugar, but finding a half-full, solidified bag, she opted instead for a splash of apple cider vinegar. She carried the mugs to the table and placed them out of harm's reach of the photos, which her mom was scattering like confetti.

"I recognize this one." Audrey held the photo to the light above the table. "This is your Uncle Thomas when he married Aunt Rose."

Erin smiled at the newlyweds. "Aunt Rose isn't wearing a gown."

"Not in this picture. She did at the church, but this must be their going away photo."

"Which church?"

"Why First Church, Easton." Audrey shook her head. "No, Rose didn't go there. I think they were married in the Presbyterian Church on South Main Street."

Erin couldn't recall such a place and said so.

"They tore it down just before you were born. The Presbyterian church is on Belvidere Road now, Pilgrim Presbyterian."

"That's a pretty church. I remember going there a few

times with my friend Maureen when I was in high school."

As if Erin hadn't spoken, her mother handed her a different photo. "I don't know about this one."

Erin took the picture and gazed at the lovely face looking straight at her, one she'd never recalled seeing before, in person or otherwise. The era appeared to be 1920s judging from the quality of the picture and the outfit the subject wore. "I don't know who this is, Mom."

"Well, then, describe it." She blew against the hot tea, then took a sip.

"Let's see … it's in black and white and of a young woman in her early twenties, I'd say. I can tell her hair is blonde. Her eyes seem light-colored, and she has a kind expression."

Audrey sat up taller. "Does she have dimples?"

Erin peered closer, wishing she had her reading glasses. "Yes."

Her mother nodded her head a few times. "Uh-huh. That's Barbara's mother."

"Do you mean Aunt Barbara?

"Yes. I've told you before her mother died in childbirth when Barbara was just a baby, well, around two years old. Her maiden aunts kept her until my dad married my mom."

Erin knew her Grammy Ott had married a widower, then about twenty years after he died, she married an old bachelor. Erin had thought he was her biological grandfather until she was old enough to understand. As for her Aunt Barbara, Erin's grandmother had raised her as her own child—the two of them as close as any mother and daughter. "So, this is Aunt Barbara's birth mother?"

"Yes. She was beautiful. Of course, I never knew her, but I used to hear about her dimples."

Erin was curious. "Who told you about her?"

Audrey shrugged. "Oh, I don't know. Maybe my mother, maybe my dad. Once in a while, he would talk about her, but not much. At times, I forget she'd even existed."

She shuddered. *I hope I never feel that way about Jim.* "What was her name?" Erin took a swig of tea and winced. The vinegar had been a bad idea, although the acidity had cleansed the stains.

"Oh, let me see if I can remember." Audrey pursed her lips and looked off into the distance. "It was something like Annette, yes, Annette, and her last name was Sitgreaves."

"Sitgreaves? Like the street?"

"And the school I went to as a girl. Her people had money."

Erin took one last look at the beautiful woman then handed the photo back to her mother.

Audrey squinted as she held the picture right up to her eyes. "This must be the photo my mother used to tell me about. She said when she and Dad first set up housekeeping, he kept this picture on his bureau."

Erin gasped. "He kept it on his bureau? Didn't Grammy mind?"

"She never said."

She couldn't help but apply the image to her own situation. If she did, in fact, end up marrying Paul, would she want to prominently display Jim's photograph in their *bedroom*? She held back a projectile "bleh." *That would in no way be fair to Paul.* Maybe the best thing to do would be to keep Jim's photo in Ethan's room. She certainly didn't want to hide Jim or the fact of him, but she didn't think she could be with Paul in the privacy of their bedroom with Jim's picture in the background. The question was, did she want to be with Paul?

Audrey handed the old box to her daughter. "You can keep these as long as you want, Erin. Maybe you'll find something interesting you can use."

"Thanks, Mom. Oh, and Connie Pierce is just about finished with your DAR application, so I'll be bringing that by for you to sign."

"Please thank her for me."

She kissed her mom's cheek and left the apartment, hoping she didn't run into Aunt Fran or any of her mother's friends since she was, once again, running behind schedule.

On the way back to Easton, she couldn't get the image of Anette's photo out of her mind. *My grandfather must've really loved and missed her.* Did he love her grandmother too, or had he mainly married her because he needed someone to look after his child? Then again, he had sisters who were taking care of Barbara. *I wonder how he felt about remarrying, loving another person as he'd loved the wife of his youth.* She stopped for a light at the bottom of College Hill near the new arts center. *Is there anything in this I can learn? After all, my grandfather did dare to start a new life even though he'd loved the old one. And so did Grandfather Peter—three times.* Whatever she decided about Paul, she was in very good company.

"There you go!" Connie accepted the signed application from Erin and smiled. "All you have to do now is get your mom's signature, have her write a check, and mail this and the check to headquarters in Washington."

A week had passed since Erin's shopping excursion with her mother, and Connie had come by the house an hour before Ethan's return from school.

Her friend's green eyes seemed lit from behind. "There's something else I did, Erin. I hope you don't mind." She produced another set of papers and held on to them as she spoke. "We've talked before about having Ethan join the Children of the American Revolution, and both of you were in favor so …" She handed the papers to Erin. "I went ahead and filled out an application for him. All I need from you is a copy of his birth certificate, some signatures, and a check."

Erin examined the document, which resembled the DAR version but with a different logo at the top. Connie went on talking, although Erin found herself unable to focus. She saw her name, address, and national DAR number, and cringed at the line stating she was the first wife of James Miles, deceased. *If Jim had lived, and I had somehow become as interested in genealogy as I am now, I would have pushed him to become a Son of the American Revolution through Samuel Miles. If I marry Paul, any supplemental apps I might fill out will say he's my second husband.*

"So, what do you think?"

Erin looked up. "Excuse me?"

"I was wondering what you thought of my idea."

"Oh, I like the application a lot. Ethan will too, I'm sure."

"Good. Except I wasn't talking about the app."

"Sorry, I was focused on the C.A.R."

"No problem. So, as I was saying, all of the George

Taylor Chapter members choose a committee to head up. Some people do more than others. To be honest, most are in name only, but we have to fill all the slots. I'm wondering if you'd be willing to be the senior society president for the George Taylor Society, C.A.R."

Her torso rose as she took and expelled a deep breath. The gesture wasn't lost on Connie.

"I know you're overworked and planning a wedding, and I feel awful asking, but please know I don't expect much. I just need to fill this vacancy, and with Ethan joining the C.A.R, you're my most obvious choice."

"What would I have to do?"

"As much or as little as you want. There are only about eight kids on the roster, not counting Ethan, and most of them are ready to age out. At that point, they'll either join the DAR or SAR, but none of them has been active, so who knows?" She lifted her hands. "We haven't had a functioning society for several years, but I'd like to do something with the group. Your responsibilities are to reach out to the membership with any activities—for example, they could be part of our Christmas luncheon and write cards to veterans. We could involve them in Easton Heritage Day or a Memorial Day parade. Some societies meet every month, but I would just like to offer at least one event a year. In addition, you would collect dues every fall. I've been doing this for five years, and I'm ready to pass the baton. It's actually quite easy, takes about two hours total, and I'll walk you through the first year."

"How long would I be doing this?"

"For the duration of my administration—another two years."

She nodded, considering. "All right."

"Well, that was easy. Thanks very much. So, what I'm thinking is …"

I wonder if Paul might have a patriot. I would like to help him find one, and we could be a DAR-C.A.R-SAR family. That is, if we become a family.

"Erin." Connie leaned across the couch. "You seem distant. Is everything all right?"

Her welled-up emotions broke free and, embarrassed, she suppressed an impulse to run upstairs and hide in her bedroom.

"Don't worry, Erin. Tears don't bother me."

She reached for a tissue from a box on Ethan's desk. "Thanks for understanding, Connie."

"You know the saying—that's what friends are for."

She had felt secure in her years-long friendship with Melissa. Now she had another dear companion in her life. *Make new friends, but keep the old …* The childhood song ran through her thoughts. Erin drew a parallel between her marriage to Jim and her relationship with Paul. Maybe this was Paul's time to be part of this season of Erin's life.

"You can tell me anything, nothing, or something in between," Connie said. "Whatever you need."

"I've, well, I've been feeling reluctant about Paul in recent weeks—not because of anything he said or did," she said quickly. "Just wondering whether I could, well, make a life with someone after Jim." Her cheeks reddened. "We were married over twenty years, and we had a wonderful relationship."

"You were lucky."

"Blessed is more like it." The words flew out of her mouth before she could stop them. "Sorry, I didn't mean to sound ornery."

"No, no. I understand. Marriage takes hard work and God's hand."

"Exactly."

"Erin, I'd like to tell you something about myself, something that's never come up before. You see, Terry isn't my first husband."

"Oh. I didn't know."

"We've only been married ten years."

"Then your son …"

"Is my first husband's. Rick and I were married right out of college, and we had fifteen years together until he was killed by a drunk driver." Her expression tightened.

Erin clapped her hand to her mouth. "How awful!"

"The first two years I just did the bare minimum to keep Mark and I going."

"Oh, so Alex is …"

"Terry's and my son. You've never met Mark. He lives in Colorado now. When I came out of that terrible season, I started getting more involved in my work and in the DAR. Life didn't seem so awful after a while. I started tasting, and enjoying, food again. And one golden day, I met Terry at a Bach concert in Bethlehem. We were immediately drawn to each other, but I felt so guilty at first, like loving Terry would be disrespectful to Rick. The thoughts and emotions weren't entirely rational, but I needed time to work them out. Fortunately, Terry was very patient with me, as I suspect Paul is with you."

Erin found every word to be a lifeline. "Did those feelings go away after you remarried?"

Connie nodded. "They faded like old jeans after a lot of washings."

All at once, she realized there'd been something else

lurking in her spirit, disturbing her. She was, in fact, afraid of losing Paul, worried she might not be able to handle the deaths of two husbands. Then again, isn't that exactly what her Grandfather Peter had endured? "Did you, well, did you ever feel afraid something bad might happen to Rick too?"

"You bet I did. To be honest with you, Erin, every now and then I still do. Last year, Terry's car got hit from behind when he was stopped at a light, and although he was fine and there were only a few scratches on the bumper, I felt as if I'd been hit head-on. I guess in the end, we need to decide whether loving again is worth the risk." The sun broke on Connie's face. "As for me, I say yes! Absolutely yes."

Erin heard the sound of the elementary kids' bus come to a stop a few houses away, accompanied by laughter and the vrooming of the engine as the vehicle continued its appointed rounds.

"What about Rick? Do you ever think about him or miss him?" She tilted her head.

"I do, but not in a present sense. How can I explain?" She looked down at her hands, resting in her lap. "He's part of a season of my life, one I deeply cherish, one I will never forget, or do I wish to. But, Erin, I don't want to live backwards. Jim will always be part of you, and in a real sense, he's left part of himself through Ethan. I've discovered you don't need to lose what you once had to move forward."

Erin smiled, quiet tears slipping down her cheeks.

"I've known Paul a long time, ever since he came to Easton. In fact, I tried to fix him up a time or two, but the right woman never came along. Until now."

CHAPTER SIX

He cast a furtive glance over his shoulder, reduced to being a small boy sneaking out of the house, unable to tolerate the constant fussing one blessed minute more. If his wife wasn't urging him to eat more pepper pot, *Frau* Hamster was directing him to take a nap. Even Susannah tended to speak to him as if he were the child and she, the parent. Only his sons, Andrew and Jacob, understood, but they were nearly always at the mills. He almost jumped out of his skin when he slipped the door open to find his servant William on the other side. One misstep and the housekeeper and Joe would be descending upon them in a jumble of German and mangled English.

Peter raised his forefinger to his lips as they stood outside in the sun-dappled greening of early April. "I don't want anyone to know I'm leaving."

William grinned. "I understand, Colonel. They still be babying you then?"

He closed his eyes. "They mean well, but I need activity, and the company of men."

"Sir, if I may have a word before you, uh, escape …"

"Of course. What's on your mind?" He took William by the elbow and steered him further down Northampton Street away from his house, which he was convinced had ears and eyes. He enjoyed finding himself in the much more familiar role of leader.

"I been wantin' to tell you, I done paid me a visit to Andrew Drunkenmiller a few weeks back."

Peter's lips parted, hungry for news of his erstwhile drummer from the Northampton County Flying Camp. "How is he coming along?"

"He still be too weak for work, but he's mending well, sir. I, uh …" He looked down at the ground and rubbed his fingers together. "I stayed for a few days to help his father. Mistress Catherine say she don't mind, but I did feel peculiar not having your go-ahead."

Peter clapped the man on the right shoulder; William had grown in his absence. What was he now, twenty? Maybe a year or two older? One usually ended up guessing with slaves, unless they'd had benevolent owners, which had definitely not been the case with William or Joe. They continued walking slowly in the direction of the courthouse. "I am pleased you went to see Andrew and helped his father. You know Mr. Drunkenmiller was none too happy seeing his Mennonite son go to war."

William gave a small laugh. "This be the truth, sir."

Peter side-stepped his agenda for the conversation to take a small detour. "How are they getting along now, and did the father treat you well during your service to him?"

He shrugged. "He be fine, sir. Not like you. Gruff. Still, he treated me fairly, and his wife be kind to me. As for him and Mr. Andrew, they be doin' well, it seems to me. No hardness there."

"I'm glad for this, glad your expansive gesture wasn't entirely lost on them." Peter recalled how William had offered to work in Andrew Drunkenmiller's place on the Mennonite family's farm so the young man could follow his convictions to serve with the Flying Camp. As they ambled along the cobblestone thoroughfare, he noticed how crowded the village had become, teaming with so many people one could become lost in a throng. For just this moment, he welcomed the anonymity.

"William, when you brought your plan to me, I gave my approval and my blessing. You did your part to secure our nation's freedom. Of course, there is another kind of freedom." A light wind fluttered around his ears and into his spirit. "I think this is the time to make you a free man."

William's expression burst wide open as he accidentally bumped into Peter's left side. Peter sucked in his breath at the dull pain shooting through his arm.

"Oh, sir, I's so sorry!" He lifted his hand to touch the tender spot, then seemed to remember what such a gesture would cost the colonel.

"Not to worry, William. I'm fine." He abruptly changed the subject, choosing to focus on the joy of the moment rather than the throbbing in his arm.

"Did I hear you right? You want to make me free, sir?"

He nodded. "I always have. Do you feel ready?"

"I sure do."

"Of course, we must make a plan." He needed to sit down and, spying a bench near Meyer Hart's store, took advantage of the chance to rest. Maybe his women were right after all to keep such a close eye on him. He patted the seat next to him. "Have you any thoughts about what you might do?"

"When I think about the future, I always have my wood workin' in mind. Maybe I'd like to be a carpenter."

William had done expert work in the village's Reformed Church building, which they shared with the Lutherans, especially the hand-carved pulpit.

"Do you think you'd like to stay in Easton?" He genuinely hoped so.

"I would, sir. I do like living here a whole lot. And then I could be near Joe, and your family, and the friends I've made here."

"How about this—after we get your papers signed, you continue to stay at the sawmill house. You are welcome to live there as long as you work for me. I will pay you the same as my other workers, not including my indentured servant. If you need lumber and time for carpentry projects, we can negotiate a fair price. I do, in fact, urge you to begin building up a carpentry business, if that's what you want."

For a long moment, William remained silent, then gave an abrupt shake of his head when a tear skidded down his cheek. He broke into a smile. "I's speechless, colonel."

"I'm happy for you, William. I do have a favor to ask."

"You name it, sir."

"The courthouse has fallen into some disrepair since Mr. Wiggins's death. Would you be willing to assist in cleaning it up? Joe could help, and I can get my sons if they're available."

"Yes sir, I's be glad to do that." William paused. "Mr. Wiggins was a nice man."

Peter responded hoarsely. "He was indeed."

He was eager to see Meyer Hart, whose family had been in Easton as long as Peter's. When he opened the door to the shop, a stranger in uniform jumped out of the way and nearly skidded into the embrace of the soldier he was talking to.

"Do excuse me," Peter said.

"Of course," the fellow muttered before turning back to his conversation.

He looked over the tops of people's heads from the vantage point of his height hoping to see his old friend behind the counter, but Meyer Hart wasn't anywhere to be seen. The place was hopping, though, filled cheek by jowl with people and the humming of their conversations. After weeks of solitude, Peter gripped his walking stick to steady himself against sudden faintness, then he grumbled, not only at his weakness, but his inability to spot one person he recognized, even if they would report back to Catherine about him fleeing the nest. He carefully nudged his way toward the counter so no one bumped his left arm.

The sales clerk continued writing something as he greeted Peter without looking at him. "*Guten morgen, mein Herr. Wie kann ich dir helfen?*"

"*Ich suche Herr Hart.*"

The young man shook his head, explaining the proprietor wasn't often there, treating Peter as if he were a fly to be shooed away.

"What about his son?" He spoke slowly, trying to keep his growing irritation from bleeding into the exchange.

The clerk looked past him to the next customer. "He will be back this afternoon."

Who even was this young man whom Peter had never seen before, who had no idea who Peter was or the deference others showed him? How strange to be in his own town and among his own people yet not be known as the leading man he was, or at least had been. If he'd been such a big noise before he'd set off with the Flying Camp, now he wasn't even a whisper.

Am I so full of pride? Have I grown too comfortable with being hailed in the marketplaces?

"Colonel Kichline!"

He heard his name above the rumbling din and followed the sound. Then he saw the waters part for Robert Levers, magnificent in his uniform. Now heads turned in Peter's direction. Levers was suddenly upon him, and Peter held out his right hand, wincing when his friend pumped with abandon. "I am so very pleased to see you out and about, but then you do look a bit peaked, my good man. I'd love to talk to you." He looked about, nodding in response to several greetings, and steered Peter outside. The two men ended up at the Bachmann Publick House where the atmosphere was slightly more subdued. Even so, a twinge in Peter's temples signaled the start of a headache.

Levers began ordering cider for both of them, but Peter raised his hand. "I'll have coffee, if you please."

When the waiter left, Levers leaned back in the chair, his posture expansive, as if he owned the place. "You're looking well overall, Colonel Kichline. How are you faring? I've been stopping by on occasion to see you but …"

"The females have been keeping visitors at bay."

Levers grinned. "I'm glad they've finally let you out."

Peter raised his eyebrows. "I let myself out."

The man who was running Northampton County's affairs guffawed, bringing his hand down on the table. Then he moved closer. "I'm not one for cossetting, my good man, but I can see the excursion to Mr. Hart's emporium has exhausted you. Give yourself time, colonel. Healing takes time."

Peter wanted to move the conversation away from himself. "I was sorry not to see Mr. Hart. Do you know where he is?"

"Ah, yes. Mr. Hart is now serving as commissar of prisoners. We're bursting at the very seams with British and Hessians. He's doing quite a nice job too."

Peter was glad his old friend had found a way to support the Cause.

"His son runs the store, along with a nephew from Philadelphia."

"And how are you keeping, Mr. Levers? I understand your duties have increased considerably."

He looped his thumbs under his waistcoat. "My family, unfortunately, barely sees me these days, but if we are to secure liberty to future generations, we all must make our sacrifices, as you have done."

"I will continue to do so as soon as I am well enough."

"I look forward to that day, and to the time when you are exchanged."

Peter looked up at the serving girl as she placed their drinks before them, another face he didn't recognize. Then he asked the question stirring his mind day in, day out. "Tell me, Mr. Levers, do you know what happened to my men, the ones who didn't make it back?" He wanted to ask after his son Peter, but he couldn't bring himself to expose his vulnerability.

He drank cider and wiped the foam from his lips with the back of his hand. "I'm sorry to say most didn't survive the battle. A few, including your son, escaped from New York with General Washington's beleaguered survivors, then they returned to their homes at the end of their enlistment in December. I do know Captain John Arndt is still imprisoned, and he was also wounded like yourself."

He sighed to himself at the mention of Peter, Jr.'s name.

"Is any attempt being made to free him?"

"Yes, I believe so, but there are so very many cases, and the procedures for parole and exchange are still being worked out."

Peter's spirit sank to the floorboards, an unfamiliar emotion he didn't much care to hang on to. "How fares the Army?" It was high time his family stopped hiding the newspapers from him.

"Winning this war is an uphill battle, my good friend, but our spirits remain strong. As Mr. Paine so aptly said in December, we are not 'sunshine patriots,' most of us anyway."

He was about to inquire about Lewis Gordon when Levers waved a man over to their table. "Hooper!"

The stocky man bearing flecks of gray in his yellow beard looked toward their table and trudged over, smiling. "Good day, Colonel Levers." He bowed from the waist.

"I'm so pleased you came in. I very much want you to meet my good friend, Colonel Peter Kichline. Colonel, may I introduce Robert Hooper, deputy Quartermaster General?"

Hooper's light-colored eyes were those of a boy during a fireworks display. "Colonel Kichline." He bowed over the hand Peter had extended. "I have long anticipated this meeting. May I say how grateful I am to see you out and about?"

"I am pleased to make your acquaintance as well, Colonel Hooper." He sensed an instant affinity for the man despite feeling naked in his own, civilian clothes.

Hooper sat across from the two men, and the waiting girl took his order.

"Mr. Hooper has come to us from Philadelphia," Levers

said.

"Is that where you're from?"

"Most recently. I have also resided in Trenton, and my family comes from New Jersey."

"And you are now in Easton?" Peter's headache spread like spilled ink.

Levers spoke up. "His immediate family lives in Saucon, but when he's in town, the colonel is staying just up the street from you, at the corner of Northampton and Hamilton Streets."

"Then we are close to each other. I live across the street and a little toward the Great Square."

"I hope we will have many opportunities to see each other."

"Colonel Hooper's immediate neighbors aren't quite as tranquil, Colonel Kichline."

"Why, may I ask?"

"There's a barracks behind my quarters, which is currently being used to house prisoners.

"You are welcome to the quiet of my home at any time, colonel." At this moment, with the headache intensifying, he craved the serenity of his abode. He closed his eyes, missing the glance Levers and Hooper shared.

"Thank you, Colonel Kichline. I would be honored to share your hospitality. You are, of course, a legend in these parts."

To his surprise—and alarm, Peter's eyes stung so he could barely focus.

Another man he didn't recognize walked over and whispered something to Levers, who stood. "I'm afraid I must be going, but I leave you two in the best of company." He shook Peter's hand first. "My dear friend, I have cherished this time with you and look forward to another visit very soon."

Peter nodded. "As do I."

After Levers departed, the two colonels spoke quietly to each other about their families, then switched to the current news, dominated by the war. He closed his eyes against even the dim light of the tavern.

"Colonel Kichline, if I may, you seem spent."

"Yes, and I do beg your pardon, Colonel Hooper. You see, this is the first I've been out on my own and for an extended period since my return to Easton in February."

Rising, Hooper put some coins on the table. "My good sir, will you allow me to accompany you to your home? I am going in that direction."

Mercifully, Hooper did all the talking on the way through the crowded street. All Peter had to do was put one foot in front of the other, which was, in fact, all he could do.

CHAPTER SEVEN

She would sit down with Paul soon and share her thoughts, which at the moment were scattered like free-range chickens. Derek McCutcheon was to call at nine-thirty, and she needed to speak intelligently. Impressed with her feature about Peter Kichline in the historical society bulletin, he had invited her to co-write his probable new bestseller, *The Unsung: Little Known Heroes of the American Revolution*.

Before her, Erin had her hard copy file on Samuel Miles, Jim's illustrious ancestor, computer and online folders, as well as her bound dissertation. A week ago, she'd electronically sent McCutcheon an outline and rough draft of her piece on Colonel Miles. Last night, she'd written some questions she had for the famous historian, and some she anticipated he might ask.

Her phone started buzzing at exactly nine-thirty, and a two-one-two number flashed onto the screen. She slid her finger to answer. "Hello, this is Erin Miles."

His mellow, renowned voice from years of TV documentaries and voiceovers was instantly recognizable. "Good morning, Erin Miles. Derek McCutcheon here."

"Good morning, Mr. McCutcheon, how …"

"Oh, but you must call me Derek. We are on equal ground here, that is, if a PhD considers me to be equal."

His humility touched her. "Of course I do! How have

you been?"

"Very well, and yourself?"

She wouldn't mention the rough start she'd had to her day, including a hassle with Ethan over dirty gym shorts. When she wondered what that smell was coming from his backpack, he protested when she pulled out the stinking red shorts and once-white tee shirt. "You can't wear these today."

"But I have to. I'll get a demotion if I'm not in uniform."

"Maybe that will teach you to clean out your backpack at the end of the week and let me wash these." She held her nose as Toby sniffed at the air.

"M-o-m! I can't take gym if I'm not in these clothes."

"And I can't allow you to wear them one blessed more time. I don't even want to know how long it's been since I washed these." She'd marched straight to the laundry room while Ethan stomped out of the door in a stink of a different kind. She shook free of the memory.

"I'm quite well, M … Derek. I'm thoroughly enjoying writing this story about Samuel Miles."

"It shows. You're bringing him to life, drawing him from a one-dimensional straight-historical portrait to a living man who underwent many trials, in addition to achieving great heights in his career."

"I'm so glad you like what I've done. I wasn't sure if I was striking the right balance between scholarship and a more literary readability, as you do so well."

"Believe me, you have done just that." He chuckled in a sort of rumble. "People might think I wrote the piece."

She felt as if she'd stepped straight onto a cloud. "I wanted to discuss my style with you, Derek. You see, I'm not sure whether you want me to try to write in my own voice or to fashion my work after yours, since this is your project." The same question that kept popping up in her life these days nattered again—where exactly did she stand?

"I've been asking myself the same thing. This is the first time I've collaborated like this. While it is my book, this is your writing. Your voice. I think at this point I'd like to have you go ahead and use your own technique with a sensitivity to the style I'm known for—well-researched, literary quality, but highly readable, engaging, sometimes even a bit punchy. Let's see how the rough draft works out, and we'll go from there. I have confidence this will be an iron-sharpening-iron experience for both of us."

"I like your suggestion." She relaxed into her home office chair.

After pointing out a couple of typos and two sections needing "more meat on the bones," McCutcheon surprised her. "The publisher and I have been discussing the project, and they're thinking this could become a series."

She sat straight up. "A series?"

"Yes. We could continue writing about unsung heroes from other periods, beginning with this one. This would tie all the people together under a specific theme, like the pursuit of independence, rather than a mish-mash of people from unrelated time periods."

Erin's thoughts swam with possibilities. "This could be an amazing endeavor, Derek. The possibilities …"

"I know, endless. Maybe even a TV documentary."

"How many are they thinking of per book?"

"Anywhere from fifteen to twenty."

She caught her breath in the back of her throat, a sound she'd only ever heard herself and her Grammy Ott make.

"If you were to do half, ours would be a true collaboration.

Now, on the present book, I'm getting behind schedule and need you to write two more profiles."

"Oh. Um, yes, of course I can do that." How she'd manage, she had no idea.

He mentioned their names, ones she didn't recognize, and added, "As you continue honing your stories about Miles and Kichline, then these other two men, focus a little more on their exploits during the conflict. I like providing an overview of these men's lives, especially their childhoods and what led them to pursue American independence, but seventy-five percent of the writing should be about their moment of glory, as it were, in the war, the thing that will define them for our readers."

The thing that will define them. What does, in fact, define me now? This book feels so right, and the idea of writing more is beyond my wildest dreams. And I also love the idea of heading up the Kichline Center, but this renovation phase is killing me. And Paul ... I want to be his wife. A zinging sensation surged through her. In a moment of surprising clarity, she knew marrying Paul was the right thing to do.

"I could do that, of course. Um, Derek, what kind of deadline are we talking about?"

"Originally, we were looking at July 1st, but with these changes, more like August 1st."

She couldn't speak around the dry ice sensation filling her throat, or the throng of emotions pelting her.

"Is that doable?"

Should she be thinking out loud? What if she said something to make him drop her? She didn't want to lose this priceless opportunity, and surely there were countless other history professors who'd gladly fill these shoes.

"Yes, I believe I could do that, although I'm ..."

"Very busy, I'm sure."

"Yes, with starting a new center for colonial Easton studies here—from the ground up."

"Big undertaking that."

You have no idea. "And I'm getting married in July." There, she'd said the words. She was getting married in July—to Paul Bassett. She braced herself for the emotional backlash she expected, but instead of a whirlwind, there was a powerful whisper of peace of the kind that passes understanding. A giggle bubbled up, which she hastily squelched, but like her friend Melissa often did, Erin's mind latched on to a tangent. *Should I change my last name? Will I be Erin Miles Bassett, or just Erin Bassett? I would like to keep the Miles, especially for Ethan's sake, but what will Paul think?* She realized this was no time to ponder such an important question. *Focus!*

"Well, congratulations, Erin. Are you marrying the man I thought was your Miles ancestor?"

"Yes, Paul Bassett."

"Good for you. Nice fellow. Well, then, is this too much for you?" He sounded wistful, a tad nervous.

"No, not at all. I'll make this work. I love this project."

She could almost hear his relieved sigh. "That's good to hear. Oh, and one more thing. I want to start paying you as you write. I apologize for not getting to this earlier."

She had wondered about how the remuneration would work but thought she might sound too money-hungry. "Thank you. I'd appreciate that."

"Would monthly be suitable? And rather than an hourly rate, I'd just like to give you a figure that seems fair for your considerable efforts, along with a portion of royalties. I'll have my publisher draw up a contract."

She nearly fell off her chair when he named the number. "Oh, yes, of course. The amount is generous, and the timing works. Thank you."

When they hung up, she realized not only was her cup running over, but unless something in her schedule changed, the waters might just overtake her.

ﷺ

Her father wiped his mouth with a napkin. "Boy, that was good. You're quite a cook, Erin."

Ethan twisted his mouth. "When she's not making weird food."

"Weird food?" Tony frowned in his grandson's direction.

"She likes to mix things up, like Froot Loops and Tabasco sauce." Ethan took a swig of chocolate milk. "Was she like that when she was a kid?"

Erin braced herself for whatever her unpredictable father might feel a need to share about a childhood when he wasn't often present.

"I don't think she ate strange food when she was a girl." He turned his dark brown eyes on Erin. "When did that business start?"

"Oh, I'm not exactly sure. When I was in college, I liked trying new things." In her answer lay a minefield—she hadn't spoken to her father once while she was at Lafayette, a season in their relationship she'd always thought of in terms of a C.S. Lewis book, *The Great Divorce*. Even this evening was a step in a new direction with her father, the first time she'd ever cooked for him, and in her own home.

She popped up from the table, grabbing her plate and utensils. "I assure you there is nothing bizarre about dessert."

Ethan also rose, gathering his dinnerware and taking his grandfather's plate. "What did you make?" He paused. "Or buy?"

"Make," she said. "Pumpkin pie from a recipe I got from one of my cooking shows."

"With whipped cream?"

"Real whipped cream. Dad, do you want coffee or tea?"

"Coffee, and since it's late, make it decaf."

Ethan followed his mom into the adjoining kitchen. "What's real whipped cream?"

"For starters, cream that is whipped." She shot him a cheesy grin.

"Like out of a can?"

"I whipped it myself."

He knit his brow. "I like the stuff in the can."

"Yes, I know. I've seen you shooting the contents into your mouth."

Ethan's face blanched. "Oh. Sorry, Mom."

Erin roughed up his hair. "You're a ten-year-old boy. You're supposed to do stuff like that."

"Almost eleven, Mom. Like in five weeks. Are you going to have a party?"

She wanted to do something special for Ethan's birthday, but she wasn't sure how to squeeze in one more thing. *Maybe I can do one of those parties where the kids do trampolines or go skating or something so all I need to do is bring a cake. Or maybe they do cakes too. Or I could have it at Crayola—that would work really well. He's not too old yet.*

"Mom, your phone is ringing. Mom!"

"Oh, right." She reached for the instrument on her kitchen desk and seeing the caller, her heart skipped. "Hi,

Paul."

"Hi, Erin. How are you?"

She noted the lightness of his voice. "I'm well and yourself?"

"Just fine. I hope I'm not interrupting dinner."

She realized how much she would have liked to have him there. "No, we're just finishing. My dad is here."

"I'll bet he's enjoying his time with you." He spoke as someone intimately acquainted with her family situation. "My friend Andy is at my place—he's also one of the stone masons on your list to interview for the Kichline Center. I was wondering if you might have some time tonight, but …"

Just what she needed. Another contractor. "We're about to have dessert. Why don't you bring him over for some pie, and we can talk—if you don't mind my dad being here?"

"That's a great idea." His eagerness reminded her of Ethan when he tore open a new pack of Pokemon cards.

They sat at the dining room table, except for Ethan who had grown bored of discussions about bricks and river rocks. Toby, however, had kept a vigil at Tony's side as Erin's father sneaked pits of pie crust. Although she wasn't crazy about her dog being fed from the table, she didn't think one night would result in a lifelong vice.

"So, where exactly is this building?" Tony asked, clearly not tracking with the plan for the old tavern's development or Erin's role in the project. She had tried to explain this to him before, but he'd never followed up with questions, just looked past her until he started talking about football or the hassle he'd had picking up a prescription.

"Just a few doors up Northampton Street from the Sigal Museum, on the same side."

"I never went to that museum, but I wanted to be there for Erin's talk. I was sick, though."

"Do you remember the Little Mister, Little Sister store?" Erin asked.

"The one with the mechanical horse and lollipops?"

She smiled to think he remembered a sweet little detail from her childhood. Her mother and Grammy Ott were the only ones who had taken her shopping for clothes and shoes. "Yes, that's the place."

"And what's happening there?"

Andy, a trim fellow on the short side, looked over stylish glasses at Tony, then at Erin. She could almost read his thoughts—*How can her father not know what's going on?*

"My dad is just getting on board with all of this," she said, her cheeks flushing. "Maybe you could explain things to him, Paul." *He's more likely to listen to a man.*

Paul gave her a soothing look. He understood. He got her.

"Well, Tony, underneath the exterior of that old store are the original walls and floor plan of what was one of Easton's most important public houses—or taverns. Erin's celebrated ancestor, Peter Kichline, built the inn back in the early 1750s when the village was just beginning to form. Some of the first court sessions were held there, and it's likely when Benjamin Franklin came to Easton during a stressful time between the colonists and the Native Americans, he stayed with Erin's family."

"Well, I'll be …!

"Isn't that amazing, Dad?"

"Lafayette College is in the process of purchasing and restoring the building to its original state, and it will become a center for the study of colonial Easton history, with Erin as its director."

"You can be mighty proud of your daughter," Andy said.

"I am."

Erin blinked back tears.

They sat in the family room with mugs of hot cider after Paul had taken Tony and Andy home. Right after Paul returned, Ethan had gone upstairs to take a shower.

"So, what did you think of Andy?"

"He's easy to talk to, and I like his opinions about how the work should progress, but also how he leaves room for other people's ideas." She added, "I didn't understand most of what he said, though. Um, Paul, I don't understand one fourth of these technicalities."

He breathed in through his nose and sat further back, gazing at her. "I wondered if you might feel like the proverbial fish out of water. Why wouldn't you? You're a historian, not an engineer."

"Fish out of water, a Kardashian at Walmart."

He smiled at her humor, then went quiet for a long moment. "In my opinion, you're far better suited to being a curator than a renovation expert."

"I've never felt so in over my head before, Paul, but I don't want Herman to think I'm being lazy or don't want to run the center." She was laying all her other cards on the table, so why not go for the entire deck? When she finished telling him about Derek McCutcheon's proposal,

Paul nodded, thoughtful.

She tilted her head. "What are you thinking?"

"I couldn't be more proud of you. This opportunity to work closely with McCutcheon is amazing. Things like this don't happen to many people. Most writers, like me, just sort of plod along and are happy to see one copy of our book disappear from the shelves every month."

"I know, and I am excited, as well as honored."

"As for the renovation—my dad always told me to play to my strengths, and his advice has helped me make pretty good decisions. When I decided several years ago to go part time with my law practice and pursue writing local history, this was a guiding principle. Maybe this could be valuable to you."

"So, writing is a strength, and teaching visitors about my ancestor and Easton's history are strengths, but deciding how to repoint 18th-century stonework is not?"

He nodded, his lips pressed together.

Her heart pounded. "What about Herman, though? What would I even suggest to him? This might be a package deal, and then what?"

"What comes to mind is the idea of turning over this phase of the project to someone with experience in restoring colonial buildings. You would still be available to advise them and make aesthetic decisions, but you wouldn't actually begin the work of directing the center until the reno was nearing completion, which will be about a year from now, at least. That would give you more time to work on your book, and …" he looked into her eyes, a shy boy. "… maybe other things."

Her spirit lifted. "Do you think Herman will go for such a plan?"

"I believe there's a good chance he will."

"And if he doesn't?"

"Then the burden will be on him and the school to come up with a better one. He's a smart man, Erin. On some level, he realizes your talents are being put to the wrong use. I suspect this is all a matter of getting caught up in the excitement of a worthy project without thinking through all the details."

Toby, lying at Paul's feet, snorted. Erin looked at Paul, and they both started laughing. When he took her hand in his rough one, she eased into his strength.

He spoke quietly. "Are you okay?"

She knew he wasn't talking about the job. "I am, Paul. Actually, there's something else I want to tell you." She dropped her gaze. "You see, I've been, well, spooked about, um, a few things. I needed to work through them."

A moment later, "And you're not any longer?"

"I am not." She met his eyes, lingering.

"That's good to hear." He rubbed his thumb gently across the top of her hand.

"Paul?"

"Yes?"

"I'm okay now, about us. I'm ready to move forward."

His face beamed from within. "Are you sure? If you need more time ..."

"No, I don't." She nestled against his chest, rising and falling with his steady breathing. "I'm glad you didn't give up on me."

He grinned, reminding her once again of B.J. Hunnicutt on M*A*S*H. "Why in the world would I do that? You're the pearl of great price."

"I've got my mind set on you" started playing on Ethan's

radio from upstairs. They smiled at each other, then Paul gathered her in his arms and sealed their bond with a kiss.

CHAPTER EIGHT

He wasn't sure what to expect as he stood at Lewis Gordon's door, although a desire to see his old friend and colleague compelled him. Despite his current drama, Easton's first lawyer had been a mainstay to Peter in the aftermath of Margaretta and Anna's deaths, a man of similar sorrows, acquainted with the grief of losing his own wife. He'd also stood by Peter when a loudmouth citizen had accused him of using his support as a member of the Pennsylvania Assembly to slow the march to independence in return for a bribe.

Gordon's long-time housekeeper *Frau* Neuss answered Peter's knock, her face a patchwork of conflict. "*Oh, Colonel Kichline, ich bin so froh, Sie zu sehen!*"

He removed his hat. "*Ich freue mich, dich auch su sehen.*"

She didn't automatically invite him in, standing there in her virtually toothless, gray-haired state.

"Is Mr. Gordon in?"

"*Ja.*" Wrinkles nestled along a downward turn of her mouth.

"Do you think he might desire to see me?"

She wore indecision like a garment.

"I see." Before he could decide what to do next, he heard a voice behind her.

"Who is calling, Mrs. Neuss?"

"*Es ist der Oberst.*"

"Speak English, woman!"

Peter aimed his words over the housekeeper's shoulder. "It's Peter Kichline, Mr. Gordon."

"Kichline, eh? Come in then."

Frau Neuss stepped aside, and Peter ducked to avoid slamming his head against the low door frame. The house lay in darkened repose as if asleep, the mantel clock ticking uneasy seconds as he encountered Gordon in the hallway and followed the bent figure into his office. He sat when his old friend waved toward the chair Peter had always occupied, then took a seat behind his desk.

"I wasn't sure if I'd be seeing you. Or if I might be welcome should I attempt to visit." His voice brandished an edge.

"You're always welcome in my home."

"Then you're in a distinct minority." Gordon struggled to light a pipe with a shaking hand, the smoke a garland about his head. "You're looking well considering."

Peter couldn't say the same for his friend, a man a few years younger than himself but looking as though he could be Peter's father. Deep lines and hoary hair had sprouted in the months Peter had been away.

Gordon's voice became husky. "I'm glad you made it back. You must've gone through hell."

"Thank you. My main concern was for my men, and now, their families."

"What was the loss for, then, Colonel?" Gordon thrust his upper body forward, the Scottish accent of his youth returning. "Weren't we all bloody deluded into thinking we could defeat the British?"

The words chilled Peter, but he met them with resolve. "With all due respect, Mr. Gordon, I believe ours is a

Sacred Cause. No matter how powerful our enemy may seem, Providence fights our battles."

He glared. "You still believe that? Well, I don't think Providence, or General Washington, are doing a very good job."

An invisible wall shot up between them. How strange to find someone else inhabiting his old friend's house, his very body. What had happened to Gordon, or was he always like this underneath? Peter rose and gently waved away a tray of refreshments. "No, thank you, *Frau* Neuss. I am just going." He turned to his friend. "My door remains open to you."

The lawyer harrumphed. "Haven't you heard? I'm under house arrest as a suspected Tory."

"Nevertheless, my offer, and my friendship, stand."

When Peter entered the glow of his own home, he encountered the females laden with baskets, wearing their cloaks and bonnets. The sight of them cheered him after the disheartening interview with Lewis Gordon.

"And where might you be headed?"

Catherine spoke up. "We're taking food and supplies to a few families."

"Would you like some help?"

His wife's eyes widened. "I don't think after going out, you're up to it."

His aching arm and a mild throb at his temples indicated he should rest, but he dearly wanted to see the families of the men who'd served him and their country at Brooklyn. He bowed from the waist. "I am at your service." Closing her eyes, she acquiesced.

For the rest of the afternoon, those they visited hailed and greeted him, a far cry from Gordon's reception. Conrad Fartenius brightened at the sight of his colonel, who took his wounded private for a short walk to the Delaware and back, reliving their happier days with the Flying Camp. Next, Peter and his family took provisions to his fallen tailor's cabin, where Mrs. Chatterfield and her two daughters received them and their offerings.

"I'd love to help at the hospital, Mrs. Kichline," the widow told Catherine. "Please do call for me the next time you go."

"Why, that's very generous of you, Mrs. Chatterfield."

"It's the least I can do for the men." She looked down, twisting her apron. "I can honor my husband this way."

Mrs. John Arndt, whose husband who continued in a New York prison, displayed a similar bent to Christina Chatterfield, except she also wanted to tend to the war prisoners. "My husband is being cared for by others, with little I can do for him directly. By helping the wounded, I feel as if I'm helping him."

Peter dragged himself across his own threshold as the shadows spread over the parlor, refreshed in spirit, though physically exhausted. Despite Lewis Gordon, patriotism was alive and well in the village of Easton.

"Come, Robert, you need to be among men just now." Peter grabbed his friend's beefy arm, interrupting the fervent pacing as groans radiated from Mrs. Traill's room.

Joe looked at the Scotsman, repeating what Peter had

told him during his son Abraham's birth nearly a year ago. "Yes, Mr. Traill, sir, this be no place for men."

Traill stopped in his tracks as if splashed by cold spring water. "You are very right, lad." He turned to Peter. "Does this ever get any easier?"

He shook his head. "I'm afraid not, my friend."

They followed Traill to the hallway and plucked their tricorns from their perches. "Where to?" the expectant father asked.

"Let's go to *Frau* Eckert's tavern for pepper pot."

"Oooooh! Aaaaah!"

Joe's jaw dropped. "Let's be on our way, sirs!"

Peter and Traill didn't need convincing.

He was pleased to see *Frau* Eckert smiling.

Herr Kichline! *Wie schön, dich zu sehen!*

"And I am very glad to see you again as well. How are you today?"

"My children and I are all right." She paused, smiling up into his face. "You are still looking thin. Are you, in fact, well?"

"Yes, *Frau* Eckert, I am well, *danke.*"

"I can't begin to thank you enough for cleaning up the courthouse. I hated to see its rundown condition. Bless you."

"I was glad to oversee the project."

She stood straighter, suddenly all business, and bossiness. "Now then, you can join your friends over there." She gestured toward a large table toward the back room's fire place. "Mr. Traill, every one of your wife's friends seem to be attending her, and every one of their *Ehemänner* are here to be fed. Just make yourselves at home, and I will bring the pepper pot and lamb."

"*Viele dank, Frau* Eckert."

"*Du bist sehr willkommen.*"

He followed Trail through the crowded public house to the back table, his recovering body and spirit still overwhelmed by so much activity but intensely grateful to be among the living. He was pleased to see not only Robert Levers, who seemed to be everywhere at once, but also Pastor Rodenheimer and George Taylor. Everyone turned toward him, Joe, and Traill as they approached.

"Hail, Father Traill!" Levers announced with his usual flair. "Come join us as we await the birth of your second child. Colonel Kichline, so good to see you." He looked down at the boy with him. "Good day, Joe."

"Hello, Mr. Sir." Then he took off toward the kitchen, presumably to see a friend who worked for *Frau* Eckert.

Levers elbowed Peter's side as he took a seat. "I think that boy needs a good lesson in English."

He winced. Would people never stop bumping his sore spot? "We are making progress, Mr. Levers. He has finally been cured of saying 'My hair."

Levers's laughter boomed through the tavern. "Sit down, sit down everyone. We are, as you can see, Easton's bachelors for this auspicious night. Tell me, Traill, how are you holding up?" Clearly, Levers regarded himself as the master of ceremonies.

Traill shook his head. "I will never get used to this."

Peter greeted the others at the table, including his old friend, George Taylor.

"Colonel Kichline, how very good to see you out and

about!" He shook hands with the ironmaster-turned-signer of the Declaration of Independence. "You are a sight for very sore eyes. I have followed your movements with the greatest of interest, as well as my earnest prayers."

Peter nodded and closed his eyes. "For that, I thank you, my friend."

"You appear a bit thinner, maybe a little grayer around the temples, but then, time and circumstance do not permit any of us to remain the same." Taylor pointed to his own silvery locks.

"I am, of course, eager to be of further service to my country."

Taylor leaned back, looping his thumbs in his waistcoat pockets. "I understand you've been paroled, awaiting an exchange with a British officer of equal rank."

"You are correct, Mr. Taylor."

"And I also understand these exchanges are mulishly slow. Let me see what I might be able to do—if there's any way I can speed the process."

"I will be most obliged to you."

Taylor harrumphed. "We need your services as much as you need to feel useful. However, we need to make sure you are well enough to be in the saddle again." His shoulders stooped. "Of course, I'm not sure how much weight I carry these days in such matters."

Peter sipped his ale, then put the tankard back on the table. "You appear to be under a strain, my friend."

"Perhaps it's the lack of strain I'm feeling. I suppose you haven't heard I wasn't reelected to the Pennsylvania Assembly," Taylor related.

"Not reelected?" This was news, and hardly pleasant.

"However, I have been appointed to our Supreme

Executive Council, which has been formed to govern under our state's new constitution."

Peter nodded. "Then our leaders have chosen well."

Frau Eckert appeared bearing piping hot bowls of her signature soup, which she personally served to the men at their table. One of her children followed with loaves of warm bread. He couldn't help but smile as she positioned an especially generous serving before him, remembering how he had dreamt of this particular meal while existing on moldy bread and maggot-infested meat.

There was still no news of Traill's baby by eight-thirty, and Peter was winding down, in need of his own home and his own bed. He'd caught himself more than once willing his eyelids to stop closing in the middle of a conversation. Joe appeared at his side.

"Oh, hello, Joe, are you ready to be off?"

"Yes, my sir."

He rose from the table. "Mr. Traill, I will be going home now, but I am available to you at any hour."

Traill got up and shook Peter's hand. "Thank you, my friend."

"I will be eager to hear of the child's birth."

"You will be the first to know."

Peter thanked the tavern keeper for the fine repast and headed out to Northampton Street, which though quiet, pulsed behind closed doors with family life, wounded soldiers, and prisoners of war. He saw a lone figure walking toward them from the direction of the ferry, a familiar figure. He suddenly forgot his exhaustion. "Peter!"

"My sir should you …"

For the first time since the battle, he ran, and nothing ached as he beheld the face of his oldest son, glowing yet mingled with unspoken heaviness.

"Father!"

They met near the courthouse, shook hands, then embraced with abandon.

CHAPTER NINE

They sat in Skillman Library's café sipping coffee, killing time until her ten-fifteen meeting with Herman Weinreich. Erin stared blankly at a sign announcing chocolate croissants and mint-flavored shaken tea. Her right foot pumped, keeping rhythm to her angst.

"What if he isn't understanding? What if he tells me to just forget the whole thing?"

Paul covered her ice-cold hand. "He's not going to tell you to forget the whole thing, sweetheart. I can't guarantee his reaction, but I've always found Herman to be a fair man with a solid dose of human feeling."

"You have, have you?"

Erin and Paul looked up to find the history department chairman standing next to their table. The normally unflappable Paul stood so quickly Erin had to steady their coffee mugs even as she tried to find any trace of the jaw she'd dropped onto the tiled floor.

"Good morning, Herman," Paul said, a little too loudly as they shook hands. "We were just talking about you."

"So I gathered." Weinreich's ruddy face carried an unmistakable hint of mirth. "Good morning, Erin."

What flowed out of her mouth sounded very much like speaking in tongues.

"May I join you, or would you like to head over to my office? I just came in for a cuppa before our meeting."

Erin cast a look in Paul's direction, unsure which venue would be the best place for the conversation they needed to have. Maybe they should just stay put. The upbeat atmosphere might take some of the sting out of any tension they might generate. "I'm fine here."

"Good. I'll just get my drink and come back."

Paul hijacked a chair from a neighboring table to make room, then he and Erin sat quietly until the stocky professor returned.

"Well, how are you two coming along?"

"Quite well," Paul said, and Erin nodded.

"What did you want to see me about? Is everything okay with the building?"

Erin looked to Paul, then began talking. "Well, things are okay with the building, but that's not what I wanted to talk to you about—what we wanted to talk to you about."

He removed the lid from his cup of tea and leaned back. "Fire away."

She dove in head first. "I don't know how to say this, Herman, I've been over this dozens of times in my head. There just isn't any easy way to ..." Seeing something like alarm in his expression, she blurted the heart of the matter. "I'm feeling overwhelmed." She quickly added, "You helped so much by relieving me of my teaching duties, but I've come to realize I'm no architect, fixer-upper, or restoration expert. My expertise in plumbing ends with unclogging a toilet, and as far as electronics go, I get confused about which light switches to use in my house." Her breath was shallow, as if she'd just sprinted from the Delaware River up to the Sigal Museum. "I'm in over my head."

Weinreich drummed his fingertips on the table, seeming to find the contents of his tea vastly interesting.

She wanted to reassure him. "I love this project, and I want to be the director of the Kichline Center. I just don't feel very good about spearheading the renovation."

When he looked up, the professor offered a crescent moon of a smile to one of his all-time favorite students. "I think I owe you an apology, Miss Erin."

She jerked back. "Oh?"

"I should have realized this wasn't your skill set. I was just so enthusiastic about the project and your being the director I didn't think all the details through. Of course you don't know anything about wiring and permits and …"

"Dry wall."

"Or dry wall." He was silent for several minutes, clearly considering what might be done. "Do you have a solution, or do you want me to come up with one?"

"I think we may," Paul said. He crossed his arms over his chest, looking relaxed. "Erin and I have been discussing the possibility of having her sort of bench-warming, watching the action, offering help when needed while someone else runs the game. Then when the project is completed, she would take over—in about a year."

Weinreich was nodding. "A year seems about right. Your plan sounds good, but I'm wondering who we would get, and if you'd want to be teaching again in the meantime, Erin."

She was ready with her response. "At this particular time in my life, not teaching is giving me freedom to collaborate on the book with Derek McCutcheon, one which, by the way, is only the first of many."

The professor's eyebrows raised. "Congratulations!"

"Thank you. I'm still pinching myself over the opportunity to continue working with him. I'm also busy with my parents' needs, and my son's, not to mention organizing a wedding."

"That's one full plate, young lady."

"Yes. As for someone to direct the renovation, I know a woman who has done this before, in Easton, and is amazing." She paused. "Connie Pierce, who's a volunteer at the Sigal Museum now and regent of the George Taylor Chapter of the DAR."

"You say she's done this before?"

"She oversaw the Bachmann Publick House renovation several years ago."

"I'd like to talk with her then." He grinned. "You have mentioned this to her?"

"Yes, and she's interested."

"Erin, I must be frank. I'm not sure what the pay would be like for you in this meantime, when you're involved in an advisory capacity only, or even if you'd be able to keep your office here. I'd have to discuss that with President Drexler."

"I completely understand, and I'm okay with not receiving pay or having an office. The McCutcheon project is more than enough, and I have a home office."

"All right, then." He sipped tea while students came and went around them, their voices making the silence between them more comfortable. "I do wonder, Erin, with this book turning into more than one project, will you even be able to direct the Kichline Center?"

She didn't want to think about that—at all. Of course she could. Couldn't she? Each represented the fulfillment of her career dreams, but she wasn't two people, just one with a lot of family demands and a new husband on the horizon. What should she say? What could she say? Her words raced ahead of her thoughts. "Naturally, I plan to do both."

Herman just looked at her, each of them knowing the best-laid plans of mice and men often go awry.

Erin was shoving the last of the darks into the washing machine when her cell phone rang in the kitchen. She didn't see Toby trolling by her feet and tripped, wind-milling to keep upright. "Really, Toby!" He regarded her impassively and followed her to the table. "Hello, this is Erin."

"Hello, Erin, this is Louise Bassett."

For a moment, she forgot what she was supposed to call her future mother-in-law. "Mrs." seemed stilted, "Louise" too informal, and "Mom" both presumptuous and premature. She'd figure out what to do about this later. "Oh, hello! How very nice to hear from you. How are you?"

"I'm doing quite well, thank you, and yourself?"

Erin went to her office, sinking into her favorite chair, Toby at her feet. "I am just fine."

"And Ethan?"

"Ethan's doing really well. He's still glowing after scoring the winning goal in a soccer match yesterday."

"How nice for him!" She paused. "Paul tells me things are working out with your impossible schedule."

"Yes, and I'm so grateful. My department head met with the college president, and they decided to go with my plan, well, the plan Paul and I came up with."

"And what is that?"

Outside, a riding mower started up. The lawn service would be doing her grass next. "My friend Connie will be taking over the restoration of the Kichline Center building, and I'll be on hand for input and public relations. Herman, my department chair, is allowing me to use my office, although I need to share with the professor who replaced me. They'll also pay a stipend."

"I don't think you could have done a better job of settling this matter. I'm so pleased for you."

Erin smiled, feeling comfortable with Louise. "The next morning I got on the scale and half expected to be ten pounds lighter. I'd been carrying such a heavy load."

"And were you?"

Erin heard the lilt in Louise's voice. "I'm afraid not."

Paul's mother sighed. "Those pounds can be monstrously difficult to shed. Of course, you don't have extra to get rid of like I do."

Erin couldn't recall a single place on Louise's frame requiring a diet or weight training. "I think you look perfect. Anyway, the wedding plans and my writing are coming along beautifully now that I'm not distracted and worried about heading up a restoration."

"Wonderful! Before I circle back to the wedding, how are your parents?"

"Pretty good. My mom's in overall good health, except for her visual impairment, and my dad, well, he's definitely slowed down since his heart attack, but he's taking better care of himself."

She nudged Toby when he began snoring in tune with some inner music.

"Well then, Tim and I have been discussing our wedding gift to you and Paul, and if you have no objections, we'd like to cover the expenses of a honeymoon."

Erin absorbed Louise's offer, then her gratitude flowed.

"What a generous gift! I hardly know what to say."

"We've waited a long time for Paul to find the right woman, and this is our way of adding our blessing. Have you decided where you want to go?"

"Not just yet."

"Well, the sky's the limit, but I doubt you'll honeymoon at the International Space Station."

Erin let out a laugh. Louis had a sense of humor.

"She what?" Paul looked like a young boy who'd caught his first fish, a big one.

"Offered to pay for our honeymoon, anywhere we want to go. She said, 'The sky's the limit,' then proceeded to say that's because she doubted we'd want to go to the International Space Station."

Paul grinned, closed his eyes, shook his head. "That sounds just like something she would say." He reached across Toby on the sofa and folded Erin's hand in his. "Even though I think the gift is extravagant, we should probably accept. They aren't usually given to big presents, so this must mean a lot to them."

"I agree, then."

"So, where do you want to go?"

"Gosh, I don't know." She laughed. "You've probably never read *Anne of Green Gables*."

"I can't say I have."

"When someone offers her a magnificent opportunity, she says something like, 'I feel as though I've been handed the moon and don't know quite what to do with it.'"

"I feel as though God handed me better than the moon

when he led me to you."

"Aww." She leaned over and kissed him, lingering. The warmth she experienced definitely put her in a mood to discuss honeymoons.

"Maybe we should brainstorm about places we'd like to go, then narrow the list."

"Spoken like a true lawyer. I just happen to have a legal pad on the side table." She reached for the yellow, lined tablet, and he grabbed a pen from the side table.

"So, what places excite you?" he asked.

"I have to tell you, I'm not much of a beach resort kind of person, like those tropical getaways in the Caribbean."

"Good! I am so not into that. I don't mind a beach, but not an all-out resort." He paused. "To be honest, I also dislike the idea of a cruise."

"Really?"

Paul nodded. "Really. Lounging like a lizard on deck after eating myself into a food coma … not for me."

"I'm relieved."

"Great!"

"I also happen to get sea sick. You know, though, I see ads for river cruises, like the ones in Europe, and I think one of those would be nice. They're not all about sunbathing and smorgasbords."

He pressed his lips together, nodding. "I think I'd like that too. I've always wanted to see more of Europe. Have you ever been?"

"Once in college, I went to Germany for a few weeks, taking a class. I didn't know then how deep my German roots were." She popped up. "I'd love to see Switzerland, where my Kichline family comes from, and England and Wales where my mom's dad's side is from."

"My Bassett family is from England, and I only ever went to Austria for a week a long time ago, skiing."

"Where's your mom's side from?"

"I think France and Holland."

She waved her arms, and Toby opened one eye. "What do you think? Do we have a plan, or should we keep brainstorming?"

"I guess we could add a few other places to the list but put this at the top." He laughed, looked down at the floor. "You may find this really strange, but I've never been to Williamsburg."

"Oh, Paul, that's a shame. Williamsburg is so wonderful. Jim and I used to take Ethan there at least once a year."

"I'll bet you have some great memories."

"Yes, I do." She smiled at him. "And I'm ready to make new ones."

He was quiet for a few minutes. "Tell me what you think of this. We could go to Europe, maybe on one of those river cruises, for seven to ten days. Then right before school starts, we could take Ethan to Williamsburg, our first family trip." He quickly added, "Unless you think he would dislike going someplace with me that was so specific to you and Jim." He looked into Erin's eyes, and as one, they echoed, "Let's ask him!"

They did, when he came home from school. Ethan listened to their tentative plans, then he was quiet for a long moment. "Where will I stay while you're on that cruise?"

"Probably with Alana and Neal. Would you like to stay with them?"

His face perked up. "That would be great!"

They were at the one-yard line. "And what about Williamsburg right before school starts?"

"Williamsburg? Like where we used to go? Busch Gardens and the water park?"

"Yup," Erin said.

"And the colonial places?"

"Yup."

"Cool. I'd really like to go there with you."

"I think we have a plan," Paul said with a smile.

CHAPTER TEN

Joe had banked the fire in the parlor and gone to the kitchen for the food *Frau* Hamster had left for the men of the house before going with the women of the house to the Traills'. Since little Elizabeth and baby Abraham were with the females, the Kichline home was uncommonly quiet, for which Peter was deeply grateful. There was so much to say to his eldest son and, no doubt, so much to hear. The last time they had seen each other had been under far different circumstances, the two of them heading into battle under a searing summer sun.

"I stopped by my house first," Peter Jr. said, "but Sarah wasn't there. I decided to come here, but then I saw you."

Peter smiled. "Much to my intense pleasure and gratitude."

Joe laid a tray before the young man with so much food the contents were spilling over the sides of a generous plate.

"Thank you, Joe," he said. "Did you empty the kitchen?"

"No, sir, Lieutenant Peter, just brought what Miz Hamster said give to us men." He looked toward Peter Sr. "Can I be doing anything else, Sir Colonel?"

"No, thank you, Joe. You've had a big day. Why don't you go up to bed?"

"Oh, all right then." He turned to Peter Jr. "It's mighty nice to see you again, Sir Lieutenant."

"And I'm glad to see you as well, Joe." He nodded

toward the tray. "Thank you." After Joe disappeared, Peter Jr. commented on his appearance. "He's shot up since I left. How's he coming along?"

"Quite well. He's showing a knack for food preparation, and he enjoys helping William with his carpentry. I have no worries about his future. I'll keep him under my roof until he's ready to go out on his own, as a free man."

"That's good to know."

As his son bowed his head in thanks over the food, Peter examined him. *Definitely thinner, but then there never did seem to be enough food for the soldiers. His hair is looking disheveled. He hasn't shaved in a few days, maybe more, his hair was always light and fine.* He glanced at the shoes. *Pathetic. I'll bet there are holes on the bottoms to match the ones on the toes.* His uniform was torn in several places, and smudged. He smelled like the courthouse pond on a hot day in July.

They made small talk while Peter Jr. ate, his father telling his own story of losing so many of their company in the battle, of being wounded, captured, and imprisoned.

"What a beastly time you all had. What about Mr. Wiggins? Did he make it?" Peter slowly shook his head. "Ah, too bad. Perhaps I should be asking who did get out alive."

Peter named names, then gave an update on the men who were recovering in Easton. The clock chimed ten. "Are you exhausted? You are welcome to stay here. Jacob has been with Andrew most nights at the mill house. Who knows when the women will return."

"I'd like that, Father." He looked down at his hands, dark under the fingernails. "*Frau* Hamster would have a fit if she saw this grubby mess sleeping under her roof."

"She would be thrilled to see you, and besides, this is my roof."

He glanced up, his blue eyes looking so much like they had after his mother's death ten years earlier, pleading, searching for an answer. "Father, there's something I must tell you before I try to sleep, something I don't know if you've heard about me."

He sat up straight, the gathering cobwebs dispersing from his mind. "I've heard almost nothing since my return—I'm just beginning to emerge from my recovery. All I know is you managed to escape after the battle and had joined Hand's Battalion."

Peter Jr. nodded, staring toward the fireplace in which flames crackled and sparks shot upward. He was quiet for so long Peter wondered whether he might have been wounded or seen or done something terrible and found talking about the experience difficult. He braced himself, praying to be wise. Finally, his son spoke. "Father, there was a good deal of confusion right after the battle, and I was … I was brought before a court martial."

"A court martial! Whatever for?" His wits scattered to the four winds. This was not on the list of possibilities. *My son, court martialed!* He wanted to keen, to run toward the Delaware and dive in, anything to be rid of the horror this news brought. He found himself panting with the exertion of his jostled spirit. He needed to calm himself, to be able to listen and not bring his own judgment into play before knowing the facts.

"Someone brought a charge against me of cowardice." His voice was both iron and thin glass.

"That's preposterous!" Peter formed a fist and slammed it into the palm of his left hand. If there was anything he knew about his oldest son, Peter Jr. was no coward. "Who would do such a thing?" The face of John Musch appeared in his mind's eye, but John Musch had been thrown out of the militia after charging Peter with using his influence to slow the Pennsylvania Assembly's march toward independence.

"I don't know, Father, but Major Pobst and Adjutant John Spangenburg were brought up on the same charges." He paused, his lips tight, nostrils flaring. "We were said to have abandoned our posts at the first sign of the enemy's approach."

Peter was out of his seat, pacing floorboards that creaked under his heavy steps. "This is outrageous! You were with me. I saw you." He muttered to himself, "'Abandoned your post' indeed." He turned to face his son, inches from his ghostly face. "You conducted yourself with nothing but dignity and valor."

"Then you're not … you're not ashamed?" His face was that of a candle whose flame had been snuffed.

"Ashamed!" The furies had been unleashed. "As if I could ever be ashamed of you." His voice caught. "I could be no more ashamed of you than I could of myself for being wounded and captured. I'd like to see the man who charged you with this outrage."

"So would I, Father."

Peter paced until he wore out himself—and his anger. Then he sat and ran his hand over his face, leaning forward. "What happened, son?"

"We were taken to some woman's home, and a court martial was set up in her dining room. There were several officers in charge and a Colonel Silliman presiding."

"Decent fellow."

"We weren't there long before they acquitted

Spangenberg and me, the charges against us being so out of line."

"I'm glad they were able to see reason. What happened to Pobst?"

"Acquitted of cowardice, but then there was an additional charge of some kind of misconduct, and I'm not sure how they ruled." Peter Jr. kneaded his fingers.

They were silent for some time, each keeping his own thoughts.

"Father?" Peter Jr. whispered.

"Yes, son?"

"What if I'm no longer respected in this community?"

Peter reached out and placed his hand on his son's shoulder. "There is no reason for such a thing to happen. You conducted yourself with the utmost bravery under withering conditions. Perhaps you were mistaken for someone else, but to my knowledge, no one under my command comported himself with anything but courage."

"Thank you." His voice was husky. "But, Father, you know how people have a way of turning things upside down. What if, what if someone should try to damage my character?"

His voice came as a growl between his lips. "Let such a man come to me!"

Peter frowned when he saw Peter Schneider standing next to his comely daughter in the downstairs hallway reaching for the basket she was carrying. Didn't he have work to do at the mills? He cleared his throat as he lowered the newspaper he'd been reading.

"Papa, Mr. Schneider and I are going to visit the prisoners," she said, eyes shining.

Peter stood, folding and placing the paper on his chair. "I should like to go with you this morning, Susannah. I haven't had an opportunity to see the conditions there or speak to those in charge."

The look she exchanged with Schneider wasn't lost on Peter. "Uh, of course, Papa."

"Schneider, aren't you needed at the mills?"

The indentured servant's brown eyes darted from his feet to the back of the parlor. "Why, yes, of course. Mr. Andrew said he could spare me for an hour to assist Miss Susannah."

"I will do the assisting today."

Schneider handed the basket to Peter, who'd expected the lightness of bread loaves and instead, felt the heft of cannonballs. What had the women packed in here anyway? "Thank you, sir." He bowed to Susannah. "Miss Kichline, I bid you good day."

She nodded, appearing to be biting her lower lip. Schneider left through the front door, and Peter reached for his hat and coat.

"Don't you need your walking stick, Papa?"

"Perhaps not today. We're only going a short distance."

"Would you like me to carry the basket?"

He swallowed a retort. "No, thank you, dear one. I can manage, although what is in here?"

She smiled as they went outside, a wind gust snatching at their head gear. Susannah pulled her cape around herself and held onto her hat. "There is bread, of course, and then pickles and beets and cheese."

He smiled down at her. "I'm happy to know you care so

much about these men."

"I know they're the enemy, Papa, but they are also German, like us, and so far away from their homes. I try to imagine how they must feel, and I am moved to help as I can."

He squeezed her shoulder with his free hand.

The prison was a block from Peter's home yet seemed to be in another realm altogether. Several dozen men filled a barracks behind Colonel Hooper's house, which stood at the corner of Northampton and Julianna Streets. The stench lifting from the stone building rose to greet them, casting Peter's thoughts in the direction of the New York Sugar House in which his men had languished. He steadied himself as Susannah led him into the dank quarters. The sound of silence greeted them, a sound of despair, yet he saw a spark of life in the eyes of the men who noticed him and his daughter enter. She nodded toward two of them.

"*Guten morgen Herr Fleischer. Wie geht's?*"

Danke. Mir geht es gut, Fraulein Kichline," said a man whose dark hair was marbled with pieces of straw.

"Colonel! Miss Kichline! Good morning!" Robert Hooper appeared before them, and Susannah took the basket from her father so the men could shake hands. "I'm glad to see you." He whispered to the side. "The men have been especially downcast today, which naturally does nothing for my own disposition."

"I am glad to be of service." Peter glanced about the jammed quarters while his daughter began emptying the contents of her basket onto a common table. He hated to let her out of his sight, but then he figured no one would be bold enough to accost a woman in the presence of her father and prison commandant. "How many men are here?"

"We have thirty-six at present. Two died this last week."

His neck hair prickled. "Sickness?"

Hooper shook his head. "More like succumbing to wounds and weakness. Thank God, we haven't had any outbreaks. Yet."

Peter understood the "yet;" fevers always found their sinister way toward prisons and hospitals. He looked to Susannah, smiling at the men who began lining up to receive her offerings. He would put a stop to these visits when the time came.

"I was actually going to come see you later today," Hooper said. "I wrote a letter to the new Commissary of Prisoners, Elias Boudinot, on your behalf requesting the expediting of your exchange. I explained how important you are to our Cause and, therefore, your case should receive priority."

"Thank you, my friend," Peter said. "I am hopeful your words won't fall upon deaf ears."

He smiled. "Somehow I don't think they will. Mr. Boudinot is a good man, although the process of exchanging prisoners is rather cumbersome. The British have been rather mule-headed about treating us as belligerents, rather than rebels. There are also complications involving the Congress's insistence upon receiving settlements for expenses incurred for the upkeep of British prisoners." He looked around at the cheering scene. "Your daughter does wonders for these men. The light seems to come back on in their lives when she appears. You have quite a young lady there, Colonel."

"Thank you," he said with a bow. "She is a pearl of great price." He cleared his throat. "I believe I'd like to join her, if you'll excuse me."

"Yes, of course. Would you like to introduce yourself to the men, or be more informal?"

He considered this for a moment. "Perhaps I will introduce myself."

Hooper waved his hand to indicate the floor was Peter's.

He smiled at his daughter. "I wonder if I might have a word before you continue."

"Yes, of course." She put her hand in front of the table to indicate the next man in line should wait.

Guten Morgen, Männer. Ich bin Colonel Kichline, wohnhaft in Easton und gebürtiger Deutscher.

At his greeting, a murmur broke out and spread over the room, then ceased as the prisoners strained forward.

Ich war kürzlich ein Gefangener der Briten und verstehe, was du durchmachst.

At the news he'd been a British prisoner and understood their suffering, the men moved closer to hear him, their smudgy faces rapt as he promised to do what he could to help them, in spite of their opposition to the Patriot Cause.

"We are, after all, made in the image of the same God, who teaches us to look after prisoners in their distress."

He didn't see Hooper turn away and blow his nose, or the looks on the faces of the grubby men. He had his own moist eyes to deal with.

CHAPTER ELEVEN

"Wow."

"Yes. Wow."

The chirpy saleswoman smiled as if she were personally responsible for the spectacular view. "I don't think there's a prettier spot in Easton."

"Or dramatic," Erin said. Was she standing on top of the world, or just feeling as if she were?

Paul squeezed her hand. "Or perfect, for us."

The panoramic, cloud-strewn vista from Morgan Hill embraced the sweep of the Lehigh Valley, from western New Jersey to the distant Poconos, the mountains the Native Americans had called "endless." This territory had been under the jurisdiction of her great-great-great-great-great-great grandfather. Had he ever stood here surveying the place her dad referred to as "God's country?" She could think of no better venue for their wedding reception, a celebration of her roots, and her future with Paul.

"One of the great things about this spot is there's almost always a breeze up here, even in July." Amanda Koloski consulted her gilded clipboard. "About how many people do you expect for the ceremony? We can set up for small and medium weddings, but I have to be honest with you, if they get too big, we can feel tight."

Erin turned from the compelling scenery. "The wedding isn't going to be here."

"It's not?"

"We're getting married at First United Church of Christ."

"At what time?"

"Six-thirty," Paul said.

"An evening reception will be wonderful up here." Amanda wrote on her pad. "And you said July 28th?"

"Correct," Erin said.

"So, a reception beginning around eight?"

She turned to Paul. "I think eight is about right."

"Or, we could say seven-thirty, and people will come ahead of us for a cocktail hour if we're still taking pictures."

"Great idea! Our receptions are for five hours, and our packages include a cocktail hour. If you follow me inside, we can review the paperwork and all your options."

Erin looked to Paul for the go-ahead to book here, and he nodded. There was no need to look any further.

They sat on the front porch with glasses of white wine, Erin having a sensation roughly like going through the car wash at the foot of College Hill while standing outside her minivan.

Paul's face lacked its usual ruddiness. "Did you understand half of what Amanda said?"

"Maybe half. I'm still overwhelmed." She sipped her wine. "Are you?"

"I'd be lying if I said I wasn't." He frowned. "What did she mean by a registry?"

A little boy from up the street rode by on his bike, his dad just behind him.

"A couple chooses a specific store or go online, and they

decide what items they need to set up housekeeping. Then people can buy them as gifts."

"Do we need one?"

"What do you mean?"

"Well, you already have a well-furnished house, and I'll be bringing some things from my place."

She'd seen his condo. "Like what?"

He looked up at the porch roof and rattled off a list. "My desk and chair, books, stereo system, shelves."

She'd never considered this before and scolded herself for being self-centered. When she bought this house, she'd been thinking only of living there with her son, but now this needed to be every bit Paul's home too, including space for an office. Besides, shouldn't they have things particular to them, not just items she'd shared with Jim? "Have you thought about where to put your office?"

"How about one of the bedrooms?"

"Will you feel too out of the way?"

"Nah. But maybe when I meet clients, I could use yours now and again, that is, if you're not."

"I think that would work, Paul."

He was on a roll. "Then again, maybe I should just rent space downtown. I did that before I started focusing on my writing and research"

She tilted her head. "That makes sense too." He'd been wanting to take on more clients, and attorneys needed their own quarters.

He reached for her hand. "I don't mind using your stuff, Erin, but I understand how choosing things together would make your house our home too. So sure, let's do a registry. How do you start?"

"We can go online and start picking out what we want.

And, uh, maybe we should do some furniture shopping together as well."

"Furniture shopping?" His brow puckered.

"Yes. I'd like to put my bedroom set into the guest room and choose a new one." She felt heat fill her cheeks.

Paul grinned. "Great idea."

Ethan opened the front door and thudded onto the porch. "What's up?"

"We're discussing a gift registry." She explained the concept to her pre-teen.

"You tell people what they want, and they buy it for you?"

"Yup."

"Cool." He flopped onto the porch swing. "Do they have those for birthdays?"

"I don't know."

"If so, maybe I could set one up for mine." Toby lumbered over to the swing, and Ethan pulled the lumpy dog up to sit with him.

"Just how many friends are you planning to invite?"

"Jake, and my cousins."

"That's it?" When Ethan shrugged, she asked, "Aren't there other friends?"

"I guess not."

She and Paul looked at each other sideways. "I thought you'd made some friends at school and church."

"Those are little kids at church."

She pressed. "But not at school." Had she been missing something? A creeping sense of mommy guilt ambushed her. She had been so distracted, but to neglect her child? Nothing else could be more important than raising him well.

Paul spoke up. "I didn't have a lot of friends in middle school either. Grade school and high school, yes, but not too much in those middle years."

"Why not?" Ethan asked.

"I kept to myself. Most kids didn't share my interests."

"Did you go to church?"

"Not too often."

"Oh." Ethan buried his face in his dog's ruff.

"What's this new school like for you?" Paul asked.

Erin's ears perked up, listening for any cues to her son's lack of local friendships.

"It's okay. I mean, the teachers are pretty nice, and I like my English class, and art, oh, and history, but …"

She wasn't sure how far to pursue this just now but decided to take the conversation as far as she could. "What don't you like?"

"Everything feels huge—the classes, the school, and a lot of the kids are, they're, well, mean."

Her voice came out husky. "Has anyone bullied you?"

He looked down. "No one does anything about it."

"Ethan, I, we, need to discuss these things."

"You're always busy. And you're so happy being in Easton. Don't get me wrong, I like living here, too, but school …"

The darkening sky breached her soul. Tears sprang to her eyes, and she couldn't look at Paul, who started rubbing her back. "I realize that now, Ethan, and I'm very sorry."

"That's okay."

"Thank you, but it's not okay. Nothing can get in the way of my being available for you."

A dog started barking a block away. Toby's ears perked up, and he growled.

"Mom?"

"Yes?"

"There's going to be a play next month at school, and one of the kids had to drop out. I'm thinking of trying out for his part."

Hope returned. "Oh, what a great idea! What play and what part?"

"'The Wizard of Oz,' and the part is the Cowardly Lion."

She smiled. "I think you'd do a fine job. You were wonderful in that skit at church."

"And remember when I had a small part in a play at my other school—I think in third grade?"

"I do."

"I think acting is really fun."

"I would go for the part," Paul said.

"I will." He smiled, and for Erin, the world started turning again. As for the bullying, she would need to talk to his lead teacher.

"Now, about my birthday party, did you get Crayola?"

"I did not. They were booked on your birthday, but I have another idea."

"What's that?"

"What about a retro party? There's a place called Bushkill Park where I used to go when I was a kid. Even then, it was a really old amusement park. There are a few rides, a skating rink, and a game room."

"I've never been roller skating."

"Then it's time you tried," she said. "I'll bet you didn't know my mother was a champion roller skater."

"Grammy? Really?"

"Really."

"Cool. We could invite her, and she could teach us how

to skate like she did."

Erin had a sudden image of her mother blindly careening around the rink, resulting in a fractured hip followed by a hospital stay, then one of the rehab centers on Red School Lane. She would call Crayola to see if they had an opening on the day before Ethan's birthday.

A twenty-something wedding gown salesclerk didn't sit well. What could she possibly understand about under-arm jiggles and muffin tops? Erin knew she couldn't trust herself if the young thing became condescending. When a woman about her own age flowed into the bridal salon, her face lighting up at the sight of Connie, Erin let out a long, steadying breath.

"Connie, dear!" The woman flew past several customers toward Erin's friend and kissed first one cheek, then the other. "Aren't you looking wonderful."

"As are you. I'd like you to meet Dr. Erin Miles, the bride-to-be, and her friend Melissa Grey. This is Deidre Whiting, owner of the salon."

There followed an extending of arms and hands, hellos and "nice-to-meet-yous." A line from an old song popped into Erin's head, paraphrased as she studied the bridal expert—and her hair was perfect. Actually, everything about her was polished, from her glittery high heels to her highlights. Erin glanced at her own hands, relieved to see her light colored nail polish hadn't started chipping.

"If you'll come with me, we'll do the consultation in the back."

Erin imagined a room filled with empty boxes and one-armed mannequins, but the reality included silver brocade club chairs, glass tables, and an open bottle of Prosecco. A plate of cheese, crostini, and fruit lay next to gilded paper napkins featuring the salon's logo, fanned of course. Deidre motioned Erin to a larger version of the chairs, something like the throne of an obscure European monarch. Melissa glanced at Erin, her eyes signaling, "Wow."

"Now, Dr. Miles, you just sit there, and we'll have a nice chat over refreshments about what kind of wedding dress you've been dreaming of." She began pouring glasses of the sparkling wine and handing them around.

"Please call me Erin."

Deidre flashed a very white smile. "Erin is such a lovely name."

"Thank you. As you know, this is my second marriage …" She made a mental note to buy white smile strips the next time she went to the drug store.

Melissa spoke up. "She's a widow."

"I'm so sorry."

"Yes, well, thank you. I, uh, had a big wedding the first time with all the trimmings. I don't want the same kind of floofy dress I wore back in the 90s."

"And what was that like?"

"A lot of lace. Very white."

Deidre raised an eyebrow. "So, you don't want a lot of lace or a white dress?"

Erin sipped the Prosecco, which tickled the roof of her mouth. "I know nowadays some women wear white no matter how many marriages or relationships they've had, but I'm a little old-fashioned." She gave a laugh. "Not to mention a little old."

She was pleased when her friends and Deidre got the

small joke.

"I understand. And there are options for a non-white bridal gown. Champagne is a lovely color, and I think it would play nicely against your complexion and hair."

Erin started twisting her napkin. "I'm actually thinking of, well, pink. Is there such a thing as a pink wedding gown?" She hastened to say, "I don't mean deep pink, but something really subtle."

"Yes, there are pink gowns, just as you describe. I'm going to show you some styles, each of which can be ordered in a blush tone."

Her heart fluttered as Deidre rose to sort through an assortment of gowns swathed in white garment bags, but she felt herself sinking as one-by-one she cast them off. Thirty minutes later, she apologized for being difficult. "I'm sorry, Deidre. These are beautiful dresses, but none of them seems right for me. There's either too much lace, too much bling, too much fabric, or not enough. I dislike the long sleeved gowns, but maybe the others show too much."

"Sometimes we need to step outside our comfort zones."

Erin bristled, but Deidre's next comment assuaged her.

"You seem to have a good sense of what you like to wear, so do you know what you want, or would you like me to keep trying to figure out what I think would look great?"

"I came in with a vague idea, and seeing these other dresses makes me more certain. I do love a sheath, and I'm fond of satin or silk, which tend to stand on their own. Something understated, but elegant."

Deidre smiled as she held up her right forefinger. "I'll be right back."

When the consultant returned, she unwrapped a bag to reveal a gown matching Erin's description to a "T."

She nearly jumped out of the chair. "That's it! That's the one!"

Melissa's eyes popped. "Oh, how beautiful!"

Connie nodded approval. "This is so you, Erin."

She tried on the dress, dazzled by how much she looked like a royal bride, especially after Deidre had put a sparkly comb in her hair and shoes worthy of Melania Trump on her feet. Erin was afraid to look at the price tag, but then again, there was no doubt this was the dress, once Deidre ordered the gown in pink.

Melissa gushed. "You look amazing, Erin."

"Paul is going to love this," Connie said.

Erin turned sideways and looked over her shoulder into the mirror. "Can I pull off the sleeveless thing?"

Deidre nodded. "Not all women after forty can, but you—definitely."

"Then this is the one." She managed to keep her cool when she learned the dress cost $2,000. She recalled the $750 she'd spent on her 90s dress, money she'd saved over the course of nine months by forsaking fast food and other clothing purchases.

Once the bridal gown was chosen, she and her friends moved on to their outfits, agreeing on deep, navy-blue dresses they could wear again at formal events. For the flower girl, Deidre showed them a girlish version they oohed and aahed over. With an hour to spare before Ethan got home, Erin offered to buy them a cup of coffee at Green Harvest where they practically drooled over fresh brownies in the case, deciding to split one.

"That shouldn't do too much damage," Melissa said.

Erin thought this was one of those nights when her head would make contact with the pillow, and she'd be gone in the twinkling of an eye. Moments after this became a reality, she bolted upwards at the sound of Toby howling from Ethan's room. She careened across her floor, bumping into Jim's tall dresser, then righted herself and managed not to inflict anymore damage to her person in the hallway lit by a street lamp. She stood in her son's doorway, the dog perched on the edge of the bed. "For heaven's sake, what's going on?"

"I don't know. He just started yowling Mom. Maybe he has to go to the bathroom."

Five minutes and one trip outside later, Erin led the dog back to Ethan's room and kissed her son good night. She climbed into her own bed, hoping against hope she'd soon drift off, but she knew in her heart, this wouldn't be happening. Jim had always had the ability to fall asleep on the couch watching TV, then wake up, wash up, and go straight back to dreamland in their bed. Not her. If she so much as dozed off for a minute in the evening, sleep would not come easily afterward.

She lay on her back and closed her eyes, trying to clear her mind. When that position felt crampy, she rolled over to her right side and removed the extra blanket. A rough toenail made contact with the fitted sheet, and she drew her foot upwards. In just a few months, she'd be sharing this bed with Paul. Well, not this bed. She wondered what kind of mattress he preferred and what his furniture style was. She mentally reviewed the mish-mosh items in his condo, including a mid-century office chair matched with an ebony Victorian desk, and a Mission-style table in his kitchen with chrome chairs. He'd probably be asking her to lead the way in choosing their own furniture. She'd always wanted a creamy white bedroom set, but what man would go along with that? Maybe they could find one that wasn't too feminine.

Erin slapped like a fish onto her back. For some odd reason, a U-2 song kept playing in her head, over and over. She wished she could extract the tune, but the earworm played on. She started thinking instead about her gown and imagined floating down the aisle of First Church toward Paul. Which led to a different set of thoughts and memories. The first time she'd married, her brother had escorted her. She'd invited her dad but not his second wife. Because there was at the time such bad blood between Audrey and Bridget, Erin could not invite the latter. It came as no surprise when her dad said if Bridget couldn't come, he wouldn't either. What about now, though? They were in a good place in their relationship. And yet … she was still closer to her stepfather. Al would be happy to do the honor, but wouldn't asking him hurt her dad? She punched up her pillow and sighed, the chorus of the music repeating in her head. She could go modern and ask her mother. People did that all the time now. She was okay with others doing so, but Erin preferred the traditional way. She would ask Paul what he thought, predicting he'd say, "Whatever you want is okay with me." The solution laying closest to her heart was asking her dad.

When had she fallen asleep? She knew she'd lain in bed a long time before she finally slipped off. But now the phone was ringing. Was she dreaming? "Hello?" Why didn't the person on the other end answer? She slid her finger across the device, but it just kept ringing. She tried again and thought she heard someone speak. Wasn't she on the speaker? No. Better lift the phone to her ear. "Hello? This is Erin."

"Dr. Miles?"

"Uh, yes. Who is this?"

"I'm Cathy Bush from St. Luke's Warren Hospital. We have your father here in the emergency room."

She blinked through a light crust. "Is he all right? What's wrong?"

"Can you come soon?"

"Yes, of course. What time is it?"

A pause. "Three-forty."

"I'll be there as quickly as I can. Please call my brother. His name is on my dad's contact list."

She hung up, clammy. She placed another call.

"Erin, what's wrong?"

"My dad's in the emergency room. They want me to come right over."

"I'll take you," Paul said. "Wait a minute, do you want me to stay with Ethan?"

"Would you please? I don't want him to wake up and not find me at home."

"You just get there as fast as you can. I'll let myself in through the garage."

"What about the bus and his lunch and …"

"We'll manage. Call me as soon as you hear anything. I'll be praying."

CHAPTER TWELVE

The sound of coughing breached the wall of his sleep, and he struggled to identify its source. Initially, he imagined himself with the remnant of the Northampton County Flying Camp, prisoners in a Manhattan church following the Battle of Brooklyn. Coughing had become as ever-present as birdsong in spring, though not as welcome. The face of his dear friend Samuel Miles enlarged to the size of a window, which he knew should not be the case, but then he found himself on the New Jersey side of the Delaware River looking west, toward Easton. The ferry wasn't in sight. Who was the ferryman these days, and where the devil was he? Peter could see Catherine limping toward the cliff, her face radiant, eyes fixed on him, but she was too close to the edge. He shouted a warning, but her expression remained fixed as she stepped toward certain doom. He tried to run in her direction, but ice encased his boots, and he could not budge. He cried out in horror as Catherine stepped into the void and plunged toward the river, which was at flood stage.

Peter bolted upright in the pitch dark, sweat glistening on his forehead, his body chilled from his soaked bedclothes. He rummaged with his hand across the mattress to feel the presence of his wife, but emptiness met him. The coughing he'd heard in his sleep continued into his waking moments. Years of serving as Northampton County's Sheriff had trained him to keep clothing on a chair near the bed in case he needed to leave the house in a rush, and now he quickly dressed, lit a candle, and padded downstairs. He followed the cough, as well as candlelight to *Frau* Hamster's quarters where he saw Catherine, her long hair spilling out of its braids, her expression pinched.

She sobbed a greeting, reaching out a hand, which he took. "Peter, dear."

He moved closer as she stood over the bed of their diminutive housekeeper, wondering how such large coughs could be contained within such a tiny frame. Then he noticed Joe lying on a mat at the foot of the bed. He swallowed around a kind of spitball in his throat. "What is happening?"

"She hasn't been feeling well the last few days."

He sighed in disgust at himself for once again being blind to the affairs of his own household. In reality, he knew very little about this woman who had moved into his home when Catherine had married him four years ago. She had seemed old then. She appeared ancient now. *I don't even know her first name.* She had been with Catherine for years, a substitute parent after her mother and father's early demise, and was fiercely dedicated to her. Initially there had been a crusty understanding between her and himself, and while she may have lived in his house, the kitchen was her domain. At least he let her think so.

He touched his wife's damp cheek then brushed past her to the old woman, Joe looking up at him with tear-filled eyes. He felt her forehead, warm as hot cider, then he struggled to find a pulse. A deep wheezing caused her chest to rise and fall—the wracking coughs reaching a temporary cease fire.

"I'll go for Dr. Ledlie." In his heart, he realized Pastor Rodenheimer would probably have the final say.

"How long does she have, Doctor?" Catherine asked, the sun asserting its presence in the hallway. Peter stood next to her, along with Joe and Susannah. Andrew and Jacob were practically living at the mill now, when they weren't drilling with the militia.

The lanky physician scratched his head, creating even more of a rumpus in his uncombed hair. "Given her frail state, I'd say a few hours, maybe a few days if she's strong enough."

Catherine nodded, wordless.

"What can we do for her?" Susannah asked in tears.

"Keep her warm, help her drink some tea or broth if she can manage. Stay with her."

"She hardly knows we're here," Susannah whispered.

"I am of the opinion you should talk to her just the same."

They sat at the dining room table eating day-old bread with butter and drinking overly-strong coffee Susannah had made after caring for Elizabeth and baby Abraham. *Frau* Hamster lay inert following a thirty-minute coughing marathon. They were as exhausted as if they had suffered the paroxysms.

"I'll check on her." Susannah rose from the table, clearing her plate and cup.

"You've done so much already," Catherine said.

The young woman smiled. "I don't mind."

Peter squeezed his daughter's hand as she brushed by, then gazed into Catherine's eyes, pale with sorrow and suffering. "I don't even know her first name."

Without a hint of reproach, she said, "Anna Marie."

He nodded. "How old is she?"

"Seventy-two." Catherine started telling the woman's story. "She was widowed in her early twenties and childless. She'd been a neighbor of my parents in Connecticut, and after her husband died, she became part of our household. She took care of me when my parents died."

"So her whole life has been about you."

"And God."

Susannah reappeared. "Mother Catherine." The look on her face said what needed to be said.

She rose in such haste she bumped the table, spattering half her coffee across the white linen cloth. Without appearing to notice, she hustled to the back room.

"I'll go get Pastor Rodenheimer."

Susannah shook her head. "You stay here with Mother Catherine. I'll get the minister. I think the children are still asleep, and I'll see if Sarah is available to help."

He'd never taken orders from his daughter. Until now. Joining his wife in the back room, he saw the *Haushälterin's* placid expression, her firm little jaw set as if forbidding any coughs to pass that way again. Catherine was holding the stiff hands, tears staining her face, both she and he watching the woman's chest rise and fall with increasing sluggishness. All of a sudden, *Frau* Hamster opened her eyes and looked straight ahead, a peaceful expression concealing her gauntness. Her eyes sought Catherine, then the old woman smiled before closing her eyes, this time for good.

A gentle breeze toyed with his hair on the hill above Easton, standing with family and friends as *Frau* Hamster's pine box was lowered into the earth. Peter well knew the pastor's reassuring words about the hope of the resurrection, having had his own heart broken by loss—his father, Margaretta and Anna, men he'd served with who would never pass this way again. Catherine sniffled into her handkerchief, and he stepped closer, hoping his presence would provide a measure of comfort. He knew losing *Frau* Hamster was like saying goodbye to a beloved mother. When the undertaker had offered his least expensive coffin for the housekeeper's mortal remains, Peter had waved him off in favor of one more suited to a family member.

The graveside service ended, and he lingered until his wife was ready to leave, then walked with the procession back to the house. Several family members and friends had joined forces to prepare a meal there.

"She was quite a woman," Robert Traill said, after filling his plate. "I think she was the only person in Easton capable of intimidating me."

Peter gave a sniffing sort of laugh. "I felt the same way when I married Catherine."

Traill clasped his hand on his friend's shoulder. "Oh, but she adored you."

His head jerked backward. "She did?"

"When you were away, she championed you. She was constantly making bundles to send to you and the men, and she demanded of everyone who came to this house to pray for your safe return."

He was quiet for a long moment. "I didn't know."

"Under that gruff façade, she had a soft heart for this family."

Peter noticed Joe sitting on a stool in the corner, his head bowed and plate of food untouched. He nodded in the boy's direction. "There's someone who's going to miss her terribly."

Traill smiled. "Oh, indeed, yes."

Pastor Rodenheimer joined them while they ate their repast. After Traill excused himself to join his wife, the minister addressed Peter in a confidential tone. "I wonder if you might have time to stop by the church tomorrow, Colonel."

"Yes, of course." Noting the furrowed brow he asked, "Is there anything wrong?"

"Let's just say there's something important I'd like to run by you."

"I'll be there after breakfast."

As he entered the church, Peter stepped aside when two men bearing sheet-draped pallets struggled past him.

"Excuse us, Colonel," said the shorter of them.

"More dead?" He already knew the answer.

"Yessir, they're dropping like flies, worse than in the winter."

He watched as they passed through the door and hobbled under their load toward Bushkill Creek and a mass grave spreading like disease itself. He wandered into the makeshift hospital, bracing himself for the smell of human suffering and the urgency of those striving to alleviate as much misery as possible. The pews had become, like those of the New York church in which he'd been confined, beds on which the wounded spent their diminished energies on the task of healing—or dying. He noticed a half dozen more sheet-draped bodies with Dr. Ledlie bent over the emaciated form of a man-child. Several Easton women moved about the sanctuary, ministering food and comfort to the wounded.

"Colonel Kichline."

He turned at the sound of his name. "Good morning Pastor Rodenheimer."

They shook hands, gazing at the setting. After a long moment, the minister said, "We're doing all we can, but daily we are losing men."

He was unable to respond in any intelligent way. "You wanted to see me."

The minister clasped his hands together. "Yes. Come with me."

Peter followed him through the jammed sanctuary to the back room where several women prepared food, bandages, and basins of water. One of them stood out, a negro Susannah's size and seemingly not much older. Pastor Rodenheimer called out to her, "Bett!" When she turned toward him, he beckoned, "Come here, would you please?" She put down the ladle she held and walked over to them with quick strides.

"Yessir?"

"There's someone I'd like you to meet. Colonel Kichline, this is Bett, who came to us, was it two weeks ago?"

"Yessir, it be two weeks now."

Peter detected a southern accent and wondered how the young woman had found herself in Easton.

"Let's go sit down. I'm eager for the Colonel to hear your story."

She gazed up at Peter, her dark brown eyes querying. They went to a couple of chairs in corner of the room. The pastor invited Peter and Bett to sit while he remained standing, arms folded across his chest. "So, Bett, tell us your story."

"From the start, sir?"

"From the start. Where are you from?"

She coiled an apron string around her forefinger. "I's from Virginny of late. Before that, Maryland where I was born."

He nodded. "Go on."

"Well, my mama and papa lived on de farm of Master Cobbs, and their mama and papa before them. Then young Master take over after de old man died, and there be a lot of debt."

Peter bristled at the thought of being enslaved, generation after generation, world without end.

"Young Master Cobbs he started sellin' us lef' and right." She dipped her chin and whispered, "I was among de first to go. I was sent to Virginny to a big plantation where I cooked and cared for the chilrun." She gazed up at the men. "Do I be talkin' too much, sirs?"

Rodenheimer smiled. "Not at all, Bett. Please continue."

She gave her head a small shake as if she couldn't imagine why two such important men would give a fig about her. "All rights then. Well, sirs, de war came, and young Master Reynold, he be a major, came home to see his folks. He'd been away afore then in de British army. He was payin' them a visit on his way up nawth to be fightin'. The big master and mistress tell him, 'Take Bett here wit you. She take care of you.' And so's I came nawth with Major Reynold, but then he be captured after a big fight. Since he also be hurt, he was brung here. I came wit him because I s'pposed to take care of him."

Rodenheimer turned to Peter. "Major Reynold died a few days ago. Bett has been keeping busy, helping the women tend to the other sick and wounded since then. She's been sleeping on the floor wherever she can find space. She has no family to return to, doesn't know what became of them."

"I'll go and speak with my wife at once."

He and Catherine stood in the same alcove of the church sharing their idea with Bett. "If you come to live with us you must understand something at the outset," he said.

"Yessir. I be listenin'."

"I have no interest in keeping slaves. There are currently two members of my household who came to us in such a condition. One has earned his freedom. The other is young, and we are preparing him to take his own place in the world. I also have indentured servants, who work for a time, then they are free to go their own way. I would like you to work your way to independence, like one of those servants, in five to seven years, so you are also ready to live as a free woman."

"Is this agreeable, Bett?" Catherine asked.

"Oh, yes, ma'am!" She clapped her hands together. "I wants to be free."

"Very good! Now, then, gather your things, and we'll take you to your new home."

When Bett didn't move, Catherine asked, "Where are your belongings?"

"I be wearin' 'em, ma'am."

CHAPTER THIRTEEN

She stood at her father's side, his face obscured by a breathing apparatus, IVs taped over his bruised arms, bags emptying their contents into his veins. She wished she could kiss his forehead or squeeze his hand, but the best she could manage was a light touch on his right shoulder. "I'm here, Dad. Allen is on the way."

A nurse recorded Tony's temperature and vital signs onto a computer. Erin watched the peaks and valleys on the heart monitor, her untrained eye sensing something about the progression didn't look right. When the nurse finished his work, Erin addressed him.

"I have a few questions. Can we speak out in the hallway?"

"Certainly."

In the emergency room's glaring light, Erin glanced at the nurse's badge, having instantly forgotten the man's name after meeting him fifteen minutes earlier. "What exactly happened, Sean, and what's my father's condition?"

"My understanding is he called nine-one-one a little over an hour ago, complaining of severe chest pain and dizziness. When the ambulance arrived, Tony was on the floor near the door, unconscious."

Erin clapped her fingertips to her lips, searching for hope in the nurse's mellow brown eyes.

"He was in a lot worse shape than he was two weeks

ago."

She grimaced. "Excuse me?"

Sean frowned. "When he had a mild heart attack. He was home in a few days."

"He was here?"

"Yes, he didn't tell you?"

Erin huffed. "As far as I know, he didn't tell anyone. Just how many times has he been in the ER?"

"I'd have to check his chart, but this is about the fourth time I've seen him, and I started working here three months ago."

How could her father not have told her? Allen probably hadn't known either, or he surely would've let Erin know. Unless there was some kind of understanding between them. But why would her father hide this from his family, or was it just her? She clawed her way back to the present. "So, he's worse now?"

"He was barely breathing on his own when he arrived, and we had to use the paddles. His vital signs are unsteady, and we've ordered a chest x-ray because there's a strong indication he has pneumonia."

Tragicomically, Erin suddenly realized she was wearing yesterday's socks and could only imagine what sort of outfit she had thrown on under her trench coat. Hopefully, she'd remembered to change her black sheep pajamas.

"As soon as we can, we'll move him into the cardiac care unit."

Just as she was about to reenter her dad's cubicle, Allen arrived, his face stretched with strain. She stumbled toward him, into her brother's arms.

"When did you eat last?" Concern etched Paul's eyebrows.

"What time is it?"

"Nearly ten."

"I can't remember."

"And what about drinking?"

She wished she didn't have to admit she hadn't had a drop of water since the night before. Her father's picking at the covers and heart-breaking moans of "Mom, Mom" had held her captive. He didn't seem to be aware of where he was or who was with him. *Thank God he had the wherewithal to call for help. If he had waited …*

"We're going to the cafeteria right now."

She spread her hands. "I can't leave him, Paul." The ICU doctor had confirmed Tony's pneumonia, along with at least two coronary blockages, which they could not correct until his condition stabilized. He had advised Erin and Allen to call the rest of the family, and she asked Paul to contact Pastor Stan.

Allen spoke. "I agree with Paul. You need to keep your strength up."

Two white-coated figures entered the room, temporarily ending the discussion.

"Are you the family?" The older physician could have passed for Tip O'Neill.

"Yes, I'm Allen, his son, and this is my sister, Erin, and her fiancé, Paul."

"I'm Dr. Nevin, and this is my assistant, Dr. Shu. Do you know if your father has a living will?"

Erin tried to make a withdrawal from her memory bank then noticed her brother nodding his head. "He made one out several years ago, and I think the hospital has a copy. If not, I know where he keeps his papers."

She didn't know where her father kept his papers. Even so, the distance she'd experienced over the years between her and Tony narrowed further in this time and place.

"Are either or both of you his medical power of attorney?"

"I am," Allen said. "His second wife was, but she passed away a year ago."

Erin wondered whether they should be having this conversation in front of her dad, even if he didn't show signs of awareness. She took a deep breath. "Maybe we could continue this outside?" Her brother, never comfortable around doctors or hospitals, didn't wait for the physician to make a move.

"How bad is he?" Allen asked near the nurses station.

"These next few hours are critical. What we need to know is what your wishes are if he goes into another cardiac event. Would you want him to be resuscitated?" He cleared his throat. "Just how far should we go to save him?"

Erin felt Paul's arm slip around her waist just as her knees went watery. She looked at her brother, who was glancing her way.

"We talked sometimes," Allen said after a long moment, "especially when his second wife was really sick. He told me he had no use for machines to keep him alive if he ..."

"He said similar things to me as well," Erin said.

Dr. Nevin looked from one sibling to the other. "Are you in agreement?"

Her neck seemed to weigh fifty pounds under the burden of deciding someone else's life and death. *Then again, God knows every day of our lives, including the last ones. If Dad goes into cardiac arrest in this condition, could that be God's way of taking him home?* She closed her eyes and nodded her ascent.

Nevin addressed her brother. "And you, sir?"

"Yes, but I have trouble saying so." Allen rubbed his forehead. "I believe that's what he would want." He paused then asked, "Are we talking minutes, hours, days?"

"Your father is as sick as anyone can get, but I've seen people pull through worse."

Allen shook his head. "I know you don't have a crystal ball, but based on what's happened before and what my dad is going through now, what do you think?"

"My hunch is hours at the least, days at the most."

"Could he become, you know, comatose, for a long time?" Erin hated the words.

"I don't believe that's likely. His body has too many powder kegs."

Allen, who hadn't eaten breakfast either, accompanied Erin and Paul to the cafeteria. The ICU nurse had promised to call if there was any change in Tony's condition, and they ate mechanically. Erin looked around the crowded room wondering which of the other visitors might be in similar situations.

"I'll call the girls," Allen said after draining his coffee cup. "They can decide whether or not to bring the kids."

"I wonder if I should get Ethan out of school. Would he be more upset not saying goodbye to his grandfather, or seeing him in this condition?" *How would that affect Ethan after his father's death just two years ago? I suppose I could ask him, let him make the decision. He's getting old enough to start making such choices.*

"I don't know what to tell you, Erin. I'm not even sure Dad is aware of us."

"At some level I think he is, but just how much, I don't know." Before she could filter her thoughts, Erin blurted, "What about Mom? We should probably let her know."

"I think that's a good idea," Allen said.

"Do you think she'll want to see your dad?" Paul asked, leaning back in his chair.

Erin looked past her brother at a wall-mounted TV looping from the faces of St. Luke's award-winning doctors to ads for a local realtor and a car dealership. "I think we should."

"I agree," Allen said.

Erin pushed her tray to the side. "I'll call her now." She wanted very much to hear her mother's voice.

She watched her mother clinging to Paul's arm while he led her slowly past the nurse's station toward Tony's room. Erin's skin prickled—she'd never seen Audrey shuffle before, and when had she started stooping? She didn't need to be reminded just then of her mother's increasing frailty and busied herself with a sober greeting, holding Audrey tightly, their bodies trembling in unison. Wordlessly, she led her mother to Tony's side, and Audrey gripped one of the bedrails with one hand while, with the other, she touched her former husband's shoulder.

"Oh, Tony. I needed to come see you. I know you're not feeling too well. Age does have a way of catching up with us, doesn't it? Audrey stroked his shoulder, crooning.

"Only yesterday we were kids, and today ... well, we have a real nice family to show for all the years."

She recalled her mother's delicate manner when Erin had gotten sick as a child, being held protectively by the arms Erin now steadied. A passing of the torch.

Audrey continued. "I know we had some hard times, but I've let them go. What's the sense of holding on to that stuff?"

Erin's eyes were a camera lens widening to take in the fullest shot. *What a huge relief to hear Mom say she forgives him!*

Tony's eyelids fluttered as if with great effort, and once open, Erin saw him taking in the sight of her mother, the love of his youth. In those dark eyes, Erin witnessed tenderness wrapped like a gift for Audrey. His lips were moving.

Audrey leaned closer, shaking her head. "I can't understand you, Tony. What are you saying?"

Erin leaned in to hear.

"I'm ... sorry."

Her vision blurred, Erin looked into her mother's moist eyes.

"He said, 'I'm sorry.'" Tears flowed down Audrey's thin face. "Me too, Tony. Me too."

Her father fixed his gaze on Erin and Allen and whispered, "I love you both. God bless you."

They were his last words.

"Mom, can I ask you something?"

Erin eased herself onto the end of her son's bed, then

Toby made an awkward leap from the floor, settling with his head on her lap, gazing up at her. *Dogs know when something has happened.* Her eyes stung with the memory of her basset hound's afternoon vigils by the garage door after Jim died.

Ethan burrowed under the comforter until only his head showed. "You didn't know Pop Pop very well, did you, I mean for a long time?"

She stiffened until her son's relaxed expression told her he wasn't accusing her of anything. "You're right, but in the last few years, my father and I made up for what was lost."

Her son pursed his lips. "Did Dad know him?"

Erin shook her head slowly. "No, not very well."

"So Pop Pop didn't walk you down the aisle when you got married?"

"No." His words struck like pricks of hail in a winter storm.

"Who will walk you down the aisle when you marry Paul?"

"I don't know. Do you have any ideas?"

Ethan looked up at the ceiling. "Well, there's always Grandpa Al."

"Yes, there is." She didn't want to think about this just now.

"Mom?"

"Yes, Ethan?"

"Do you think Dad will get to know Pop Pop in Heaven?"

She smiled down at him. "I think there's a good possibility. I mean, Jesus tells us he'll make all things new, and that includes relationships.

Ethan nodded, seeming satisfied.

"I'm really glad I got to know Pop Pop, and Paul did

too." He sighed. "I do wish he'd been able to come see me in the play." Not only had he won the part of the Cowardly Lion, but according to his director, Ethan was a natural.

Erin's mind wandered past the four walls to the funeral home where she'd stood that evening in a receiving line with her son between her and Paul. Allen had been on her left, the first person visitors greeted as they streamed past floral displays and the casket. Erin had depended on hearing her brother say the names of some relatives she no longer recognized, having not seen them since her youth. She also held close to her heart an image of how natural having Paul beside her had felt, as if he'd been in her life a very long time.

"I really loved Pop Pop," Ethan said, breaking into her thoughts.

Judging by the many people who had come to the viewing and funeral, Erin realized her father had been the object of much affection. This knowledge satisfied her.

She may have had her issues with Tony, but others had seen a different side of him.

"There sure were a lot of flowers. Did you see the one from that guy you're writing the book with, the guy from TV?"

"All those flowers were beautiful, and I really appreciated Dr. McCutcheon's kindness to us."

"He must be really nice."

"He is."

"Mom?"

"Yes Ethan?"

"I love you."

"I love you too." She kissed his forehead and watched as he turned off the light.

CHAPTER FOURTEEN

If not for the striking resemblance to his own muscular body and Margaretta's eyes and mouth, he might not have recognized his middle son. There was something disquieting about Andrew's expression as they stood across from each other at the grist mill, the grinding stone playing its tune in the background. He wondered where young Schneider was, bristling at the image of the indentured servant strolling down Northampton Street with Susanna. Most likely, Peter's youngest son Jacob was just across the creek at the saw mill.

Andrew opened the conversation. "Thanks for coming to see me, Father. I'm pleased to see you regaining your strength."

"Yes, I'm feeling quite well these days."

"You look a lot better than when you first came home."

Peter grinned. "Was my appearance that bad?"

"Let's just say the real you was buried under layers of snow and ice …"

"And a beard and dirt and vermin."

"You looked wonderful to me, Father, to all of us." Andrew coughed into his upper sleeve. They each spent a long moment studying their hands. "There are a couple of things I'd like to talk to you about." He gestured toward two rugged chairs, and as Peter settled in, he pulled out his pipe while his son began unloading the contents of his mind.

"I know things are going badly for our Cause, but I'm as committed to independence as I ever was. I see those men suffering in our church with their wounds and illness, and I just can't think of much else than taking up their mantle and getting the job done." He gazed into his father's eyes. "Do you understand?"

"Completely."

He smiled crookedly. "You're probably itching to get back into the fight."

"You know me well."

"And Mother Catherine is probably trying to keep you at home."

Peter nodded, then blew out a puff of fragrant smoke. "For now."

"The thing is, Father, I need to be ready for whenever my unit becomes active." He pressed the tips of his fingers on one hand, then switched to the other. "I think Jacob is in the same situation, and I need to know whether or not you're in a position to run the mills. Naturally, your health is uppermost in my mind."

"I can begin putting my hand in more as I await my parole."

"What happens after you get paroled, though? Will you be off fighting again?"

Peter clenched his teeth on the pipe stem as he gazed across Bushkill Creek toward his other mill. "I am ready to do anything I can."

"I understand." A brief silence swathed them. "There's something else, Father. Maybe you're aware of this already, but in case you're not, well, do you know Mr. Levers has been throwing his weight around a lot?"

Peter had guessed as much judging from a grumble

here and an oath against Levers there. The man could be exasperating, but he was loyal, and as committed to the Cause as anyone he'd ever known, including himself. "He has a lot of responsibilities."

"I know, but the way he conducts himself, as if he's the king and emperor rolled into one." He created a fist with one hand. "Isn't that what we're fighting against?"

Peter needed details in order to make a judgment. "Is there anything specific?"

"One of many issues is how he's been procuring supplies for the army. One of the Moravian millers told me last week Levers came to buy grain for the army, paying no attention to the needs of the local people, who also need to be fed. In addition to demanding most of what the man had, Levers paid with nearly worthless Continental money."

He breathed out slowly. "Has he taken much grain from us?"

"A lot. Because I'm sympathetic, I comply and accept his form of payment, but, Father, the Moravians are trying to be neutral, and I don't feel right about the way Levers pushes them around." He paused. "Do you understand?"

"I do." He recalled the previous summer when he was charged with the unpleasant duty of confiscating guns from the Moravians for his troops. They had willingly submitted, and he allowed them to keep enough weapons for their own protection. Right on his heels, though, George Taylor had gone to Bethlehem and taken what was left. Peter hated gray areas. Give him black and white any time. He also despised in between phases . Action and advancement were his bread and butter, not uncertainty and discontentment, or deprivation without any indication life would end up being any different than when they'd first begun.

"Is there anything to be done about Mr. Levers?"

Peter cocked his head. "I could try to talk to him privately, appeal to his better nature if you will, but Andrew, he does have jobs to do, often unpleasant, thorny jobs."

"Yes, I realize that." He sighed. "Sometimes just talking things over helps."

"I'm always here for you, son." He wondered whether he should express what lay on his mind like his new housekeeper's leaden dumplings.

"You seem lost in thought, Father."

He smiled. "You know me well. Perhaps you can shed some light on a situation for me."

"I'll be glad to try." He crossed one leg over the other.

"Our Susannah. She, well, she's growing up so quickly, and I can't help but … I see her a lot with Schneider." He felt as if he'd fouled the air between them and immediately regretted indulging his suspicions.

"She's quite the young lady, beautiful, smart, patriotic. A number of local men find her company desirable."

He chomped on the pipe stem and growled. "I see."

"Schneider's a good fellow. Very hard working, honest, a man of good character. Eager to make something of himself. He attends services regularly and would do anything for us."

Still, an indentured servant? What if the young man had baser motives, like getting in good with one of Easton's wealthiest families? He hated thinking such things, but this was about his dear Susannah.

Andrew continued. "I wouldn't worry too much, Father. Girls her age can be quite fickle."

"Yes, well, thank you, Andrew." He rose. "I'll get more involved here. You're not to worry about getting called up.

Everything will work itself out."

He walked to the forks where the rivers met to clear his mind, to focus on something more powerful and lasting than himself. If he followed the Bushkill to where it tipped into the Delaware, he'd be less likely to run into anyone than if he went by way of Centre Square. As he set out, four soldiers bearing pallets drew near, accompanied by Pastor Rodenheimer.

He stopped to greet them. "Good morning men, Pastor." The men paused. "How many have died?"

The soldier in charge spoke up. "This is our third trip today."

"Where exactly are you interring them?"

"Just upwards of the creek bank." He indicated the direction with his thumb.

"A mass grave then?" Peter asked.

"I'm afraid so, sir. There's just no time for separate burials, nor space at the church cemetery."

Peter guessed a lack of sleep had caused the dark smudges under the minister's eyes. "At least I can give them a decent service," Rodenheimer said.

"I was going to stop by the church later today to visit the men."

The minister motioned for the soldiers to go ahead. "I'll be with you shortly." He addressed Peter. "I wouldn't do that if I were you, Colonel Kichline. I'd also keep your wife and daughter from visiting until this scourge passes."

His arms prickled. "What exactly is happening?'

"At first, I thought scarlet fever, but the men aren't

presenting the usual symptoms. Dr. Ledlie suspects a different kind of contagion, and the sickness has spread quickly." He looked into the distance toward the soldiers bearing their burdens. "So many have died."

"What can I and my family do to help?"

The dark eyes flashed, then dimmed. "As I said, stay away. You're just getting back on your feet, and the ladies shouldn't be exposed to this."

"But the men will need food and supplies."

"Just leave the packages outside the church door."

"Do you know if the prison has been affected?"

"I'm not sure, but I wouldn't be surprised. I haven't seen Mr. Hart lately, or Colonel Hooper. They would know, of course."

Peter put his hand on the parson's shoulder. "Are you keeping yourself?"

A sigh and a softening of his expression replaced his gruffness. "As well as I can."

"Perhaps not well enough, my friend. I suggest you get more sleep for starters."

"I can only try, Colonel. There's so much work to be done."

"I will keep you and the men in my prayers, as always."

"This is a great comfort to me, sir. Thank you."

He stared at the round ball he'd forked, wondering what on earth he was about to put into his mouth. The item had obviously been fried to a crisp. He attempted to strain impatience from his question. "What is this, Bett?"

She hovered over Catherine's shoulder as she placed

a platter full of sliced ham on the table. Ham he could recognize, but biscuits—again? He missed *Frau* Hamster's dark *brots*. A man could get a good chew out of sturdy German bread, but *biscuits* fell apart when he all but looked at them.

"Oh, sir, these be hushpuppies. Ain't you ever had 'em?"

"No, Bett, I can't say I have." He bit into the food, the size of a large hailstone, steam rising from the center. Soft. Chewy.

"Well, sir, they be made of corn meal and fat, a little sugar and salt, fried nice and crispy. Major Reynold was crazy for 'em."

Another food made from corn. Grits in the morning, cornbread in the afternoon, now cornballs at night.

"Do you like it?"

He had to admit they weren't bad.

"These are delicious, Bett," Susannah said.

"I wanna puppy!" Elizabeth reached across the table with her pudgy hand, and Catherine placed one of the bread balls on her plate.

He liked the hushpuppy well enough, but this southern cuisine was taking some getting used to. Maybe the climate down there made people eat strangely.

If he wasn't already out of sorts over the sight of dead soldiers unceremoniously layered one on top of the other, watching Peter Schneider deliver firewood to their home and linger at his wife's invitation downright irritated him. How many nights had this been now? At least two, and this only Wednesday. How much wood did they need in late spring anyway?

While Susannah and Schneider taught Joe the fundamentals of chess, Jacob sitting nearby, Peter brought himself to a simmer in his favorite chair. He kept going back to the same passages in his book after his mind wandered like the pigs around the courthouse. He might have spoken instead to his wife, but she'd taken Elizabeth and Abraham up to bed. At nine o'clock, he could stand the situation not a minute longer. "I'm going for a walk," he announced to the room.

Schneider popped up from his chair so quickly he bumped the game table. "Oh, I beg your pardon. Forgive my clumsiness!"

Susannah smiled at him while she put the figures back into their places. "Please don't trouble yourself. I'll set this back up."

"If you will excuse me, I must be going."

"We can finish the game tomorrow."

Schneider's eyes darted from her to her father, gathering his cloak and hat in the hall. "Perhaps. Good evening, Miss Kichline." He bowed and walked into the hallway. "Colonel Kichline, I wonder if I might accompany you as I head back to the mill house for the night."

The last thing he wanted. Then again, maybe he could speak his mind to the young upstart. "Yes, Schneider, feel free to join me."

They walked in silence past a few houses, some candlelit, others in repose. The young man spoke after an uncomfortable silence. "Sir, I believe I owe you an apology."

Peter looked down at him. "For what may I ask?"

"I have been much in the company of your family recently, and I fear I may have presumed upon your hospitality, somehow overstepped."

His glacial heart started thawing. "Yes, I see."

"I can't help but feel comfortable with all of you, and you have been so kind. But do forgive me, sir."

"There is nothing to forgive." While they were at it … "You seem warm-hearted about one family member in particular."

Schneider's face paled. "Oh, sir, I never meant to …"

"And she is clearly fond of you."

"I did nothing to … perhaps I've been too helpful, but I … wanted to help, to protect …"

They stopped in front of the courthouse where Peter attempted to put the fellow out of his misery. "You are an ambitious young man, Schneider. Tell me, what do you hope to do in the future?"

"I'd like to settle in Easton, sir, because this place has become home to me. I'd like to own a business and be successful, not just to enrich myself but to better serve others."

Peter sensed there was no guile here, no pretense. "Which is why you came to America?"

"Well, sir, you see, I was born here."

He stopped in his tracks. "Oh. Perhaps you told me before, but I seem to have forgotten." Schneider had come to the mills around the time Peter had been organizing and leading the Flying Camp. No wonder he didn't recall much about the young man.

"I'm not sure if we ever spoke of my background."

"Where, then, were you born?"

"Near Lancaster, sir. My father came to America from Germany in 1744, part of a large Mennonite contingent. He and my mother did quite well for themselves. Actually, they ran a gristmill too, and my father became deeply involved as a leader in the church and community." He smiled to himself. "My father believed in pouring himself out for the benefit of others. He just didn't realize when he had reached the bottom of his own reserves."

Peter had a feeling Schneider meant this both in a physical and financial sense.

"When he died, my brother apprenticed himself, and then, I followed suit, coming here."

A light breeze toyed with the hair around his ears. "You were educated then?"

"Yes, sir, and I continue to read every chance I get. I want to be able to make a better life for myself and for my future family." Red blotches on his face replaced his earlier pallor. "I do know my station now, and I assure you of my honorable intentions regarding all your family."

Peter looked into his eyes, man to man. This could easily have been himself when he was a young man, after his father died, but circumstances had favored his family. Schneider came from a good home that had known hard times. Still, he wasn't ready to give the go-ahead regarding Susannah and spoke around the tacit issue. "Let's just see how your indenture progresses." He hoped his meaning was clear. "In the meantime, you're welcome in my home, and if you'd like to borrow my books, just ask."

Schneider nodded, his face solemn. "Thank you, sir."

CHAPTER FIFTEEN

She tugged at the bottom of her tee shirt unsure where to begin. Erin pictured her Grammy Ott's bedroom with its old-fashioned dresser and mirror, could almost hear the music of the little silver box her grandmother had always kept there, gleaming against a snow white lace doily. Did anyone besides the elderly even use doilies anymore? Erin had no use for them, something her mother couldn't begin to comprehend. Erin had been comfortably acquainted with every single object on her grammy's dresser top, a faux tortoise comb and brush, a crystal catch-all tray, a small porcelain lamp with a defective switch. Erin had even been allowed to go inside her relative's closet on rainy days to peruse all the neat little boxes in which Grammy Ott kept her costume jewelry.

Her mind wandered again, to her mother's apartment, which, like Grammy Ott's dresser, Erin knew as well as if she lived there herself, including the location of Audrey's important papers, bills, stamps, even money for the downstairs laundry. By contrast, her father's desk was uncharted territory, a howling wilderness, its only familiar aspect, his blocky handwriting. She wondered if Allen had a better feel for these contents. Noticing an unlabeled prescription container, she discovered a slew of old pennies inside. Were they worth anything? Should she and Allen try to sell them, or had they meant something special to her father?

Why had Allen suggested she clear out the desk? *Maybe because he and Paul are helping move Dad's furniture to my Cousin Mark's house.* She heard Tanya and Alana talking and laughing in the kitchen while they cleaned out cabinets and the refrigerator. Hefty trash bags littered the small apartment, filled with items her father would never need again and no one else wanted, slippers white with athlete's foot powder, dusty VHS tapes of *Bonanza*, a corroded flashlight. A few bags were being marked for the Green Drop, and every now and then residents of the apartment complex stopped by to take whatever appealed to them. When she realized there was precious little she wanted, Erin's stomach quivered. In truth, the only thing she ever desired from Tony was his love. Toward the end of his life, he'd provided his only daughter with a treasure she would always keep in her heart.

Erin blew a puff of air through her lips as she took a seat at the desk and picked up the first file, containing his life insurance policy. The next one dealt with his pension. Since she had no idea what to do with them, she rummaged through the stack for something that might make sense of the whole, like her father's will. Allen had overseen the funeral expenses and burial, which their father had prearranged using some insurance, but were these policies separate ones?

Her left eyelid began twitching when she spotted a folder marked "Last Will and Testament." She extracted the yellowing document, seeing he'd made this fifteen years earlier, a time when their relationship had been distantly polite. As she read, the activity in the kitchen faded. Tony had stipulated his second wife as executor, and in the event of her death, Allen would step in. Half of the estate was earmarked for Bridget, with the other half divided between Allen and Erin. A tear slipped down her cheek as she realized her father, though hardly close at the time he wrote this, was trying to do right by her. The will also specified if Bridget preceded Tony in death, his estate would be divided between Allen and Erin, "share and share alike." He designated his war medals and other related items also be divided equally between them.

She folded and placed the onionskin paper back in the envelope, then into its folder. As executor, Allen would need to handle any legal matters, so she set aside a pile just for her brother to go through. She discovered an address book and flipped to the back to see if her name was there. "Erin Pelleriti Miles." Underneath he'd recorded her birthday, Jim's name and birthday, then Ethan's. Her Lansdale address stood out to her as a memorial to her former life, while the College Hill information Tony had written in a shaky hand brought her to the present. There was no record of her anniversary. Over the years, she'd been careful not to say too much to him about her wedding or the anniversaries that followed. She didn't think her dad had ever sent Jim a birthday card, but Tony had at least known the date, and he'd faithfully remembered her and Ethan's special days over the years. Warmth filled her to know she had always been deep in her father's heart, if not directly in his life.

"Before we pick Ethan up at my mom's, I'd like to take a side trip," she told Paul after the full day of sorting and cleaning. She was bone-weary but satisfied, because, with all hands on deck, the apartment had been emptied in a single day. Allen had promised to go through the legal files and had arranged to meet the building superintendent on Tuesday morning for a final inspection. Everyone exclaimed over how quickly the process had gone, but then Tony had done a deep cleaning after Bridget's death, and he had lived simply afterward. She'd been amazed to discover her dad had only owned three pairs of shoes, not because he couldn't afford more, but because he didn't see the point of possessing more than he needed.

When they got into the car and buckled their seat belts, Paul started the engine then reached for her hand. "I'm guessing this has been an emotional day for you."

She nodded, grateful for his concern. "Yes, it has, but I'm okay. There's a sense of closure. I'm especially thankful for the time Ethan and I had with him up here." She added wistfully, "And that you got to know him."

Paul's brows creased. "He never really knew Jim, did he?"

"They met a few times, but there was such stiffness between them, as if they never really got past an introduction. Jim knew how deeply my dad hurt me when I was younger, and I think he was always protecting me and Ethan. I think my dad sensed this, and he ended up keeping his distance. He always seemed a little intimidated by Jim."

"Are you at peace with that?"

"Yes, I think so. In this season of my life, I got to know my dad all over again, and Ethan became close to him." She smiled. "You got to know Dad too."

"Tony was a nice man. Sure, there were still some rough

edges, but people often mellow when they get older."

The engine's smooth hum in the chilling twilight soothed her. "That was true of him. After Bridget began accepting me, and he gave up drinking, our relationship started changing for the better. Ethan made life more joyful for us too. They both really doted on him."

"Did that bother you?"

She frowned. "Why would it?"

"Because he was receiving what they never gave you when you were a kid. Also, Ethan never knew their harsher sides."

Erin gazed into Paul's eyes, liking the compassion mirrored in them. "I'm glad for their sakes they had a grandchild who only knew their better natures. Why stew over things you can't change? Why not forgive and move on?"

"Forgive and forget?" He cocked his head to the right.

"Forgive, yes, but I don't think you ever forget that kind of pain. The memories become less vivid, though. I believe in putting relational brokenness in God's hands and leaving it there. He knows what to do with the pain."

He leaned over and kissed her cheek, the sweetness filling her with tenderness. "So, where did you want to go? You said you wanted to take a side trip."

"Oh, right! I'd like to show you where I grew up, the house I lived in when my parents were still together." She spoke the words softly, feeling suddenly shy.

"I'd love to see it. Just point the way."

When Paul pulled out of the parking spot, she directed him to take a left on South Main Street. "The house isn't too far from here, maybe two or three miles. Funny, when I was a kid, I didn't realize how close the P'burg suburbs were to town. They always seemed like different worlds."

"How so?"

"Town was where my grandparents were, where the working class people from the factories lived. The suburbs, which really aren't suburbs like in Philadelphia, were quieter. There was a cornfield behind our house, for goodness sake! In town, there were twin houses on tiny yards, but where I grew up, people lived in Cape Cods and traditional colonials, and we had a lot of land to roam around."

"I'm beginning to understand. We just passed out of dense housing, and here's a stretch with a trail."

A mile later, she directed him to turn left over a Depression-era cement bridge. "We're crossing over the Morris Canal, but when I was a kid, we called it the crick."

Paul laughed. "I thought cricks were sore spots on your neck."

"Not in P'burg in the 1970s. Okay, turn right over this other bridge. See that playground on the left? That's where my friends and I spent our summers. One of them lived in a house a little further upstream, and we used to go to the canal and playact." Her face reddened. "We would make up scenes from *Gilligan's Island*. Isn't it funny? I was always the professor."

He laughed. "I am not a bit surprised, however that show was before your time."

"Not in reruns. We watched every episode. Do you know if they ever get off the island?"

"I'm not sure." He frowned. "Probably."

"Anyway, in the summers we had programs at the playground. I remember one year there was a teacher who led it, and I had the biggest crush on him. He drove a

Mustang."

They both smiled as she directed Paul to hang a left in a few blocks then pointed out the window. "Okay, that's my house, right there."

He slowed the car. "Nice place. I can see why you enjoyed growing up here. And there's your cornfield."

"At Halloween, we used to pick dried corn and husk the kernels into bags. Then we'd go tick tacking in the neighborhood."

"What, may I ask, was tick tacking?"

"Oh, you haven't lived if you never tick tacked." Erin laughed, pleased to be sharing her childhood memories with Paul, yet sad never to have brought Jim here. But then, she'd been denying part of herself. Now, she was embracing the whole package. She continued. "At night we would go around and throw handfuls of dried corn against people's windows, then run like heck when the porch lights turned on."

His voice rose. "And this was allowed?"

"Today, people wouldn't dare do such a thing, but back then most of the neighbors expected it, had done it themselves when they were kids." She stared at the house, pleased the owners were taking good care of the place.

"How long did you live here?"

"From about the time I was three until I was in fifth grade, when my parents divorced."

"That must've been so hard for you and Allen."

"He was already in high school, so he pretty much kept his friends, but I left my closest ones behind and started over in a new school. In town. I always wished we could've stayed here, but my mom couldn't afford it on her small salary, and my dad wouldn't let us live there if he was out of the picture. My grandmother took care of me after school, made dinner, helped me with homework, so we moved to a house to be near her." After a pause, she said, "Let's go see the school I went to. Then we can pick up Ethan."

"Lead on."

She guided Paul up the central street through the neighborhood and back onto the main thoroughfare. "My dear friend, Jennifer Fritz, lived over there." She pointed to the right, to a cluster of houses lining the road. "I found her on Facebook a few years ago, and we've discovered we're distant cousins. We were always close, but neither of us suspected we were that connected." She pointed to the left. "Okay, slow down if you can." She saw him look in the rearview mirror—no one was behind them. "There's Shimer School."

"Shimer is a familiar name in this area's history."

"Yes, and believe it or not, I'm related to the family."

Paul smiled. "Of course you are. It looks like the school is closed."

"I'm not sure when or why that happened, but I feel sad seeing it like this. The school was so alive when I went there. I loved it."

As they drove past, Paul asked where to go next.

"Up to Still Valley, then we'll get onto Route Twenty-Two West, which will take us back to my mom's."

"I think your childhood was pretty wonderful, at least parts of it."

"You're right. I had a beautiful home, good friends, teachers I adored, a great place to roam and play. I feel blessed to have had that."

Some moments passed as purple twilight streaked the sky, brushing itself against the mountains in the background. She had reopened a book she hadn't read in many years, sharing its contents with the man she'd be spending the rest of her life with. Even so, she was closing a volume of her life after bidding her father a last goodbye. She gazed out the window. *I'm glad the ending of that story was a happy one. I'm ready to move on.*

CHAPTER SIXTEEN

In the stone house at Hamilton and Ferry Streets, they sat before a fire with their port and their pipes, Peter silently contemplating whether he was growing old at the speed of his dear friend. He and George Taylor were roughly six years apart, yet the latter's thatch of gray hair and the lines charting his face seemed to separate them by more than two decades. At least to Peter. Although his prison ordeal had aged him, he was now wearing his clothes, rather than his clothes wearing him. Catherine had just noted the color returning to his face, and the progression of silver threading his hair, still thick at fifty-four, had taken a temporary hiatus.

"I understand you've been under the weather," Peter said, warming to the blaze and the conviviality of a man he'd long known and highly regarded.

Taylor released a puff of smoke, clasping his pipe with his right hand, gazing at Peter. "My public life is drawing to a close, my friend. I couldn't handle the Council meetings any longer and resigned."

"Oh, I didn't realize your condition prompted you to take such action."

"I wanted you to hear this from me first. I'll continue overseeing the production of cannon shot for the army, but other than that, I must stay close to hearth and home."

At least he wasn't abandoning the Cause, not like Lewis

Gordon.

"What about you, Colonel? I hear you've been itching to get back into the fight."

"As I am but a young buck, sir, yes, I suppose I am."

They shared a laugh until its genial notes flickered into the flames.

"I haven't stopped pushing for your parole, nor will I, but are you up to further service?"

"I may not end up bearing arms against the King, but I would like to have the option of going wherever Providence may lead. And yes, I am feeling stronger with each day."

Taylor nodded his head. "I understand you've been taking up a collection for some of our prisoners and wounded. A worthy undertaking. Is this a general collection, or specific?"

"Specifically the funds are for the relief of our good friend, Captain Arndt, still imprisoned in New York along with Colonel Miles, who is yet awaiting parole, as well as other Flying Camp members who have had a particularly hard time since returning."

"How is young Mr. Fartenius?"

"Coming along, I am pleased to report, Mr. Taylor. His wife and daughter have been running the stable, and Peter Junior and his Sarah have been helping out as they can."

"Better include him in the collection." Taylor's face reddened. "It's a crying shame our Congress doesn't do more for our soldiery. Goodness knows I did all I could to promote their welfare, but the truth is, they were operating on a budget as thin as my housekeeper's potato soup." He put the pipe on an end table and reached into his pocket for a wallet Peter noted was rather thick. Taylor pulled out more than half its contents. "Here you go, my good friend.

Unlike Congress, I have some means to share with these deserving troops."

Peter accepted the cash, noting this was British currency, not the almost worthless Continental money. These funds would go far. "I thank you very much for your generosity."

"Don't mention it. While you're out doing good, Colonel, I wonder if you might drop by the prison. Our Colonel Hooper was back in Easton yesterday on his rounds, and when your name came up, he mentioned a need to speak with you."

"Yes, of course." His blood stirred with the possibility of an actual assignment.

Taylor's smile crinkled his eyes. "Will they never leave you alone, sir?"

"I hope not."

"Old Reliable."

Peter grinned. "Speak for yourself."

"Colonel Kichline!"

"Colonel Hooper, how nice to see you." Peter strode up to the officer, noting for the first time just how prominent his forehead was. Perhaps this was because Hooper's hair had begun a northward retreat. "How is your family?"

"Quite well, thank you. And yours?"

"The same." He thought twice, recalling how baby Abraham's nose seemed to be constantly running, yet the boy seemed in overall good health. Elizabeth was a sturdy little toddler, and for the most part, his family had managed to avoid the grip of disease since his arrival.

"Which is more than I can say for half these prisoners."

He looked toward the dismal compound, the building appearing as weary as its contents. "This winter has hung on so stubbornly, and in these cramped quarters, well, most of these men haven't fared well." Hooper closed his eyes, shook his head.

Peter frowned at the patches of snow hanging around the village this late into spring, his mind picturing soldiers carrying cloth-covered bodies for a mass burial. He had difficulty reconciling Easton's sweeping vistas and peaceful meadows with the stark reality of war's aftermath. While he mended in the company of his family and friends, filling his stomach with nourishing food, prisoners of war struggled to survive a block away. "Have you lost many?"

"Five more since I was up here two weeks ago." They observed a quiet pause. "By the way, Colonel, some of the Germans have been trying to tell me something rather urgent, but I can't understand a word. I thought perhaps you could translate."

"I'll be happy to." This was a small bit of service that he was pleased to perform even for Hessian soldiers. Did he harbor ill will toward these men who had been pawns in powerful men's hands? These captured soldiers did, after all, come from his homeland, and they suffered intensely. The words of his Lord came to him just then, "Father, forgive them," and he took them very much to his heart.

Peter walked side-by-side with Hooper past his stone house to the prison barracks where the rank odors of filthy, ailing British and German prisoners assaulted his senses. He found himself silently praying the ancient words, "Lord, make me an instrument of your peace." As he did so, his gaze fell upon a man huddled in a corner, his naked arms clutched around his knees.

"Fowler, get me one of those Hessians who have something to tell me."

The young private, his own uniform fading and threadbare, sprang to action. "Yes, sir." Moments later he returned with a fellow on the short side, who gave the appearance of having once being stout, and young. Maybe just weeks ago. A place like this could cause a rapid decline in the heartiest of constitutions. "Colonel Hooper, Colonel Kichline, this is Dietrich Schmidt."

"If you don't mind, I'd like to speak with him privately." Peter tilted his head toward the door. "Outside if you will."

"Yes, of course." Hooper leaned closer. "Would you like an escort?"

Peter assessed the bedraggled prisoner and pursed his lips. "That won't be necessary, thank you. We won't go too far."

Hooper leveled his gaze at the German. "Schmidt, you are in the presence of a very distinguished man." Although the prisoner clearly didn't understand a word, the meaning registered in his eyes.

Peter addressed the POW. "*Guten morgen, Herr Schmidt. Ich bin Colonel Kichline.*"

The prisoner's eyes sparked through their crustiness, and his posture straightened. "*Guten Tag, mein Herr. Ich bin sehr dankbar, dass Sie zu mir gekommen sind.*"

Peter nodded as a way of accepting the man's obvious gratitude. He went on to inquire what Schmidt and his fellow prisoners wanted to communicate to Hooper. "*Ich verstehe, dass Sie versuchen, etwas Wichtiges mitzuteilen?*"

"*Ja wohl, mein herr.*"

"*Komm mit mir,*" commanded Colonel Kichline.

Schmidt looked toward Hooper for the go-ahead, and

the colonel made a small wave with the tips of his fingers. "Yes, go ahead."

The other prisoners gaped at their mate's sudden good fortune, then again, maybe not.

The prison was a short walk from the cemetery, and although the expanse of graves might not have been the most preferred backdrop for a suffering prisoner of war to spill out his heart, no one would bother them there. Besides, the sloping view of the village and the rivers couldn't help but inspire. Schmidt followed a few paces behind, and when they stopped at the crest of the hill, Peter gestured toward a boulder, bare of snow, large enough to accommodate them both. When Schmidt hesitated, Peter said, "*Bitte, nehmen Sie Platz.*"

Schmidt gave a small bow and lowered himself to a sitting position at a respectful distance. He began all at once to thank Peter again for the opportunity to speak freely. Peter returned to his earlier thoughts. This soldier had come to the colonies with the express purpose of siding with the British to overthrow what they considered a rebellion. The prisoner at his side may have been responsible for the deaths of Patriots, maybe some of Peter's own men. Nevertheless, Schmidt was a captive now and not faring well. He sized up the young man, wondering just how old he was. Peter couldn't even determine his hair color, so like feathers he was reminded of Nebuchadnezzar in the Bible. He smelled of sour straw, and his once-proud uniform had been reduced to wrinkles, rends, and dirt, his well-crafted boots, badly scuffed and mud-encrusted.

Peter took on the manner he'd often used as a sheriff and judge. "Where do you come from, Schmidt?"

"*Ich komme aus Offenheim.*"

A slight chink cut through his armor of suspicion. "That is next door to my birthplace, Kircheimbolanden."

Schmidt's mouth formed a perfect O. His eyes came to life, and in them Peter wondered whether he was seeing gladness or remorse. The soldier asked Peter when he had come to America. "I came with my family to Pennsylvania in 1742 at the age of twenty." He paused. "How old are you Schmidt?"

"*Neunzehn.*"

In speaking his age, the young man seemed to have regained a modicum of his youth. He had a story to tell, and Peter found he was eager to listen. A nineteen-year-old German lad didn't often have his own say about the course of his life. "How did you come to be in the military?"

Schmidt gazed toward the hills of New Jersey, the ferry boat just then crossing the Delaware. "I am one of six sons and four daughters, and since my family had little means, my prospects were poor. My only chance to make something of my life was to join the army." He gave a tight laugh. "Not that I had much choice. Our prince had much to say about taking our young men and accepting payment from the British for our services."

The snow around his heart melted. Peter's family had never been financially compromised. He'd known the benefit of their means to come to America with something of a head start, whereas this young fellow had had few options. This was exactly the sort of tyranny he had fought against in battle and would continue to do so.

Schmidt continued. "I arrived here early last summer."

So he was at Brooklyn. He frowned. "How were you captured?"

"During the winter encampment, Continentals harassed us on a regular basis, and they caught several of us."

Peter fixed his eyes on the ferry boat as it moored on the Jersey side, its passengers stepping off carefully in the swift current. There was something he had to know. "I was at Brooklyn." Schmidt's face drained of all color. "I was wounded by a Hessian, and imprisoned." He looked straight into the startled eyes. "Did you engage in any cruelty toward American patriots?"

The youth's hands shook. After some hesitation, he said, "I did as I was told, sir, but I did no harm beside that."

Several moments passed. "What is it you wanted to talk to me about, Schmidt?"

The prisoner gulped, his Adam's apple prominent against his gauntness. He seemed to have trouble getting started, following Peter's revelation. His teeth chattered.

"You may speak freely, Schmidt."

"I, I have great admiration for your people and your country, sir." He shook his head. "I do not admire the British." His voice dropped. "Or even some of my fellow soldiers. I am not a person for harshness." He twisted his hands. "There are a few of us at the prison who have been talking a lot about, well, I, uh, we would like to know if there is any chance for us to be one of you, to fight in your cause."

The breath seemed to go out of Peter's lungs. He hadn't been expecting this. He said nothing for a long time, then he got up, took off his coat, and draped the woolen garment around Schmidt. The young man looked up, wide-eyed, objecting, beginning to peel the cloak off, until Peter's steady hand held the coat fast to the German's shoulder. "Keep it, Schmidt. There's someone I want you to meet."

He found Robert Levers at *Frau* Eckert's tavern, bent over a sizable book, his forehead creased, right hand tattooed with ink.

"Colonel Levers, I'd like to introduce you to someone."

He looked up, blinking a few times before focusing on Peter and the young prisoner. "Good day, Colonel Kichline." He stood to shake their hands, frowning at the young German.

"May we speak with you? This is an important matter."

"Yes, yes, of course." He indicated the chairs across from him. "Please excuse this mess. I am figuring out the payroll."

This was hopeful. Maybe the Congress was fulfilling its duties to the soldiery after all. Peter got right to the point, explaining who the German was and what he and six of his comrades were proposing. Levers pressed his lips together, his head bobbing up and down as he listened. When Peter finished, he stared at Schmidt. Then, "So, you want to join our Cause, do you?"

Peter translated, and the fellow nodded, determined.

"This will not be easy, I assure you. Our own men are suffering privation as they fight for what they most earnestly believe in. Are you prepared for such a life?"

After Peter explained, Schmidt nodded, resolute. Then he said, "We have come to love America and what it stands for. We are familiar with hardship, sir. We are ready to suffer more to become Americans."

For this, Levers needed no translation. "I'll draw up some papers," he said.

CHAPTER SEVENTEEN

"I'm glad you like the chapter." Relieved was more like it.

"You've done a fine job, Erin. I like how you used your article for the historical society as a jumping off point, then branched out to include aspects of Colonel Kichline's story you didn't have space for previously."

Derek McCutcheon's familiar bass lulled her, a voice known across the country as a narrator of historical documentaries and audio readings of his bestselling books. Although she was familiar enough with him by now to be on a first-name basis, the reality of collaborating with the man on his new book still unleashed jitters.

He continued. "Just address those changes we discussed, and this chapter will be ready to go. Then you can focus on Colonel Miles."

"Thanks to you, I feel my writing is getting stronger," she said, wondering immediately if she should have confessed such a thing.

"I'm not so sure I have anything to do with it, Erin. You came to this project with considerable skills that I believe are, as you say, getting stronger."

She heard a smile in his voice. *What a nice man, comfortable in his own skin but not all wrapped up in himself either.* There was one more thing she wanted to say before ending the call. "My family and I are so grateful for your beautiful floral tribute."

"You are quite welcome, my dear."

She appreciated the fatherly tone more than he could know.

"How are you faring in these weeks since your father passed?"

"I'm doing pretty well, thank you. I have my moments, but I'm glad he had a long life."

"Be patient with yourself. You'll find the coming weeks bring both hills and valleys."

She knew this all too well. She was, after all, a widow acquainted with grief.

Her bags were packed, she was ready to go. Almost. Consulting her list on her cell, she checked off "toiletries, shoes—flats, heels, sneakers for the fitness center—two suits, two dresses, two gowns, white gloves, a hat, my pin case." Something was missing. "Vitamins!" She went to the kitchen and started sorting supplements for Friday, Saturday, and Sunday. She'd be meeting Connie at one-thirty for the drive to the annual DAR State Conference in King of Prussia, which gave her forty-five minutes to chill. Paul would pick up Ethan after play practice, and he would spend Thursday and Friday nights with his soon-to-be-stepfather. On Saturday, Paul would drive Ethan to his grandparents' Lansdale home to spend the night with them and his buddy Jake, while Paul attended the state banquet with Erin. She couldn't wait to show him off, hoping he'd like her new gown as much as she did.

She poured a glass of iced tea and went to her study. Toby

took up his spot at her feet after she sat in her recliner and checked her email. A message from her ancestry account caught her eye, an invitation to join a free service called "My People." She read aloud, "'Discover who you're related to, from celebrities to historical figures, presidents to pals on social media.'" Erin made haste to download the app, eager to venture into the wider world of her family history. Once it was installed, she went through the paces, jiggling her right leg as she waited for the initial results.

A banner appeared at the top of the screen, "Relatives," with an icon to the right for categories including social media friends, actors, artists, authors, explorers, historical and military figures, US Presidents and First Ladies. Toby's snoring and the sound of the garbage truck on the street faded as she waited for the first connection to appear.

"Well, how about that!" She grinned when Andy Griffith's face appeared. Underneath she read, "Andy Griffith is possibly your eighth cousin, two times removed." She discovered by clicking on "Relationship," the app linked her family tree to Griffith's, through a common ancestor, Michael Schenk, born in the late 1600s in Switzerland. A notice at the bottom of the family trees gave her a choice of a thumbs up or a thumbs down as to whether or not she considered the information to be accurate. As far as she could tell from her family line, this was a thumbs up.

Completely absorbed, she found three other connections, one to her childhood friend, Jennifer Fritz, her fifth cousin. She also discovered her eighth cousin, once removed, was none other than Debbie Reynolds, from which Erin guessed would also make Carrie Fisher her cousin. "Whoa! What's this, Toby?" Her dog's indignant expression was lost on her. "I'm related to Amelia Earhart! Let's see, sixth cousins. I wonder if the path is correct." The family tree appeared correct up until the common ancestor, someone she'd never heard of. "This is so cool!"

The exhilaration continued as Erin turned up relationships with First Lady Rachel Jackson, Stonewall Jackson, and Henry Wadsworth Longfellow. She couldn't help but wonder if somewhere in her past, there'd been a *Mayflower* descendant, maybe even a US President. Since the app updated frequently, she couldn't wait to uncover the next batch of relatives.

At the ringing of her doorbell she flew across the hall, finding Connie looking her fresh and polished self. "Oh, Connie! Just wait until I tell you what I've found!"

They were at the Northeast Extensions' Quakertown Exit when Erin clapped her hand to her mouth. "Oh, Connie, I'm so sorry! I've been completely monopolizing the conversation."

Her friend's eyes crinkled beneath sunglasses. "I'm enjoying hearing about these new discoveries you're making."

"That's nice of you to say. I'll sit back now and give you a chance to talk."

She paused then said, "Things have been going very well at the Kichline Center."

"Please tell me what's happening."

Connie pulled down her sun visor when brightness spilled onto the windshield. "I finished grant applications for the state historical register of places and the DAR."

"Are our chances of getting them good?"

"Very good, I think."

"I'll bet they were time-consuming."

Connie shrugged her shoulders. "You were quite helpful, and generous with your time given all that happened with your dad."

"The work gave me something else to think about."

"Well, my friend, you also had your book to do and a wedding to plan, so thank you again." She passed a moving van. "Demolition has begun, and the workers are being extra careful not to upset the integrity of the original structure."

"Do you think they'll find anything, like in an archaeological dig?"

"I don't know if they will, since the building has been worked on at various times over many years, but if they do, you'll be the first to know."

Erin smiled to herself, visions of coins, pottery shards, and old papers filling her imagination. Maybe there would even be something related directly to her Grandfather Peter.

Their conversation turned to the DAR state conference, and since Connie had been to several others, Erin picked her brain for information.

"The conference itself begins officially on Friday evening," Connie said, "but during this administration, we've started doing a state book club on Thursday. The last one was successful, so we're doing another this year. The author will be there to speak and do Q and A, followed by a book signing."

"And what about Friday morning and afternoon?"

"This is when the vendors have a chance to set up, and there's a tour in the afternoon."

Erin consulted the conference schedule she'd downloaded. "The tour is after lunch, which is on our own, and will be at the Museum of the American Revolution in Philadelphia. Do you think you'll go?"

"I'd love to, but I promised to help the juniors set up their table. They always have a lot of merchandise to sell, and this means lots of hands on deck."

Erin had an idea. "I've been to the museum twice, and I wouldn't mind filling in for you. That would give me an opportunity to meet some of the younger Daughters."

"Really?"

"Really. Let me do this."

"You'll get no argument from me. Thanks, Erin."

As she skimmed the schedule, she noticed there would be a memorial service on Saturday after lunch. Her stomach clenched as she revisited her father's funeral not yet a month ago. This was one state conference event she'd sit out.

Just shy of a hundred Daughters attended the book club event in which a retired professor from Maryland had given a compelling look into the lives of the women who were at Valley Forge—from Martha Washington to the camp followers. They had endured a lack of proper food and sanitation, the rigors of nursing the sick, including amputations without benefit of anesthesia, and being far from their homes. Erin thought she might like to become more involved in serving active duty military and their families, as well as veterans, through the DAR.

After Q and A, a crowd converged upon the book table,

including members of the Valley Forge Chapter. Filled with joy, Erin embraced them, their perfumed hugs mingling on her jacket. A tall woman with a commanding presence greeted Connie as they drew nearer to the author.

Connie shook her hand. "How good to see you, Susan! What a great event tonight. She was so engaging!"

"I'm pleased too." The woman scanned the buzzing crowd with a smile.

Connie introduced the woman to Erin. "Susan, this is my friend Dr. Erin Miles from the George Taylor Chapter. Erin, this is Susan Hess, the State Book Club chairman."

Erin extended her hand. "I'm pleased to meet you, Susan."

An eyebrow raised. "Doctor, did you say?"

"I'm a historian at Lafayette College."

Connie spoke up. "Erin is currently writing a book about forgotten patriots with none other than Derek McCutcheon."

Susan's grey-green eyes expanded. "The Derek McCutcheon?"

"Yes. The book will be coming out this fall."

"This could make a great book for next year's conference. Would you be interested?"

"Oh, yes, very much so." Erin's heart fluttered.

"Do you think Dr. McCutcheon might be willing to come?"

Connie was practically jumping up and down. "Oh, Erin! Wouldn't that be great?"

She knew Derek was in great demand for national appearances and didn't know whether a smaller audience would be worth his time. Then again, if he were to come, they could fill twice the space. "I would need to ask him."

"Please do. Although nothing is official at this point, we could set the ball in motion." As if remembering her manners, she added, "Even if he's unable, would you consider presenting?"

Erin didn't take offense. After all, no one knew her writing outside of Easton. "Yes, I would. Thank you for the honor.

Erin leaned closer to Connie to be heard above rousing music as younger women, all dressed in white, paraded two-by-two into the ballroom, bearing the US and various other flags, their pinkies linked. "Who are they?" she whispered.

Connie spoke into Erin's ear. "Pages. They're personal attendants to the state regent and officers, and VIP guests from other states."

"Why do they hold pinkies?"

She smiled. "They're pinky pals so they stay together, shoulder to shoulder."

Sydney Stordahl from the Valley Forge chapter grinned in Erin's direction. "It takes a while to learn all these traditions."

Erin inhaled, eyebrows raised. "They are lovely, though."

Once the pages had entered, state dignitaries and guests proceeded down the center aisle to enthusiastic applause. Finally, the Pennsylvania State Regent, a radiant woman on the far side of middle age, entered to cheers suitable to an A-list movie star. She took her time getting to the platform, then called the assembly to order.

"Daughters and guests, welcome to the Pennsylvania

State Society, Daughters of the American Revolution Conference. State Chaplain Ilene Linder will bring us the invocation."

Erin stood through the prayer, Pledge of Allegiance, American's Creed, and the National Anthem, finding herself swathed in goose bumps. Then came the "posting of the colors," when with great solemnity, the flags were placed into floor mounts. As the state regent brought greetings from the National Society, Erin thought her first wedding hadn't been this decorous, nor any of her graduations. For that matter, the only event she could think of rivaling the pomp and circumstance of this one was a Presidential inauguration or a state funeral.

As the state regent brought greetings from Pennsylvania's governor, Erin whispered to Connie, "Why doesn't that one page sit?"

"As long as the state regent stands, she stands. When the regent sits, she sits."

Tough job.

The evening contained a long series of greetings from this society and that organization, including the Sons of the American Revolution, Children of the American Revolution, the hotel manager, the mayor, a smattering of state representatives, and state and national officers, some who took their allotted few minutes, others who warranted the use of a long shepherd's crook to pull them away from the microphone.

At one point, the state regent announced the doors would be opened. "What's that about?" Erin asked her friend.

"If anyone needs to leave, now is the time."

"You can't leave before then?"

"If you must, but once the state regent has entered, no one is to use the center aisle."

Erin gaped at Connie. *This is all taken so very seriously!*

"By the way, Erin," her friend whispered, "make sure your cell ringer is turned off. There's a twenty-five dollar penalty for any device that rings during meetings."

She quickly reached for her evening bag and turned her phone to "mute."

After the opening ceremony, Erin followed a crowd to a receiving line and quickly slipped on a pair of kid gloves her mother had worn to her prom, happy to be thinking of Audrey here and now. *She would love all of this.* She grinned to herself. *On the other hand, Dad would be shaking his head. He was so not formal.*

"What happens now?" she asked Connie.

"This is our opportunity to meet all the dignitaries who came tonight. We shake hands, say a word or two, and move on. The receiving line goes quickly."

Erin shook the Colorado state regent's hand first. "It's nice to meet you. Thanks for coming."

"Pennsylvania is lovely. I'm honored to be here."

And so the line went, until Erin came to the state book club chairman, whose eyes brightened at the sight of her.. "Dr. Miles! I want you to meet our state librarian, Kenna Cole. Kenna, Dr. Miles is a history professor who's writing a book with none other than Derek McCutchen."

"Nice to meet you, Dr. Miles."

Erin felt a nudge at the small of her back.

"I've asked her to consider doing our book club next

year."

"Oh, wouldn't that be wonderful!" Kenna's starry eyes matched her necklace.

Another nudge, this time harder. Erin turned around to see a line of pages whose job it was to keep the line flowing. Her nudger frowned. "Please move along."

"They are talking to me," Erin said. "I won't be rude."

Susan Hess seemed to realize she was holding up progress and making Erin pay the price. "We'll talk some more this weekend."

Erin managed to smile as she met other state VIPs, but by the time the line ended, she smoldered while relating the incident to Connie.

"Those pages take their jobs very seriously," she said with a laugh. "My guess is you were the victim of one newly-minted. Come on. Let's get some wine and dessert.

She definitely needed chocolate.

CHAPTER EIGHTEEN

"My, but it's good to see you, Phoebe."

As a young woman, Peter's niece had arrived in Easton to keep house for him after his first wife's death. She'd also captured the affections of the village's school master, William Hanlon, who now served a cluster of churches across the river in Sussex County.

Phoebe removed her hat and cloak, handing them to Bett, Joe standing just behind her as he had always done with *Frau* Hamster. She looked down at the girl gazing up at her. "Oh, my! Is this Elizabeth?"

The toddler flashed a gap-toothed grin. "Yesh."

"You are becoming quite the young lady. I hardly recognized you."

Catherine touched her daughter's shoulder. "She is growing so quickly I'm hard pressed to keep her in the right-sized clothing and shoes." She paused. "Phoebe, I'd like you to meet our housekeeper, Bett, who has recently come to us. Bett, this is our niece, Mrs. Hanlon. Joe, you remember her, don't you?"

"Yes, ma'am." He bowed to Phoebe.

Bett curtsied. "Pleased to meet you, ma'am."

"And I am happy to make your acquaintance, Bett." She smoothed back windswept hair as she said, "You are practically a man now, Joe."

He blushed as Bett spoke up. "I'll bring some

refreshments."

As they made themselves comfortable in the parlor, Phoebe took up the reins of conversation. "Uncle Peter, you are looking almost robust. Are you feeling better then?"

He smiled, affection swelling his chest. "Yes, my dear, I am quite well. Under the ministrations of Catherine and Susannah, I have returned to health."

Phoebe frowned as she exchanged a look with Catherine. "And where is Susannah?"

"Off doing her work among the wounded," he said, none too happily. "We've all just recovered from an illness that laid low everyone in our household, and Susannah couldn't wait to return to the soldiers."

Phoebe's mouth curved downward. "Our little parishes experienced a similar outbreak a few weeks ago, and William was at home for several days. Fortunately, the children are back at their school again, but, well, I needed to see you because I have something …"

At the sound of coughing drifting down from upstairs, Catherine's face blanched. Elizabeth spoke up, her head bobbing up and down. "Baby's sick."

Phoebe turned to Catherine "Has he not recovered from the illness?"

"Abraham has had a much harder time. I'd better go to him. Please excuse me."

"Me go too?" Elizabeth yanked her mother's skirts.

"Stay with me, little cousin." Phoebe held out her arms to the child, who went right to her.

After Catherine departed, Peter said, "I'm afraid she hasn't fully recovered either. She's up at all hours taking care of him. We all help, but she insists on being with him then as well."

"What does the doctor say?"

Peter lifted his hands, palms up. "The sickness is harder for babies to overcome." A knot filled his gut.

"I will keep Abraham in my fervent prayers. We must remember babies are also resilient." She paused, exhaling. "I do have some rather sad news, Uncle Peter."

He was instantly on the alert. "What might this news be, niece?"

Her face stretched, making her look older than her not-quite three decades. "I'm afraid my Aunt Catherine has died."

Peter's jaw dropped. "My brother Andrew's wife? When? How did this happen?"

"She died a month ago at home. I didn't know until I saw Uncle Andrew yesterday."

He struggled to sort through the morass. "Andrew is here?"

"He's at an encampment near our home."

"Why didn't he let us know sooner?"

"I asked him the same thing. He was in northern New Jersey with the army, and he didn't get back home to Bucks County until several days after Aunt Catherine's death. Most of the family, including Uncle Charles, were bedridden at the time. They had all they could do to make final arrangements while caring for the sick among them. He was awfully sorry you didn't know." She twisted a hankie. "I would like to have been there for her. She and I were quite close."

"Yes, I know. She was a good woman. Do you know what took her life?"

Phoebe seemed to hesitate. "She was sick for a few weeks, then began to recover just as everyone else in their household fell ill. With Uncle Andrew off fighting, she had her hands full and succumbed." She whispered, "He's quite stricken."

"Who's minding the children?" He leaned forward, ready to spring to action.

"Grandmother and Grandfather Koppelger have taken the youngest, and the older ones are caring for themselves."

His thoughts swam in circles, as if being dragged through a fast current. "How long will Andrew be in the area?"

"I think they'll be there for a few days at least."

"I must go to him."

"Perhaps you could accompany me when I return— tomorrow if that suits you?"

"Yes, of course. We'll be happy for your company."

Bett arrived with a tray as Abraham let loose a pathetic coughing jag from upstairs. No one said a word.

He sat with his younger brother inside Andrew's tent, smelling an ashy scent. At the end of April with crocuses poking hither and yon through patches of snow, the men in Andrew Kichline's company warmed themselves, as well as fed their stomachs, by the campfires. Something about his sibling's appearance disquieted Peter. Andrew, always slighter of build and fairer haired, seemed darker somehow, his face furrowed like a farmer's field. The blue-gray eyes conveyed sorrow Peter found difficult to look upon. *Maybe I appeared the same way after Margaretta died. And Anna.* The memory of his own grief encouraged him to comfort his brother with the same comfort he had received, from

God and others.

After a long silence, Andrew spoke, his voice husky, eyes pleading. "How did you cope, Peter?"

"I don't remember much about the first couple of months after I lost Margaretta, just that I wandered as if caught in a heavy fog. I could only take one step at a time. Gradually, I began to see more clearly again."

"I can't believe you went through this twice." Andrew paused, tight-lipped. "You survived. I suppose I will too."

"You will, brother. Our heavenly Father gives grace and strength to go on."

Andrew nodded, looking down at his hands. "I only wish I had been with her. That's the part I find hardest to bear. She needed me, and I …" His voice broke.

At that moment, a soldier appeared at the tent's entrance. "Colonel Kichline, I'm sorry to disturb you." His eyes widened when both Peter and Andrew answered in tandem, "Yes? What can I do for you?"

Peter looked at Andrew, and the two brothers shared a low-key laugh, which lifted some of the heavy burden they'd shouldered moments before.

"I'm sorry, sir, but, well …" The young soldier was clearly flummoxed.

"Private Shotwell, I'd like you to meet my brother, Colonel Peter Kichline of the Northampton County Flying Camp."

Shotwell gave a crisp bow. "Sir. I'm pleased to meet you."

"The pleasure is mine, private."

"Is the matter you bring urgent?" Andrew appeared in command of himself again.

"It can wait, sir."

"Very well. I'll find you when I finish here."

"Yes, sirs." He bowed as he backed away, as if in the presence of royalty.

Peter smiled. "See how easily laughter can return? Life won't always be full of pain."

"I'm very glad you came to see me. Perhaps I was wrong in leaving my family after Cath—" He paused. "I suppose I could have asked for a leave of absence, but to me, she was already gone. What more could I do?"

"I understand."

"Mother and Father Koppelger are looking after the younger children, so I know they're in good hands. I just hope I did the right thing. My country needs me too."

Peter had a feeling his brother wasn't asking for input or advice, just giving voice to his thoughts. He wanted to give Andrew the space he needed to work through these things without trying to fix or correct. The sounds of men talking as they went about their business permeated the dwelling and after a few minutes, Peter brought up a far different matter.

"I wonder, Andrew, how your recruitment has been."

His brother ran a hand through his unkempt hair. "I've struggled to hold on to my men. We have some deeply committed soldiers, but others get discouraged and want to go home. They say they'll return to the ranks if needed to defend Bucks County. I haven't had desertions, but very few have stayed after their initial recruitment ended."

Peter offered his brother a crooked grin. "Could you use ten more soldiers?"

At least momentarily, Andrew's grief faded. "Indeed! Do you have ten men to give me?"

"I do. In fact, you may be the answer to their prayers."

Andrew, though no skeptic, had never fully shared his

brother's wholehearted faith. "I'm not sure I've ever been the answer to anyone's prayers."

"Oh, but I disagree, on several counts. Presently there are ten young German men in Easton who are eager to join the Cause."

The blue eyes constricted. "Perhaps you'd better explain fully."

"I have spoken with these men at length. Each of them speaks only German, having recently arrived in America by way of involuntary service to Britain."

The light dawned. "Hessians?"

"Yes, all of them prisoners, young men who came at the behest of rulers who dictated the terms of their lives. Now, they see what America has to offer, especially in breaking free from British rule, and they want to fight to make this a reality. They want a better life, and they are willing to fight and die if necessary to make this happen. I have permission from authorities in Northampton County, myself among them, to find a place for these men. They require a commander who speaks their language, and that is where you come in."

Andrew was leaning on his elbows, stroking his chin. "This could work very well, Peter. And the timing is perfect. I'm not going to be in this area much longer."

"I can have them ready in a couple of days. We need to outfit them in some way."

"I don't have much, but we have enough arms, and I can scare up some clothing. What do they possess?"

"Very little. I will say, however, each of them has a fine pair of boots. Between the two of us, we should be able to outfit them."

Peter could almost see the inside of his brother's brain

at work. "You know, we might be able to use them not only as soldiers, but as spies. With their knowledge of German, they could easily pass through Hessian ranks to glean information."

"I've had similar thoughts, and I know they will do anything they can to help. They've already signed oaths of allegiance."

"I like their dedication." Andrew looked deeply into Peter's eyes. "Thank you."

He knew his brother wasn't just referring to the Hessians. "You're welcome."

CHAPTER NINETEEN

At six-thirty, Connie had been up for an hour, fixing coffee in the room's tiny machine, showering and blow drying her hair, looking flawless. This woman obviously woke up, up. Erin felt grubby by contrast. She loved mornings, but rather than dive in headfirst, she dipped herself into them one toe at a time. Rousing herself through a shower and makeup application, she felt readier for conversation as she pulled her red suit from the closet. "So, the first thing we do is a breakfast, right?"

Connie was arranging her copious ribbons on a suit jacket the color of daffodils. "Yes, this is the Cameo breakfast."

She was still working out DAR lingo. "Do women wear cameos or something?"

"The members of the society do."

Erin craned her neck to see if her friend was wearing one. She wasn't. "So, what exactly is this group?"

"The Cameo Society is for women whose mothers, daughters, nieces, or aunts are also DAR members. It's to promote generational involvement in DAR. There's a simple application to join, and there's a pin to wear."

She couldn't help but laugh. "Naturally! There seems to be a pin for every occasion." Not that she minded. Having never been a Girl Scout, she rather looked forward to filling her blue and white ribbon.

"Once your mother's app is approved, you can join."

"What does being a member entail?" She didn't think she could swallow another bite of activity.

Connie waved her hand. "Mainly a breakfast meeting at our state conference."

That she could manage.

Erin spooned yogurt on top of her quiche Lorraine, then sprinkled Tabasco sauce over the food. Why was everyone staring at her?

"Yes, my friends, you can dress her up, but you can't take her out," Sydney joked, relieving some of Erin's embarrassment.

She decided to dial back her food mash ups for the duration of the conference, at least publicly, but the incident left her wondering … *If I behave like this at forty-seven, what will I be like at eighty?*

The morning business section commenced at nine o'clock sharp with a musical prelude, followed by the entrance of state officers with their pages. The state regent called the meeting to order, then the chaplain gave her invocation, and visiting dignitaries led them in the Pledge of Allegiance, the American's Creed—which Erin had just about memorized—and "God Bless America." A long, slow progression of minutes and reports began, with each presenter admonished to observe the time limit.

"They're quite strict about how long people speak,"

Connie whispered to Erin. "We have timekeepers who tell the person to stop if they go over."

When an image of a page with a huge gong presented itself to her, Erin covered her mouth to keeping from laughing. She wondered if she were the only one who saw the humor in some of these rules, although truth be told, she rather liked the pageantry and protocol. After all, she'd been the little girl who once pretended to pour imaginary tea into china cups with white-gloved hands at a DAR meeting. She smiled at the memory, her arms tingling at the realization of a dream come true. Here she was, at the Pennsylvania State Society Daughters of the American Revolution, because she was one of them, because her Grandfather Peter and her Grandfather Charles had laid everything on the line to create these United States.

She followed the schedule in her conference booklet, amazed to see the morning session stretched to eight pages. After each state officer gave a report, Pennsylvania's chairmen of national committees presented theirs. A few left her numb, but one captured her attention, about Alpha Bravo Canine, an organization dedicated to raising and training service dogs for veterans suffering from PTSD. The chair of the committee appeared at the lectern with one of the dogs, a chocolate Lab named Gus.

Erin's attention held for the next two reports, then flagged when state chairmen issued nearly two dozen awards with every recipient photographed with the state regent. She wasn't sure she'd be able to keep her eyes open when her lids took on a mind of their own, but mercifully their leader called for a ten-minute break. She woke fully up to a virtual tide of Daughters flooding from the room, spilling into the hallways. Erin sensed where everyone was heading and, having drunk three cups of coffee, decided the brief trek to her room would take as long as waiting in one of the lines trying not to hop from foot to foot.

In the latter part of the morning meeting, Erin didn't think she could handle another report and whispered in Connie's ear, "Is it okay if I leave for a while?"

"Sure. These reports do go on and on, but each one is necessary."

Guilt stabbed her conscience, but Erin decided she needed a longer break than those ten minutes an hour ago had afforded. To her delight, she was not alone. Out in the hallway, several Daughters talked to each other in low voices, and shoppers crowded the exhibit room. Apparently playing hooky was okay. After all that sitting and listening, she needed some retail therapy, as well as a new tote bag to carry her haul. She found one she liked at the Juniors table, then she bought a C.A.R. tee shirt and pin for Ethan and a DAR umbrella for herself. She also ordered a Korean War commemorative pin for her ribbon in honor of her father's service, holding back tears as she slipped her card through the credit device. She found a friend from the Valley Forge Chapter selling silk scarves to benefit the Bell Tower at the George Washington Memorial Chapel and bought one for herself and one for her mom. She entered raffles for five different baskets created by individual chapters around mostly patriotic themes—her favorite being Byers Choice figures of George and Martha Washington and Benjamin Franklin. She also purchased an assortment of pens, key chains, ball caps, and mugs. If only she could've found something suitable for Paul. She glowed at the thought of him. Once the meetings were over, he would come for the state dinner.

Erin behaved herself at the National Defense Luncheon, resisting the urge to mix cream with pepper and pour them over a Caesar salad. She even managed to stay awake for an interesting presentation by a USO representative, which went a tad long. The business session resumed at two-thirty, while voting occurred in a side room for two hours. Erin stayed at the meeting long enough to hear reports from the Valley Forge and George Taylor Chapters, then left to vote for state officers. Every part of her body and mind craved a place to go and think her own thoughts. Still, this was her first state meeting, and she didn't want to miss anything important, or be rude. She went for an iced tea at the hotel café, then returned to the ballroom for the last thirty minutes, feeling slightly more refreshed. Connie got involved in a conversation with someone from Gettysburg afterward, so Erin took off for a short nap. Before drawing the curtains and lying down, she reached into her snack bag for some dark chocolate with sea salt and dipped it into a container of creamer she found next to the coffee maker. Within minutes, she'd eaten the entire bar and gone through five little cups. *I definitely need a nap.*

"So he's doing all right then?" She'd been texting Ethan, but he'd mostly responded in emoticons.

"More than all right." Her mother-in-law's voice sounded even cheerier than usual. "I'd call him to the phone, but he's outside with Al and Jake putting in a zip line."

"A zip line!"

"Yes, and I'm just hoping Al doesn't monopolize their time."

Erin huffed a laugh. She could just picture Al in a helmet zipping several feet above the lawn while amused neighbors watched from second-floor windows. "When did my guys arrive?"

"They got here just before supper last night, and since Ethan wanted Asian food, we went to a hibachi place. He got a kick out of the chef's antics with knives and flames."

"I'll bet!"

"This morning I made a full breakfast, and they've been bouncing from one activity to the next ever since."

"Thanks for filling me in. I haven't had time to check my emails or see if anyone called."

"They keep you pretty busy then?"

She nodded. "This is the most intense conference I've ever been to, but I've enjoyed myself. I've met Daughters from across the state, and even though the business meetings drag at times, I love learning about the wonderful things the society does, especially for veterans."

"I know Paul is looking forward to seeing you. What 'til you see him! He looks so handsome."

Tingling, she asked, "When did he leave?"

"Oh, I'd say a half hour ago."

"I'd better get cracking then!" Erin checked her watch, alarmed to discover her nap had stretched to forty-five minutes. After ending the conversation, she bustled to the shower, deciding her hair only needed a few tweaks, rather than a full shampoo. Connie entered the room while Erin was applying her makeup.

"It smells good in here!"

"I love the hotel's body wash. I didn't use all of it in case you want to try some."

Connie sprawled onto her bed. "I'm toast."

"I can be finished here in a few minutes or use the room mirror to finish my makeup."

"Take your time, Erin. I need to close my eyes for a minute or two."

She opened the door to find two handsome men on the other side, both wearing expectant expressions. For a moment, she couldn't seem to locate her voice, taking in the sight of her tall, grinning fiancé in a dark blue suit with a tie and pocket square in her dress's pale blue. How had he known? She hadn't described her gown to him, or had she?

He breathed her name. "Erin." Paul's eyes made a polite sweep of her. "You look beautiful."

"Thank you." She felt middle-school-dance shy. "I like your suit."

"Paul! Terry! Don't you men look handsome!" Connie rushed toward the door, waving them into a room cluttered with the detritus of garment bags, empty pantyhose containers, hangers, and dry cleaner's plastic.

"What a beautiful dress, Connie," Paul said, then abruptly looked back at Erin, kissing her cheek.

Terry grinned. "I'd say we made out pretty well."

They were seated at a table toward the back with four other couples, two from George Taylor, the rest from Valley Forge. The state banquet had begun with the usual ceremony, but there seemed to be a lighter note in the transformed ballroom, lent by the feeling of a job well done. Pots of tulips and hyacinths, along with balloons in matching shades promoted the festivities, and a wooden birdhouse lit inside by tea lights graced each table.

"What is the American's Creed?" Paul pointed to the item in the program bulletin.

"We say it at every meeting," Erin said.

"There seems to be a lot of ritual."

"There sure is, Paul, but I'm finding I like these traditions." She smiled at him, and he squeezed her hand.

A Daughter named Tina Ference introduced her husband as her "HODAR" as a band started playing an oldie Erin couldn't identify.

Paul's eyebrows raised. "HODAR? What is that?"

Tina lifted her chin. "'Husband of DAR.'"

"Who also happens to be an SAR," Connie said.

Paul pressed his lips together, closed his eyes. "Let me see. Bob is a husband of a DAR, but also a member of the Sons of the American Revolution?"

"What about you?" Bob asked, while the waiters placed artisan salads in front of them.

"I'm not a member, if that's what you're asking, but…" he turned to Erin, "I did find out something quite interesting."

"I'm all ears."

"My mother called the other day to tell me she found some old family photographs. Her grandmother was wearing one of those DAR things, and she was all dressed up." He pointed toward Erin's ribbon, a small model Sydney had encouraged her to buy for formal occasions so the bigger one didn't weigh down her dress.

She burst into a smile and waited for him to continue.

"I went online and was able to trace her back to a patriot."

"Oh, Paul, how exciting!" Connie's face lit up as she produced her cell phone from a tiny purse. "If you give me her name, I can look her up in the DAR database."

"Oh, uh, sure."

While he gave Connie the information, the others nibbled their salads. Moments later, she located a certain record. "I found Sarah Bennett, and her, rather your, ancestor was a Jacob Shepherd. Let's see …" She scrolled. "Oh, here it is! Oh, wow! He was in the Continental Line at Brandywine, Germantown, and spent the winter at Valley Forge!"

"Bingo!" Erin cried. She hugged Paul sideways. "Valley Forge!"

When the backslapping and merriment began to settle, Bob offered to help Paul fill out an SAR application. "Yes, I'd like that." He smiled at Erin. "Then I can be a DODAR too."

She playfully slapped his shoulder. "HODAR."

Erin laughed when the state regent kicked off her heels and started tearing up the dance floor with her husband. Just a few hours earlier, she'd been presiding over a solemn business meeting with timekeepers, pages, and a rather ominous-looking gavel. Here and now, however, Madam State Regent resembled a teenager at her senior prom. So did many of the other Daughters, entering the joyous fray. One rather diminutive woman in a tasteful, black sequined gown, was doing a semi-John Travolta, her double chin lifted, while her juniors applauded.

Connie leaned over to Erin. "When we party, we party."

"I'll say!"

The band finished the number from "Saturday Night Fever," switching to a familiar Beach Boys hit, the singer sounding very much like Mike Love.

"Shall we?" Paul held out his hand, and Erin felt its familiar roughness. She didn't know what kind of dancer he was, curious to discover. She was a decent hoofer herself, but she hadn't partied since Jim's death. She smiled as she recalled the last time they'd danced together, at his cousin's wedding six years earlier when little Ethan had wowed everyone with his grown-up-looking suit.

"Earth to Erin. Come in please."

She looked into his eyes. "I'm ready to dance."

CHAPTER TWENTY

When he left the Sunday service at the courthouse, his memory carried him back to the days before the church was built, when this place had served both as a temple of justice and a temple of the Lord. Pastor Rodenheimer had moved worship back to the Centre Square site until the contagion at the church passed. Peter inhaled deeply of the mid-May morning air, containing the sweetness of blooming trees and flowers while ignoring the impinging odors of pigs and sheep at their stations in and around the pond. Even those filled him with a joy of being alive, of being home. Winter was indeed passing, and he prayed sickness would fade with the last of the frosts.

Out of the corner of his eye, he noticed Susannah talking to Peter Schneider, who in Peter's mind, stood at a respectful distance despite the unmistakably glowing gaze. He sighed, feeling his chest rise and fall. He was becoming resigned to his daughter's burgeoning womanhood and the prospect of an assiduous indentured servant as a suitor.

"Colonel Kichline!"

He turned to the right and saw the welcome face of Michael Gress, a Williams Township farmer, church elder, fellow soldier and prisoner in New York. "Mr. Gress." His smile came instantly as he reached out and clasped the man's hand. "How very good to see you! I've been wondering how you've been faring." As far as he could tell, Gress seemed his hearty self, minus a few pounds and the addition of graying around his temples. Peter bowed toward the man's wife and tipped his cap. "Mrs. Gress. I am delighted to see you as well."

She curtsied. "Colonel Kichline. You appear to be well again."

"I am, thank you. The ministrations of my wife and family have been a sweet balm to body and soul." He patted Catherine's arm as she extended her hand to Elizabeth Gress.

"The same has been true for me." Gress gave his wife an appreciative smile then looked around. "This is the first I've come to town since our return. My wife has insisted I stay as close to home as possible and regain my strength."

"A wise woman to be sure. How is Mr. Gress Jr.?"

"He, too, has been on the mend, a little slower perhaps than myself since he caught sickness in March."

A scene playing itself out several yards away broke into Peter's joyful reunion, and he became aware of disapproving stares toward the same direction. Robert Levers had positioned himself at the opposite side of the courthouse door than Pastor Rodenheimer, greeting parishioners as if he were the minister. Peter searched Rodenheimer's face and saw a sliver of what appeared to be awareness of the situation, as well as a certain upturn in his mouth. While the congregation met the pastor with smiles and handshakes, stone faces and forced hand clasps were Levers's lot. Mary Levers stood dutifully by her husband's side wearing a tentative expression, her large eyes wider than usual.

What does he think he's doing?

"He's in charge of practically every other aspect of running the town," Gress said, "I guess he figures the church is under his jurisdiction too." Contempt tinged his words.

A number of people gaped at the flagrant display of disrespect toward the pastor. Just then Robert Traill sauntered into their midst, glancing at Levers over his shoulder. His wife broke away from him, carrying their baby, joining the other wives in conversation.

"So, now he's the minister too?" Traill fixed his eyes on the Williams Township resident. "Good to see you, Mr. Gress. How are you?"

"I am pleased to see you as well, Mr. Traill." Gress shook his head. "I guess he's not busy enough sticking his nose into every farmer's business in these parts."

Traill grimaced. "So I've heard."

"What's been happening?" Peter asked.

"Mr. Levers regularly comes to our farms to procure whatever items he deems necessary for the troops."

This didn't seem so bad since, after all, this was the man's job. Only a year ago, Peter was knocking on doors collecting firearms for the troops—a thankless business.

As if reading Peter's thoughts, Gress provided additional insight. "I know he must do this, sir, and I and every patriotic farmer in Williams Township is glad to help however we can, but the problems are, number one …" Gress held out his index finger. "He takes more than we can give, leaving us to scrounge for our own families." He added his middle finger to the first one. "Number two, he pays way under market value for what he takes and gives us Continental currency, which I'm sorry to say, we all know is worth about as much as a three-legged horse." Out came digit number three. "Third, he takes more from the German farmers than the English or Scotch-Irish."

Peter frowned. "You're saying he shows favoritism to

non-Germans?"

"That is exactly what I'm saying."

Traill gave a low whistle, looking meaningfully at Peter. "I think we need to pay Mr. Levers a visit."

In fact, he would rather take on a unit of Royal Dragoons single-handedly.

A slender man of indeterminate age met him and Traill at Levers's residence near the county jail, a fellow so new he gave no signal of recognition. Almost in spite of himself, Peter chuckled when he realized the fellow reminded him of an effigy he'd seen of King George in Philadelphia, in which the monarch, in clothes too big for himself, displayed long, dangling arms and a vacant expression.

"What can I do for you?" His manner was brisk, his lack of good manners not sitting well with Peter. Apparently civility ended at this doorstep.

Before Peter could open his mouth, Traill growled, "We're here to see Mr. Levers, *son*."

The soldier squared his shoulders. "Mr. Levers is a busy man."

"So are we." Traill muscled his way past the flustered guard, who squawked, crow-like. Peter entered the front room, which had been turned into an office where two other troops worked at tables. Candlelight strained against the foggy morning, and Levers's face was pressed to a paper on his desk as he spoke to a soldier at his left. "Is this all you got from Mr. Esser?"

"Yes, sir. I tried my best." The soldier grunted. "He's not an easy man to intimidate."

"No, *Herr* Esser is not." Levers gave a scornful laugh. "These Germans aren't to be trifled with, yet we have to remind them now and again who's in charge here."

Peter and Traill gaped at each other, disbelief mingling with disgust and anger.

Levers gave a sharp look in the direction of the man who'd met them at the door. "Yes, what is it, Private?"

"Mr. Levers, I told them you were busy." The young body appeared to be vibrating. Levers noticed Peter and Traill and stood, offering what passed for a smile. "Good day, Colonel Kichline, Mr. Traill." He gave the impression gout would be more welcome.

The aide's eyes popped at the sound of "colonel."

Peter extended his hand, finding Levers's grip strong.

"Gentlemen, what a pleasant surprise." He looked at the man beside him. "Private Kanary, I'd like you to meet two of Easton's most distinguished gentlemen, Colonel Peter Kichline and Mr. Robert Traill."

Something about the introduction set as poorly as one of Bett's oil-soaked hushpuppies. "And this is one of my aides, Private John Kanary. This is the distinguished colonel who led our brave soldiers at Long Island last summer."

The soldier began bowing and muttering something intelligible.

"At ease, Private Kanary. And where do you come to us from?"

His face brightened. "Well, Colonel, my mother was born in New York, but her father took a job in Philadelphia when I was two years old, so I grew up there until I was eight, and my father's job ended because of a dispute with the boss, and then I went back, with them of course, to New York, but I mean Albany not city of. I stayed there until I married my wife, who is from Sussex County, New Jersey, and moved to be closer to her family of farmers."

Peter closed his eyes against the onslaught of the obtuse life story.

Traill was more direct. "What kind of greeting do you call that?"

"Well, I was told by my grandfather, or was it my uncle, back in New York, Albany, not city, that when you meet someone, you should help them get to know you."

Levers stepped in. "Remind me, Private Kanary, to have a talk with you later today."

"Oh, yes, sir, of course, sir. I look forward to talking with you, especially when you're so busy and I know you have to go …"

"You are dismissed!"

The private saluted, bowed, and backed out of the front door.

"I think you'd better have a long talk with that one," Traill said.

Levers grinned. "If I can get a word in edgewise. At first he's tight-lipped, but just get him started …" He invited them to sit down on chairs flanking his desk, Peter disliking the way the seating arrangement forced him and Traill into physically subordinate positions.

"We've come on rather important business, Mr. Levers," Peter said.

Levers sat in his leather chair, no doubt imported from a fine Philadelphia furniture establishment. "So much of the affairs of these times are important."

"Yes, and you're in the middle of it all." Traill's sarcasm seemed to bounce off Levers.

"I have been given a good deal of responsibility."

Peter detected weariness beneath the self-important veneer, and a right hand betraying a tremor so slight only the observant would notice.

"Perhaps too much," Traill said.

Levers sat taller, his eyes narrowing. "What do you mean by that, Mr. Traill?"

Peter broke into the exchange. "As I well know from hard experience, Mr. Levers, one man can do a great deal, but he can only do so much. He is, after all, one man."

"Where is this going, Colonel Kichline?"

Peter leaned forward to lessen the distance between them. "Perhaps you should let those who have their own jobs do their own jobs." When Levers's face remained blank, Peter spelled out the situation for him. "Everyone knows you hold an important position, Mr. Levers. There is no need to flaunt. Humility is a necessary component of the best leaders." He paused for a moment, observing Levers's changing expression.

Traill barged into the conversation. "In other words, let Pastor Rodenheimer greet people after church. What you did the other day didn't sit well."

"With you?" Levers blurted, his face reddening.

"With anyone, sir."

The soldiers in the room looked in their direction, then abruptly down at their work, their quills scratching against the temporary silence.

Levers smirked. "You came here to tell me not to greet people after church."

"No, Mr. Levers," Peter said, "we came here to advise you to show more humility after church by not standing in the place of our pastor."

"Was he offended then?"

"Mr. Rodenheimer is an unassuming man, but he looked rather surprised at your show. Many others expressed their aversion, however."

"Is that all?"

"No, Mr. Levers, that is not all," Traill said. "There have been reports of you and your soldiers taking more than is due you from our farmers, of paying them unfairly, and treating those of German extraction with a decided lack of regard."

Levers's lips pinched together, his face aflame. "I have been appointed by Congress to procure food and supplies for our troops, Mr. Traill. These are deserving men who are putting their lives, their fortunes, and their sacred honor on the line to win independence, and you would deny them the meager goods I am able to supply from these fattened farmers who wouldn't give so much as a stick of hay or a cup of milk if they weren't forced to do so?"

Peter's temper flared, and he took two deep breaths to keep hot words in check. "Mr. Levers, every patriotic man, woman, and child in Northampton County is doing everything possible to feed and clothe our troops, often at great personal sacrifice. They do not need to be strong-armed into giving. Can you deny your men have been forceful and insolent against the German population?"

Levers kept silence.

"I thought not. There is a fine line, sir, between doing an unpleasant job with the authority placed upon you and thrusting your weight around unnecessarily."

The soldiers in the room continued to appear engrossed in their paperwork. Peter would have preferred conducting this interview in privacy, but Levers had forced their hands.

Traill had the last word. He rose from the chair and

bent forward, speaking in a low voice. "I advise you to remember, Mr. Levers, no one is indispensable."

CHAPTER TWENTY-ONE

Being with Paul filled her with joy. Being with him in his fifteen-year-old Mercedes hurtling down the Turnpike's Northeast Extension at a cool eighty, not so much. Then again, the speedometer didn't always work. Not long ago she'd driven him to the airport for a quick visit to his parents', and when she backed out of his driveway, the brakes hadn't engaged. She'd shrieked, "The brakes aren't working!" while bracing herself for an inevitable crash. Why wasn't Paul freaking out? They could be dead in a matter of minutes, depending on traffic.

"Oh, they do that first thing in the morning." He'd actually yawned while saying this.

"Paul!"

"Yes?"

"I can't make the car stop!"

"Just pump the brake a couple of times. Once the juices start flowing, they're fine."

The episode had left her shaken. "I need you to get these brakes fixed." She didn't add, "Or I will never drive this car again." This was tacitly understood.

"My mechanic said the systems are just old, and you only need to pump the brakes a little."

Once she retrieved her jaw from the fraying floor mat she said, Paul."

"Yes?"

"Get a new car. Soon."

As of this day, however, he hadn't made up his mind what kind of car to get, another Mercedes? A Beemer? Perhaps an Audi or VW. He said he preferred German engineering because of the tight, fast feel of the road. She wasn't surprised—Paul was in possession of a seriously lead foot. On this particular day, she'd offered to take the minivan to Philadelphia, but he said "The Benz is easier to park." She found herself praying extra hard to get there and back in one piece.

She needed to take her mind off the antediluvian vehicle. "Have you been to the Pennsylvania Historical Society before?"

He nodded. "While I was at Penn, which was a long time ago. I've been eager to go back, but most of my book research has been within Northampton and Lehigh Counties."

"I went when I first started researching Samuel Miles." She smiled. "And here I am digging deeper into his life. Derek wants me to describe his service as mayor of Philadelphia and what came afterwards. My dissertation focused on his early life and the war."

"I'm sure you'll find a lot of interesting information today."

"And you'll get to research this possible Patriot ancestor. You said Jacob Shepherd was from Bucks County?"

"I think his family came from Bucks, but I've found records in Philadelphia as well."

"Bucks was once part of Philadelphia County, which you already know. Maybe they lived in Philadelphia when they first came, then went to Bucks."

"I'm hoping to find out when his family got here and

218

sort out Jacob's dates."

When they had looked into the man's life online, they'd come across two other Shepherds in the same area. Their family trees had become tangled, with the two Jacob Shepherds being married to the same woman and no documentation to back up the connections.

"I think we'll be able to uncover at least some of the mystery today," she said. "I do hope you find you're a descendant of the Jacob Shepherd who's a proven patriot." Sydney Stordahl had double-checked the DAR database and confirmed what Connie had found after a quick search, that he'd served at the Battle of Brandywine, then wintered at Valley Forge.

"I hope so too." He pulled into the left lane to pass a Mini. "And what discoveries have you been making on that ancestry app?"

She grinned. "If they're correct, I'm many times cousins with Grover Cleveland, Dolly Parton, and King Edward II."

Paul made a chuffing sound. "That's quite a spread."

"Just think, you may be marrying royalty."

He pressed his hand against hers. "I know I am."

Midday dazzling sunlight, after spending hours in dimly-lit archives, pouring over microfiche and reference books, sent Erin for her sunglasses. She and Paul stood on the sidewalk, adjusting not only to the brightness but Locust Street's pervasive clamor. Their morning research had yielded a gold mine of information, including original letters Samuel Miles had written as mayor of Philadelphia, plus Paul's confirmation that proved Patriot Jacob Shepherd was, in fact, his six times great grandfather. "Now I just need birth, marriage, and death certificates for the most recent generations for my SAR application."

"We'll be quite the patriotic family—DAR, C.A.R, and SAR!"

"Too bad there isn't a Dogs of the American Revolution."

Remembering her son's creation when she was joining the DAR, she said, "No, but there is a Monkeys of the American Revolution."

He frowned. "You can't be serious."

"You are too gullible, Paul Bassett! I'll explain over lunch."

"All that research has made me hungry," he said over the roar of a SEPTA bus.

"My grandmother used to say head work was harder than physical work." She smiled at the memory. "I'm not sure if that can be proven scientifically, but I'm with you."

There were several nearby options, but they didn't appeal. "Let's go someplace quieter, more special," he said.

"City Tavern."

"Good choice!" He pursed his lips, thinking. "My guess is we're about ten blocks away."

She wasn't wearing her best walking shoes.

As if reading her mind he said, "I think we're too hungry for a brisk walk before lunch. Let's get a cab. I don't want to mess with a bus or subway."

"You won't get an argument from me."

A twenty-something woman in colonial garb led them to a small, second-floor room with a fireplace and view of the rear grounds. After she handed them menus, a man came over and filled their pewter mugs with ice water. Neither she nor Paul opened the bill of fare right away, preferring to bask in the ambience, transported back to the eighteenth century.

"I haven't been here in years," he said. "I half expect to see Thomas Jefferson walking through the door."

"Or Peter Kichline." She grinned. "I'm amazed to think he ate here, probably many times as a delegate to the Provincial Convention, and member of the Pennsylvania Assembly."

"This was the tavern of choice for those men. He likely dined here with Samuel Miles."

"I'll bet he did. I'm amazed they knew each other so well, and I married one of Miles's descendants." She shook her head in wonder.

A waitress appeared, rosy and plump, looking the part of a tavern wench, except for a small turtle tattoo on the underside of her left wrist. "Hi, I'm Sarah, and before you take a look at the menu, I'd like to go over our specials for today."

After scrolling through a half dozen items she concluded, "Finally we have Virginia Ham and Oysters, as well as Beef Olives, which do not contain actual olives. The name is a reference to the technique of rolling and stuffing the meat, like an olive. It's served over rice." She paused. "I'll be back in a few minutes."

Two tables away, the woman's ham and oyster dish smothered in heavy cream had grabbed Paul's attention. Erin, on the other hand, disliked even the smell wafting over. As for her, she wanted West Indies Pepperpot Soup for starters, but had trouble deciding between Chicken

Breast Madeira or Beef Olives for her main course. When the waitress returned, she said, "I'll have the Beef Olives."

"A good choice. And for you sir?"

"I'll go with the Pepperpot followed by the Virginia Ham and Oysters."

"Wonderful."

Oh, well. She looked up, handing over her menu. "Do you still serve Thomas Jefferson's sweet potato biscuits?"

"We certainly do. And Sally Lunn bread."

"Bring them on!"

"Would you like anything to drink?"

"Iced tea," Erin said.

"I'll have a glass of shrub." Paul closed and handed his menu to the waitress. He gazed at Erin. "You're looking thoughtful."

She exhaled. "I hope you don't mind my saying this, but I'm remembering other dining experiences here."

He smiled. "With Jim?"

She nodded, looking out a window. "This was one of our favorite restaurants in the city. Even before I knew I was descended from Patriots, I felt the atmosphere was part of who I was."

"Sometimes we know things before we know them."

She gave a small laugh. "I think you're right."

He reached over for her hand. "You never need to worry about mentioning Jim to me. I almost feel as if we were friends—I'm sure I would've liked him a lot."

Her eyes filled. "Thank you."

The waitress walked over bearing a pewter bread tray. "The sweet potato biscuits were Thomas Jefferson's favorite."

"And they're mine as well." Erin had an idea. "Do you sell these—I mean to take home?"

"I'll ask our baker. How many were you thinking of?

"About a dozen."

"I'll check."

When she left, Paul handed the breads to her. She selected a warm biscuit and scooped butter from a pewter "butter dome."

"I like to serve refreshments when Pastor Stan comes for our meetings, and he's coming tonight."

"That's right, he is. I hope they have enough for us to buy. Isn't this our last session?"

She nodded her head. "I've enjoyed talking with him. How about you?"

"He's asked some good questions and helped to prepare us for blending our lives."

"He wanted us to think about our finances and your relationship with Ethan for tonight, but in all honesty, with my dad's death and the DAR conference, I haven't."

"Which is understandable." He chewed and swallowed a piece of bread. "I have."

"I'd like to know your thoughts."

"Well, he asked whether we wanted to maintain separate checking accounts or to combine them, and also to think about our assets, like insurance and money market accounts."

She leaned back into her chair as another waiter presented relishes and explained each one. Erin knew she'd have a good time mixing them up. When he left, they passed around the food, then fell back into conversation. "So, what do you think about our accounts?"

"I know we're older, and this is your second marriage, and people often keep their funds independent, or at least some of them, but I prefer sharing everything. Maybe I'm old-fashioned, but I think when people get married, they become one no matter how old they are." He put his fork down and tented his hands. "If you have yours, and I have mine—that doesn't feel right to me somehow. What do you think?"

Her shoulders relaxed. "I would agree. I think we should combine our accounts. There's no mystery that way, no secrets. I also want to put your name on the house so it belongs to both of us."

"Are you sure?"

"Yes, unless you mind having your name on a mortgage." She arched her eyebrows.

"Not at all. We should also discuss our overall budget, considering our two incomes.""

"Do you think Pastor Stan will help us with that?"

"Doubtful. He's about the general ideas, and then we find ways to do the specific."

"I really like the idea of a budget. Jim and I tried a few times, but we never stayed on track for long. Sometimes we didn't know what we had or how much we owed. I dislike financial confusion."

"Me too. We can also decide who pays the bills."

The waitress brought their soup, and when she left, Paul quietly prayed over their meal. Then, picking up his spoon, he asked, "Do you like paying bills?"

"I like getting them out of the way." She smiled. "But that was my job before, and I'll do it again if you like."

He licked the outside of his lip where soup had splashed. "Boy, this is good!"

She took a spoonful and rolled her eyes. "The best. Even better than my Grammy Ott's."

"I won't tell her." He grinned.

Erin reached for the relish and put a dab into the soup. Paul gave a laugh and said, "That's my girl!"

She almost hesitated to bring up the next subject because there hadn't been any problems so far. Not doing so seemed irresponsible though. "We also need to talk about your relationship with Ethan, which I happen to think is strong and positive. He likes you a lot."

"We've become fairly close."

"I'm so glad. When I was at conference, were there any discipline issues?"

"Not really. He did balk when I asked him to take the dog out, and getting him up the next morning wasn't what I'd call easy, but he wasn't uncooperative, just being a kid."

"Do you feel comfortable disciplining him?"

He pinched his lips together. "I think so. I see you taking the lead most of the time because he's your son, but I will always back you up. If I think you're wrong about something, I'll tell you away from him."

Something about this didn't sit well. She wanted him to share discipline, like she had with Jim, and that meant sometimes she took the lead, and other times, Jim did, whatever the occasion required. She explained this as Paul listened.

"I think I understand what you mean. I want to strike the right balance with him, and you. We probably will have to work this out as we go, and have lots more conversations."

"I'm comfortable with that."

"Ethan is a great little guy, and I'm looking forward to being his stepdad."

"That makes me really happy. By the way, are you okay with him calling you Paul?"

"Sure. I don't want to force anything."

On the way home, Paul discussed things he'd been discovering about the Kichline building in Easton. "I wanted to earlier, but we were talking about other important matters."

"What's happened?" She'd been seriously out of the loop since her dad's death.

"I went with a small group of archaeology students at Lafayette to make sure we didn't cover over anything or miss anything of importance in all the layers when construction begins. We mostly found some broken pottery shards …"

She clapped her hands, wide-eyed. "How exciting! What else?"

"Not so much material things, but I've also been going over records at the courthouse, and my hunch has proven correct. I believe Peter and Margaretta Kichline sold the license and rights to the tavern to the Eckerts, as well as its accoutrements, but he and his family stayed in the building, turning it into their residence on all the floors."

"So, he didn't live somewhere else in Easton?"

"Not In the center of the village. He did have a good deal of land elsewhere, and when he first came to the area, I think he built a home in the vicinity of Twenty-fifth Street, where his son eventually built his own tavern. But I think he just had this one residence in Easton proper, along with the quarters at the mills, which other people lived in."

Her eyes twinkled. "Where's your badge?"

"What badge?" He looked over at her while he drove.

"You're quite a detective."

CHAPTER TWENTY-TWO

He relaxed in his favorite chair, Elizabeth on his lap, warmed by her innocence as he read to her from the Psalms. The child's brown and yellow-speckled eyes gazed into his face, her lips parted, head resting against his chest. He smiled at her through the opening words of Psalm 33—"Sing joyfully to the Lord, you righteous; it is fitting for the upright to praise him"—but tripped and stuttered his way through the rest. During those dreary six months in prison, he'd dreamed of a scene like this, visions mixed with such yearning they formed an invisible cord pulling him forward, toward Easton, toward family. Reading to his little girl brought not just its own consolation, but a renewed hope in a time of intense uncertainty.

Except for Washington's victory last Christmas evening, the army had had little to cause to celebrate. The war had become cat and mouse intrigue, the Continentals badly outmatched in every possible way—numbers, experience, provisions, uniforms, armaments, supplies—all except for one thing. Washington's motley army had heart. Bloodied and bruised as their Cause was, he'd witnessed the resilience of men who believed liberty was worth dying for. His deepest fear was losing this greatest of assets if Congress didn't do a better job of caring for the soldier's needs.

If only he could get back in the fight, command a unit, scout, spy, anything to assist the patriots. His right foot started tapping against the floorboards as he reminded himself he truly had no right to complain. He was, after all, free and assisting his remaining soldiers in their small village, along with the sick and wounded. He slept each night in his own comfortable bed next to his lovely wife while his friends, Arndt and Miles awaited their parole.

"Papa."

Elizabeth's voice brought him back to her. "Yes, my dear?"

She pointed a chubby finger at the Bible. "Read."

He smiled. "Yes, of course."

He heard Catherine's footsteps clicking toward the hallway and she appeared carrying a small bundle wrapped in twine. Despite the scorching heat of late August, she looked fresh and crisp. "Well, isn't that the sweetest scene?"

He grinned like a schoolboy. "We're reading from the Psalms."

"I would've thought Locke or Rousseau." She raised her eyebrows.

"We'll tackle them tomorrow. Where are you off to?"

"To see Sarah."

His mirth was wind-driven chaff. "How is she doing?"

"Struggling."

His daughter-in-law's pregnancy hadn't been going smoothly, and he feared there might be a second miscarriage.

"Bett is taking care of Abraham. If you need to go out, she can watch Elizabeth too."

"I'm not going anywhere." He immediately regretted his choice of words.

Shortly after Catherine's departure, he heard someone at the door, but little Elizabeth had fallen asleep, and he didn't want to wake her. Fortunately, Joe came in from the kitchen to answer the summons. Peter strained to hear who the caller might be. A moment later, Joe appeared, standing tall. "Colonel, sir, Colonel Hooper is here to see you."

"Thank you, Joe." He spoke just above a whisper so as not to awaken his daughter. "Please come in, Colonel."

"I'll bring somethin' cool to drink," Joe said, and he hurried away.

Hooper cocked his head, entering on tip-toe. "I hope I'm not interrupting anything."

"I was reading to her, and she nodded off. Have a seat."

The burly soldier sat, smiling. "She reminds me of my little one."

"How old is she now?"

"Not quite two." Hooper reached for a handkerchief and wiped his brow.

"The same as Elizabeth." He paused while the mantel clock chimed the ten o'clock hour. "When did you get back in town?"

"Late last night."

"And how are things going?" How well he remembered being on top of every bit of news not so long ago.

Hooper inhaled sharply, his shoulders lifting, eyes looking downward. "About the same as here. I've really struggled with these Moravians."

"I take it they refuse to abide by the Militia Act."

His friend nodded. "They won't join, which is understandable given their beliefs, but they won't pay the fines either."

Peter breathed out, nodding. He had always respected

their position, but in return, he expected them to give and take as well.

"They don't seem to take seriously enough losing their rights as citizens if they don't abide by the law."

"We've had our challenges here as well," Peter said.

Hooper looked up. "Gordon?"

"He declines every opportunity to sign the Oath of Allegiance."

Joe entered quietly and placed a silver tray with cold apple cider and lemon cookies on the table between the men. He poured drinks, then bowed and left.

"Thank you Joe."

"Gern welcome, sir."

Hooper frowned. "What did he say?"

Peter laughed quietly, and Elizabeth stirred in his arms. "He speaks an exotic blend of German and English. He started saying 'you're welcome' in German and finished in English."

"As long as they can practice their religion peacefully, these Moravians, Mennonites, and Quakers aren't disloyal so much as neutral. But Gordon on the other hand ..." He paused, taking a long drink of cider. "He seems to have given up on our Cause, and that sets a bad precedent." He gazed at Peter. "Has he actually turned Loyalist?"

"I haven't had much contact with him recently, but I have the impression he's more discouraged than anything else."

"Discouragement isn't exactly unique to Mr. Gordon." A deep furrow appeared between his brows. "I do have some news to share, Colonel Kichline. Intelligence we've gathered leads us to believe General Howe is going to make a move toward capturing Philadelphia."

Peter's eyes opened wider. "Philadelphia!"

"Yes. Imagine if they caught our capital." He leaned forward. "Talk about discouragement. Then again, we're going to do everything in our power to prevent that."

Peter's heart sank.

He watched Peter Schneider bend over the wood he'd brought to the hearth as he stacked the boards almost geometrically. Then he glanced at his oldest daughter, who was stealing glimpses of the servant while she read aloud with Joe. Peter yawned, overcoming the urge to go all out, arms flailed, mouth wide open in his chair. He was, after all, not alone. From upstairs came the unwelcome sound of Abraham coughing again. The baby seemed to go from one cold to another since the weather had turned chillier at night, and Peter could tell from lines permanently forming on his wife's forehead, Catherine was concerned.

"I'll go to the baby," she said, rising from her chair.

Unexpectedly an urgent knock sounded at the front door, and Joe hustled to see who the caller was. "Hello, sir Colonel. *Kommen Sie* inside."

Peter got up at the sight of Robert Levers, looking as lathered as a horse after a strenuous climb. "Colonel Levers. Please come in."

Levers paused for a moment and glanced up the stairs as a fresh wave of paroxysms drifted from the baby's room. "I'm sorry if I've come at a bad time, but I must speak with you at once, Colonel Kichline."

Susannah sprang forward. "You stay here, Mother Catherine. I'll go see about the baby."

"Thank you, dear."

"Come in, Colonel Levers." Peter waved him into the parlor.

"May I bring you anything?" Joe asked.

"No, thank you."

Peter nodded toward the servant, who left the room. "Sit down, my friend. Something is on your mind."

"I'll just be going then," Peter Schneider said, but as he began to leave, Levers held up his hand.

"Please forgive the late hour of my visit. I come on a matter of great urgency. Colonel, I wonder if you might be available for a special assignment."

Although he'd been forcing himself to stay awake moments earlier while reading from Pope, Peter came to full attention, as though he'd just jumped into the refreshing Bushkill Creek. *An assignment?* He was ready to take on the King's personal guard. "Why, yes, of course," he said.

Levers's eyes swept the room. "I am expecting a package to be hand delivered to me by a personal courier in Bethlehem. I need the most reliable person I know to get this and bring it back as soon as possible." He stared straight at Peter. "You are the most reliable person I know."

"I will be happy to oblige, Colonel Levers." He didn't want to look at his wife, unsure what she might think about such a mysterious mission.

"I beg your humble pardon, my lady, but I wonder if I might have a private word with your husband."

Catherine looked from Levers to Peter, who gave an affirming nod. "Yes, of course. If you need me, I'll be upstairs."

Levers addressed the servant. "Schneider, I suggest you stick around, just not in this room."

"I'll be in the kitchen if you need me."

When they were alone, Levers leaned forward, eyes blazing, voice low. "I just got word, Colonel Kichline, of General Washington's defeat at Brandywine, not far from Philadelphia." He stared as if searching for Peter's reaction. "Traill's down there now with the Fifth Pennsylvania Battalion in the defense of Philadelphia."

The situation must be especially urgent or Robert would have told me he was leaving.

"The British are poised to capture our capital, and Congress is preparing to evacuate. All its papers must be protected from the enemy, and Representative John Adams is making arrangements for their safe keeping. I need you to rendezvous with the person in charge of these government documents."

The weight of the news bore down on his spirit—the British were about to invade their capital! Ignoring the knot forming in his gut, he refused to indulge in foreboding. "I will gladly help. Who is in charge of the operation?"

Levers scratched his chin, and Peter noticed the man hadn't shaved for at least a few days. "Mr. Adams is overseeing their evacuation. The entire mission is so secretive only I am aware of the objective. You are to go to Bethlehem at once to meet with him."

"How will he know who I am?"

"You are to identify yourself by wearing a sprig of green in your hat."

He nearly burst out laughing, the reaction fueled by absurdity and irony. Instead, he smiled to himself, remembering when he'd been ordered to wear "a sprig of green" before. "Civilian clothes or military?" he asked.

"Definitely civilian."

"When is the courier expected?"

"Any time tomorrow, which is why you must set off at once." Levers lowered his head, a proud man humbling himself in the face of a dire situation. "Please tell me you'll do this."

"Of course I will. Do you prefer I go alone?"

"Oh, yes, my friend. It is essential you take no one with you or let anyone know where you're going." He looked toward the upstairs, his meaning not lost on Peter.

Catherine isn't going to like this. While he hated to leave a sick baby or his wife, he could make this small sacrifice at a time when their independence from Great Britain hung in a precarious balance. With Andrew and Jacob at the mills, Peter would instruct Schneider to keep a close watch on the household. Levers was speaking, and Peter once again focused on what he was saying.

"I'm afraid time is of the essence."

"I will make haste then, Colonel."

He rose and shook Peter's hand. "Good luck to you, my friend."

"I appreciate the opportunity to make myself more useful."

He rode through the night, a solitary figure on the road to Bethlehem, his company crickets, foxes, raccoons, the occasional owl, his thoughts. He could see the face of his brave but clearly frightened wife as she helped him pack a satchel and provisions, not knowing where Peter was going or how long he would be away. Her lips had quivered when he kissed them goodbye, her eyes brimming with love and not a little fear. Susannah had thrown her arms around him and squeezed tightly, declaring her love for her Papa as if she were her little sister's age and not nearly a woman. Schneider had shaken his hand and solemnly promised, "I will take good care of them. You have nothing to worry about." Joe and Bett had waved, Bett dabbing a handkerchief to her eyes.

Through the long night, when sleep threatened to overtake him, he reminded himself of them, the heart of his own heart next to his beloved God. He could manage one sleepless night.

He arrived at the Sun Inn as crimson and purple smudged the eastern sky, his horse appearing ready for an overdue rest, himself a study in dishevelment. Before he went inside, he cut his identifying sprig of green from a boxwood and lumbered up the steps, opening the door to the sound of the bell tinkling above its frame. Inside, a young man swept the floor. Peter's mouth watered at the fragrance of bacon and fresh bread as a familiar figure strode into the hallway.

"Why, Colonel Kichline! I didn't expect to see you here today."

"Good morning, Mr. Hellerich. How are you keeping?"

Jost Hellerich reached over and shook Peter's hand with vigor. "I am quite well, thank you, and very pleased to see you. I heard you had been wounded and captured in the fighting last summer. I'm so happy you're home again."

"Thank you. I'm awaiting my exchange."

Hellerich nodded, smiling. "So you can get back into

the fight?"

Peter grinned. The man knew him too well.

"What brings you here so early? You must've ridden all night if you've come from Easton." Hellerich's eyes studied Peter from wind-blown top to muddy bottom.

"Yes, I did." He felt suddenly ready to sit. "I am to meet someone here today."

"Oh?" Hellerich shifted from one foot to another.

"I'm afraid I can't identify him." He trusted Hellerich but didn't want the innkeeper to be privy to information about John Adams's rescue of the government's documents.

The tavern owner closed his eyes, nodding. "Of course. Come in and sit down. Let me get you something to eat—or would you like to wash up first? I have a room you can use."

He was concerned if he saw a bed, he might be tempted beyond his ability to endure an opportunity for a nap, which could easily turn into full-blown sleep. "If you would, please, I'd prefer some breakfast."

Hellerich led him to a table next to a fire another servant was stoking. Then he leaned closer. "If there's anything I can do, I am at your service."

"Thank you, my friend. I will." He leaned back, at ease, knowing he wasn't entirely alone.

CHAPTER TWENTY-THREE

"Yes, Mom, I'll pick you up at nine-thirty. No, there isn't lunch afterwards, just a meeting starting at ten." She looked over her shoulder at Paul, sitting at her kitchen table scribbling on a legal pad as he looked back and forth to his laptop. "Sure, we can get something to eat afterwards. And you need groceries? I thought Allen took you this week. Yes, I forget things too. Okay, Mom, I'll see you in an hour. What? Yes, I'm wearing a dress. Most of the older women wear pants. You can stay at our house afterward and go to Ethan's play with us tonight. Okay, see you soon. Bye."

Erin exhaled, then sipped her stone cold tea.

"Audrey must be excited," Paul said, smiling.

"This is a big day for her—getting inducted into the DAR, seeing her grandson in a play. She reminds me of when I was getting ready for proms." She changed the subject. "And how is your car shopping coming along?"

"Pretty well." He picked up his pen and began pointing at his notes. "I found a 2018 M Class for sale by owner in Bangor, looks clean on the pictures. Lower mileage. Good price. I wasn't thinking of an SUV though. I've always driven a sedan. There is one in Palmer Township, also a good price and a 2017 model, but the mileage is a little higher." He pointed to the screen. "Here's a car that checks all the boxes, except for the color."

Erin leaned in for a closer look. "It's nice, but you don't

seem like a dark green kind of guy."

"I'm not, but maybe I could be."

"Uh, Paul?"

"Yes?"

"Dealers have used cars too." This process of buying a car from a private owner was new to her. Jim had never bought a used car, always a new one straight from the showroom, under warranty.

"I actually do have a couple listed here." He looked down briefly at his notes. "I'll check them out too, but sometimes you can do better one-on-one with a private seller."

"I suppose so, but there are more risks that way, too."

"If I find the right one through a private seller, I'll have Denny, my mechanic, go over it stem to stern before writing a check."

"Sounds like a plan." She looked up at the wall clock and gave a start. "I'd better get dressed, or I'll be late picking my mom up, and she does not tolerate lateness, believe you me." Erin nodded toward the family room where Ethan was playing a video game. "Please make sure he stays within his time limit."

"Will do. I plan to take him car shopping with me today."

"He'll love that! Just make sure he gets to school in time for the play." She bent down and kissed his temple. "And now, if you'll excuse me. . ."

Audrey bent her head toward Erin and whispered, "What am I supposed to do?"

Erin sneezed, the result of a member's veil of rose-based perfume in the Parsons-Taylor House's small gathering room. Although the Daughters were all talking, Audrey's voice seemed to rise above the others, at least for Erin.

"Connie will call you to come forward, introduce you, then the chaplain will lead you through the oath of membership."

"Do I have to memorize anything?" She twisted a tissue almost to shreds.

"Not a thing. You'll just answer 'I do' to the questions."

Audrey's fading eyes sparkled. "I'm not getting married, am I?"

"Only to the DAR."

"I am delighted to welcome a new member today, the mother of our own Erin Miles." Connie smiled in Audrey's direction.

Erin reached for the package she'd squirreled away in her tote bag, away from her mom's prying eyes.

"Erin, would you please escort your mom to the front?"

She pressed Audrey's upper arm. "It's time."

They covered the few steps and stood facing the group of a dozen ladies while Connie made introductions.

"Ladies, I present to you Mrs. Audrey Owen Pelleriti, whose Patriot Ancestor is Colonel Peter Kichline, whom we know so much about because of his prominent role in Easton history. Cheryl, will you please administer the oath?"

"Audrey, please raise your right hand and respond in the affirmative to the following questions."

Erin was glad Cheryl Bonebaker spoke loudly.

"Do you promise faithful loyalty to the Bylaws of the

National Society Daughters of the American Revolution, the Pennsylvania State Society and the George Taylor Chapter, God being your helper?"

"I do."

"Do you promise faithfully to uphold the Constitution of the United States and to respect the Flag of the United States of America, God being your helper?"

"I certainly do," Audrey said, accompanied by a series of chuckles.

"Do you promise that at all times you will promote the objectives of the National Society, which are historic preservation, education, and patriotism, to the best of your ability, God being your helper?"

"I do."

Erin found herself crying soft, proud tears as the chaplain concluded the ceremony with a prayer.

Cheryl reached out her hand. "Audrey, welcome to the George Taylor Chapter and the Daughters of the American Revolution."

"Thank you," Audrey said, reaching for a tissue.

Connie slipped next to Audrey and held the hand Cheryl had just shaken. "This is an especially happy moment for me because these two ladies have grown so dear to me. As you know, I am currently overseeing the restoration of the Kichline building in preparation for its opening as a colonial history museum, which Erin will curate. Just last week, a team of professionals uncovered something I'd like to show you."

Erin's left calf tingled as she watched her friend produce what appeared to be an old utensil.

"This silver spoon has been under layers of dirt for over two hundred and fifty years." She held the object at eye level. "There is the slightest trace of engraving on the stem, but someone at the Sigal Museum has determined the presence of the initial 'K.'"

Erin blew her nose into her grandmother's handkerchief, the one she always took to DAR meetings and events.

"Audrey, this spoon mostly likely belonged to your ancestor, Colonel Peter Kichline, and as a memento of your becoming a Daughter of the American Revolution, I present it to you on behalf of the George Taylor Chapter."

Connie handed the spoon to Audrey, who accepted the artifact with an unsteady hand, several people taking photos to Erin's delight since she wasn't in a condition to take any herself. She reached behind her back and produced a bouquet of coral tulips, hugging her mom while more flashes bounced off the room's historic walls. When the meeting ended, people crowded around her mom, one of them Erin's high school friend, Christa Arndt Harcus, who hugged Audrey with abandon.

"Oh, Mrs. Pelleriti, I am so happy you decided to join our chapter! And I'm just thrilled for your present. You must be over the moon."

Erin knew her mother's grin, an expression portending one of Audrey's famous—or infamous—quips. She braced herself.

"I felt like the President of the United States. I don't know how I can defend our country against all enemies, but having this spoon makes me feel like I could."

She took her mom to a celebration lunch at Williams, Audrey's favorite place to dine, and texted Paul before they went inside. "I want to see if he and Ethan can join us."

"Where did you say they went?"

"Paul's looking for a new car, well, a new used car, and he took Ethan to see a couple."

"I think it's great how the two of them are getting along."

"I keep waiting for a shoe to drop on their relationship, but so far, so good. I think Ethan appreciates how Paul isn't trying to replace Jim."

Audrey pressed her wrinkled hand on top of her daughter's. "And no one could." Then, "What's wrong with Paul's car?"

"The brakes. The alternator. The fuel pump …"

"Sheesh!"

"I know."

Erin helped her mother inside the restaurant where the seating hostess broke into a smile.

"Well, hello, Audrey! How are you?"

"Real good. Is that Sondra?"

The middle-aged woman bent down. "Yes, it is."

"This is my daughter, Erin. She's a professor at Lafayette."

"Hi, Erin. I just love your mother."

"I do too."

"How about one of these front booths? I know you like to sit up here."

"I'd like that," Audrey said.

As she and Erin scooched into place, the seating hostess placed menus in front of them.

"I have something to show you, Sondra." She reached into her purse and brought out the spoon, wrapped in a velvet pouch. "This belonged to my ten times great-grandfather, Colonel Peter Kichline." She lifted the object so the woman could see better.

Erin bit her lower lip, trying to keep words of correction from spilling out. *He's your five times great grandfather.*

"Oh my, is that ever old!"

"I became a Daughter of the American Revolution today, and they gave this to me. My greatgrandfather was a colonel in the war, and this was found during a dig where he lived."

"Where did he live?"

"Easton. Just north of the Circle."

"Well, that is very special, Audrey. Congratulations. My grandparents came here after World War Two, so we haven't been here long." She paused. "Your waitress will be right over."

Erin decided she wanted the salad bar and a bowl of chicken noodle soup, while her mother ordered her signature grilled cheese with French fries. They sipped iced tea and chatted while Erin tucked into a plate of marinated tomatoes with strawberry Jell-O.

"I want to thank you for helping me get into the DAR, Erin. You worked real hard."

"Believe me, Mom, I'm happy I could bring you on board."

"Wouldn't Grammy be busting her buttons?"

Erin grinned. "You bet. She'd be proud to know our family's history. And now, dear mother, we need to order some pins for you."

"Like the kind you wear?"

"Yes.

"Do they cost a lot?"

The waitress brought their soup, and Erin slid her salad plate to the side. "Pins aren't cheap, but they make great gifts for birthdays and holidays."

Audrey picked up her spoon and dipped into the soup, then blew on the food to dissipate the steam. "What pins should I get?"

"I think we'd get you a starter set—the DAR insignia, chapter bar, and ancestor bar." She was already scheming about telling her family they could help buy the set for Audrey's birthday.

"I'd like wearing them." She took a spoonful of the soup. "This is good, like Mom used to make. Speaking of spoons … I'd like to add this new one to my collection."

Erin winced. Her mother's spoon assortment consisted of kitschy souvenirs and garage sale finds, hardly fitting company for a family heirloom. "Mom, how about if we buy a shadow box from a craft store and display the spoon by itself? Something this special deserves to stand alone."

"Great idea. Would you pick one out?"

"I'll be happy to." Her phone buzzed, indicating a new text message.

I'M GLAD YOU HAD A GOOD TIME. I BOUGHT A CAR. ARE YOU STILL AT WILLIAMS?

YES.

A few seconds passed, and the phone droned again.

WE HAVEN'T EATEN YET, AND ETHAN SAYS HE'S STARVING. CAN WE JOIN YOU?

YES, PLEASE.

WE'LL BE THERE IN TEN.

Audrey told her story in full when the guys arrived, and Erin wished she'd give Paul room to talk about his adventures. He didn't seem to mind, however, nodding and offering one and two-word comments as he and Ethan bore down on hamburgers all the way.

Suddenly, Audrey lifted her hands. "Just listen to me! I haven't let you get a word in edgewise. Erin says you bought a car."

Paul's face brightened. "Sure did! Ethan helped me choose, didn't you?"

He gave a thumbs up. "What a cool car! You can even make phone calls and text on the instrument panel."

Audrey frowned. "You should drive when you drive, not talk and text. People get in accidents that way."

"When will you get the car?" Erin asked, trying to head off further unpleasantness.

Paul beamed. "How about now?"

"The car's outside, Mom."

Erin turned her head to look out the windows. "Which one?"

Ethan nearly deposited the contents of his chocolate milk onto his grandmother's lap in his haste to show his mom. "See that red pickup truck?"

Erin nodded. "Yes."

"Paul's car is right next to it."

She peered more closely in the direction her son was pointing. "A black Mercedes SUV?"

"The very one." Paul grinned, a Cheshire cat. "Low mileage, all the bells and whistles, one owner, a woman going to live with her daughter in California. Now that I'm about to become a family man, I figured it was time to get a bigger vehicle."

His comment touched her heart, and she squeezed his hand. "Sweet. Um, what happened to your other car?"

Ethan bounced up in his seat. "You wouldn't believe it, Mom! We pulled into the driveway, and the brakes just gave out. Paul almost slammed into the garage!"

Her heart hammered. What if this had happened on the road? She felt like chewing him out for driving such a wreck, but then what would the point be?

"I called a tow truck. I'll try to get some money for parts "

She slowly blew out tension. "Well, then, do you have a name picked out?"

Her son grimaced. "No names, Mom."

"We always enjoyed naming our cars, Ethan. What about Mr. Scott?"

"Mo-ther. That is so not cool anymore."

She and Paul exchanged a look. Where had the little boy gone?

Family and friends gathered at the front of the auditorium to wait for the young actors. Erin held a vibrant balloon bouquet for Ethan, who had knocked her socks off with his portrayal of the Cowardly Lion. *I might be prejudiced, but I think he stole the show.*

"Excuse me, but are you Ethan Miles's parents?"

Erin looked into the earnest face of the twenty-something director, who reminded her of a younger version of Connie. "I'm his mother, this is my fiancé, and this is Ethan's grandmother."

The woman shook their hands, all smiles. "That young

man has an acting gift."

Audrey thrust out her tiny chest. "He gets that from my side of the family."

Giddiness bubbled in Erin's chest. "You think?"

"Oh, yes. I've been around acting most of my life, and I recognize talent when I see it. Ethan is the real deal."

CHAPTER TWENTY-FOUR

He was a man of sleepless diligence, but not even he could resist the lulling effect of sun-spangled windows. The warm glow proved as mesmerizing as a hearth fire following a long trek through an autumn wood. His eyelids seem to have sprouted weights. Up and down, his head bobbed, only to jerk skyward. How long he acted out this particular comedy he didn't know, but had the tavern been full, he would've been the entertainment.

Jost Hellerich bent over the man he'd known for more than a decade. "Colonel Kichline."

He bolted upright, arms clutching the sides of his chair. "Yes?" Had Adams arrived and found him loafing?

"Sir, you need to get some sleep."

Peter looked into moss-colored eyes, whose expression reminded him of Catherine's whenever he'd pushed himself too hard. He wrestled with an urge to argue his case. "Thank you for your concern, Mr. Hellerich, but I must be at my post."

"I have prepared a room for you near the stairs, and I will wait right here on your behalf." He paused. "I believe, Colonel, you are wearing this, ugh, *strauch*, as a *zeichen*." He nodded toward the greenery adorning Peter's tricorn.

"*Ja*." He nearly blushed at being so obvious, but those had been his instructions.

"If you would, please, I can put a *strauch* in my hat so

there will be a point of contact for your messenger, should you be resting when he arrives."

Peter realized he desperately needed sleep when an image of Hellerich, his headgear embellished with a giant bush, burst on his mind. Chuckling to himself, he acquiesced. "The minute he comes?"

Hellerich smiled as if he were reassuring his youngest child. "The very second."

"You won't leave this room until I return?"

"No, sir, I will not, except to find a bit of *strauch*."

"You won't let on to anyone what is afoot?"

The tavern keeper held up his right hand. "I will not."

"Very well, then." Peter hoisted six feet two inches of dead weight from the chair. "I will wait until you get the greenery." While Hellerich went on his mission, Peter rolled his shoulders, then his head. He noticed two farmers talking in a far corner, a piece of paper laid between them, likely a bill. They paid no attention to Peter, and he called none to himself, for once glad he hadn't been recognized as in previous years when most people knew the sheriff. The dampness in the room where the fire burned low brought about the familiar ache in his upper left arm. Hellerich quickly returned sporting an unmistakable yet understated bit of vegetation. Peter nodded approval.

The innkeeper gave a small bow of his head then pointed to the room. "Rest assured, sir, I will take care of this."

"*Vielen dank.*" Peter found the chamber with the covers turned down and curtains drawn. Although the sun asserted itself against the window, he was glad for its bright intrusion so he wouldn't lie there until doomsday. He placed his hat on an end table where he could grab it in a hurry. Not bothering to remove his boots or any clothing, he stretched out on top of the covers on a bed made for someone three quarters his height. With his feet dangling off the edge, he was asleep nearly as soon as his grateful head sank into the pillow.

"Sir? Colonel Kichline."

"What?" he muttered.

"Colonel, I think you'd better come downstairs."

His eyes abruptly opened. "Mr. Hellerich."

"I believe the man you're waiting for has arrived."

Peter's feet hit the floor before he was fully awake. "Thank you, my good man." He reached for his hat, making sure the green sprig was in place.

Hellerich scratched his chin. "Your fellow is a rather scraggly sort. About thirty."

Peter followed the owner downstairs. Waiters hustled to provide food and drink to a disheveled clientele, a few of which had fallen asleep where they sat. He consulted his pocket watch—nine-thirty-four. Hellerich nodded in the direction of a sharp-featured farmer who looked like he'd been struggling to earn his daily bread. His thin hair dangled to his shoulders, his face and clothes were awash with road grime, yet he maintained an impression of strength. As he lifted a tankard, his glance fell upon Peter, who saw the brown eyes move up to Peter's hat. A spark of recognition, yet where was John Adams?

Peter walked up to him. "Good day."

The man nodded his head, took a long draught of his drink, and placed the tankard on the table. "Won't you join me?" He motioned toward an empty chair.

251

"Yes, thank you. There seem to be few available seats this morning." When a waiter came for his order, he said, "I'd like a pot of tea, sausage, and bread." He looked to his companion. "What would you like?"

"The same, please."

"Yes, sir. I'll bring them straightaway."

The young fellow disappeared, and the farmer continued playing out their drama. "You from around here?"

Everyone born and raised in the area knew who Peter was. "Yes, I come from Easton. And yourself?"

After a pause, he said, "Lately from Philadelphia."

Peter detected an accent belonging to New York, maybe New England. "There's a lot happening in the city these days." The fellow's eyes locked onto Peter's. "What brings you here?"

"I have business to attend to." His hand shook slightly when he lifted his tankard.

Grateful for the chatter of other patrons, Peter stepped into the conversational water. "Are you alone?"

"Yes, sir, I am."

"I also have come to Bethlehem on business, representing Mr. Robert Levers."

His eyes enlarged. "I am acquainted with Mr. Levers, and Mr. Adams." He looked meaningfully at Peter's hat. "I see you're fond of the green."

"Yes, but only on special occasions."

The waiter brought their food much quicker than expected and although he wanted to get right down to business, he decided to let the drama play out while they ate. He bowed his head to say a silent grace, and when he finished discovered the messenger was already halfway through a sausage. He decided to take a risk. "By the way,

I'm Colonel Peter Kichline."

The fellow's eyebrows raised, then his Adam's apple bobbed up and down as he swallowed. "I am pleased to make your acquaintance, sir. I am on business for Mr. John Adams of Massachusetts, late of Philadelphia. I have come by way of Bristol."

He chewed a biscuit slathered in honey, then chased the food down with Hellerich's strong tea. "I once had the pleasure to meet Mr. Adams while serving with the Pennsylvania Assembly." Peter noted the tension releasing from his companion's shoulders and color returning to his sunken cheeks. How long had he gone without proper nourishment? Had General Washington's proud army been reduced to this? He thrust out a long leg as he eased back into his chair, careful not to become a tripping hazard.

"I'm here to inform you of a change of plans."

Peter's back stiffened. "Oh?"

"Yes. I came to bring you up to date about the situation, so you weren't waiting in vain." He paused. "We are to meet the rest of the party in Easton."

"Very well, then. I'll be glad to accompany you after we finish our meal."

"Thank you." He dove into his food, seeming to hold himself back from acting like a ravenous pig.

"Might I ask your name?"

He nodded, chewing. "Hall, Lt. Phineas Hall."

I'll make sure Bett and Catherine fill his belly when we get to Easton. "I am glad to make your acquaintance, Lt. Hall."

"I do apologize for the inconvenience."

Peter waved his hand. "I am only too happy to be of service." After a few moments of silence, he spoke again.

"Do you know these other people?" His eyes moved in the direction of the chock-a-block Sun Inn.

"Only a few, sir. Do you see that man and his son?"

Peter had noticed them earlier. "Yes, Lieutenant."

"I was part of a wagon train they joined five days ago along the route from Philadelphia. They were on their way to Northampton Town via Bethlehem, but they encountered some trouble as we climbed the last hill into town." Hall seemed to regret each word for taking him away from his meal. "One of their wagon wheels broke."

Peter prodded him. "Are they on a mission as well?"

Hall nodded slowly. "One of his neighbors is with us, and he'll finish the journey while the wheel gets fixed."

Sensing he could get no more out of Hall, he wolfed down the bread, imagining his wife's puckered brow. Surely, he thought, she would understand his haste.

Peter waited for the stable boy to bring his stallion, taking in a refrain of whinnying, snorting, and hoof stomping. A pang tore through his chest when he noticed another horse's strong resemblance to Abelard. He'd lost her during the Battle of Brooklyn, never knowing her final fate, but guessing she'd either perished or been commandeered by the British or Hessians. Maybe she still lived.

The stable boy apologized. "I'm sorry for the delay, sir."

"Take your time, son." The holdup would enable him to investigate what was happening several yards away where a man and a boy labored with three other fellows to transfer something from the back of their hobbled wagon to a replacement vehicle. The temperature hovered somewhere in the low sixties, he guessed, not warm enough to account for sweat beading the brows of two men standing in the wagon. He wandered over to them.

"Good day, gentlemen. I'm Colonel Kichline, though you would not know by my present outfit. May I be of assistance?" The boy looked from Peter to his father who said, "Thank you, Colonel. We'd be grateful for another hand."

The men in the wagon slid a large crate toward the back, and Peter reached out to take one end, the heft of the object causing him to grab with more effort than he initially thought would be required.

The men uttered non-words as they strained to position the crate, the boy and his father concealing the object with piles of straw. As they alighted, bits of stubble sticking to their hair and clothes, the man clapped his large hand on the lad's shoulder.

The boy stared at the covered box. "I wanted to finish the job."

"I know you did, son, but we got the bell this far. Mr. Leaser will protect it."

Peter finished brushing straw from his own clothes and stepped over to them, sniffing more than hay. As a former sheriff, he couldn't help but try to figure out this mystery. "Did I hear you say 'bell?'"

The boy's mouth dropped nearly to his knees.

"Don't worry, son. Colonel Kichline can know." He transferred his glance to Peter. "With the British preparing to occupy Philadelphia, several of us farmers volunteered to remove a number of bells from the city so the Red Coats can't turn them into bullets and cannon balls. We're headed to Northampton Town to secure them in a church."

The farmer's son smiled, his upper body quivering. "May I tell him Father?" When the man nodded, the boy addressed Peter. "Colonel, the bell you just helped us with is the most famous of all—from the State House."

The bell that had tolled liberty for all the land.

Peter nodded because he couldn't find his voice.

CHAPTER TWENTY-FIVE

She jumped when her cell phone blasted the Loony Tunes song, muttering, "That Ethan!" Toby wrapped a leg across his head when the ringer continued playing. "Oh, I just need to finish this one sentence …" Her concentration broken, she saw Connie was calling. "Hi, there."

"You sound breathless. Did I catch you at a bad time?"

"Uh, yeah, sort of."

"So sorry! I was wondering, can you stop by the Kichline building around lunch time?"

With a glance at her watch, she nodded, then realized Connie couldn't see her. "Uh, sure."

"See you then!"

Erin tapped the red phone icon and turned back to her computer screen. "Ah, yes, this one sentence doesn't quite fit the tone of the paragraph. I remember thinking at the time I wrote this I'd have to deal with the problem later." She looked down at Toby, who had resumed a more relaxed position on the floor. "I'm trying to transition from Grandfather Peter's life in active military service to his continuing support of the Revolution when he was paroled."

She tapped the top of her pen against her teeth, stared out the window at a squirrel straddling the bird feeder, and filling with a revelation, wrote as one inspired. She continued for the better part of an hour, then sat back in her chair and removed her reading glasses. "Toby, I feel as though I'd just finished a symphony." She rose, stretching. "I could use a Coke. And a veggie burger topped with some of Ethan's chocolate cereal. Uh, maybe for a snack. I'll be meeting Connie soon."

Her nostrils tickled at the fresh sawdust covering every surface, fine particles hovering like miniscule stars. The reno of the Kichline Tavern was in full swing, and Connie needed immediate feedback.

"I know you're trying to finish your manuscript, but the architect needs to know where you think your office should be."

She failed to hold back a sneeze, and dove into her bag for a tissue.

"God bless you! This dust gets to me too."

"With everything gutted, I find picturing my office difficult."

Connie nodded. "I know something that may help you." She led Erin past two hard-hatted workers to a table at a window overlooking Northampton Street. "Here's the general plan of what the place will look like. On the first floor, visitors will feel as if they've just entered an eighteenth century tavern. We've drawn inspiration from the Bachmann, figuring there might be some similarities to things like fixtures and fireplaces, and the size of doors and windows."

"Good thinking."

"Then upstairs will be rooms with collections pertaining to Easton's colonial history. Your office would make the most sense there, at least I think so."

Erin leaned in for a closer look at the plans. "What's the other option?"

"At the back of the first or third floors."

"I like the idea of having my office be part of the story. Then again, offices and collections in one area make the most practical sense."

"I'm thinking the third floor would be a good bet for administrative spaces. You'll have an assistant, and any interns or volunteers need a work room. Then there will be supplies to store."

"The third floor then." Erin punctuated her comment with a vibrant sneeze.

"Bless you! Let's go outside. Do you have time for a coffee?"

"Sure. I'm almost finished with my final edits for Derek. I just need one more look, then I can mail them."

"Do you mean email them?"

Erin laughed. "Derek is old school. He wants a physical copy and an electronic one."

"I'd give the man what he wants. You must be so excited—a book with Derek McCutcheon, your wedding, and the Kichline center!"

Erin's enthusiasm lasted all of fifteen minutes, until her friend made an innocent remark. "I'll bet Ethan is looking forward to the end of school."

She was a parrot. "The end of school?"

Connie sipped her latte. "Doesn't the school year end in a couple of weeks?"

She felt like crying. "Honestly, I don't know if I'm coming or going. After my dad died, I just got through life for the first few weeks. Then I've been focusing so hard on the book and the wedding, I totally forgot about the summer." She gave Connie a plaintive look. "What am I going to do?"

"Good morning, Erin. It's Derek."

"Well, hello." She put the phone in the crook of her neck and continued clearing off the breakfast dishes. "How are you?" She hoped Toby wasn't underfoot.

"Quite well, especially after reviewing your chapters."

She felt a smile stretching across her face. "Oh, I'm so glad."

"I've made quite a find in you, my friend. I couldn't be more pleased."

"Thank you. It's been a pleasure to do this project with you."

"I do have one more favor, if you would care to indulge me. I do realize, of course, you're about to get married, and also have the Kichline building to think about."

Erin's left calf tingled. *Please, Lord, not one more thing.* "What did you have in mind?"

"The galleys will be ready in a couple of weeks, and while my editors do a top notch job, I would be pleased if you would also take a look at the proofs and see if anything is amiss."

She sat on one of the chairs. "I would be happy to." This wasn't so bad.

"Great! I'll have the publisher send a copy to you." He harrumphed. "No doubt they'll be electronic."

She leaned over her son's shoulder. "How's the book report coming along?"

"Okay. This subject was better than the last one, so I'm having an easier time thinking of things I want to say."

"What's this one about?" She sat on the couch near Ethan's desk, wincing at the layer of dust covering pencils with teeth marks and no erasers, and a waterfall of books and papers.

"We were supposed to pick a Civil War general and write—what's that called when someone writes his own story?"

"An autobiography."

Toby sauntered over and rested on her feet.

"Oh, okay, then. I'm writing as if I'm the general, telling my story."

"So, who did you pick?"

"His name is Joshua Chamberlain."

Erin reached back into her memory. "Wasn't he from New England, Maine I think?"

"That's him. Anyway, I really like him, and I like writing as if I'm him. I feel a little like you must feel when you write about my Grandfather Peter and Grandfather Miles."

She smiled. "I'm glad you get to feel that way too."

Ethan turned away from the monitor. "Uh, Mom, I've been thinking about something."

"What, oh favorite son?"

"I know we have plans for our vacation, like you and Paul are going on a honeymoon, and we're all going to Williamsburg, but I was wondering. . ." He looked down, rubbing his lips together, seeming hesitant. "Is that everything, or is it possible to do something else?"

"I'm glad you brought this up, Ethan. I've been wondering what your summer is going to look like, what you want to be doing."

His mouth popped open. "I've been thinking the same thing! How weird is that?"

"I hear a lot of your friends already have plans."

"What friends?"

She'd touched a sore spot. Ethan was still only associating with his cousins, and Jake from Lansdale. Only rarely did he mention a girl or boy who'd been in the play with him.

"Oh, kids in general. They get out of school and go straight into summer camps."

Ethan frowned. "I don't think I'd like that."

She relaxed into the sofa, pulling her feet up and covering them with a throw, displacing the dog. "When I was a kid, we used to have a good time in the summer. The local playground had activities, and my parents had a pool. I mostly hung out with my friends."

"What about vacations?"

"We took a lot of day trips."

"It sounds like fun."

She smiled at him. "I think we were better off without cell phones and all these electronics. We had to do relationships and make a lot of our own fun."

They were silent for a long moment. Then Ethan said, "Mom, I like how you did summer. Do I have to go to camps and stuff like that?"

"First of all, it's a little late to register you, and second, I'm not a fan of keeping kids organized all summer long. However, I think Vacation Bible School and the library's reading program would be good activities."

He popped up. "Oh, like we did in Lansdale?"

"Yes."

"I like that a lot. There are so many books I have on my list."

"You have a reading list?"

He pointed to his head. "Up here. Mom, do you think I could go back to Lansdale for a week and go to VBS with Jake?"

"I think spending a week with your old friends would be nice. You could always stay with your grandparents."

"Great! Oh, and there's Heritage Day."

"Right. Do you want to be in the parade again?"

"You bet. I'll march with those soldiers again." He paused. "Um, there's something else." His cheeks reddened. "I was wondering if maybe just you and I could go on a trip."

"Just the two of us?"

"Yeah. I like Paul a lot, but I just wonder if we could do something alone."

Sensing he had something specific in mind, she coaxed him. "Is there a trip you'd like to take before Paul and I get married?"

"I'm really interested in the Civil War, and I'm wondering if maybe we could go see some of the battlefields."

"What a great idea!" Her son was learning to love history. "I think there may be tours you can take, like bus trips where you have a guide and spend a certain amount of time at each battlefield."

"I could start looking them up now!"

She lowered her gaze. "Don't you have a paper to write?"

"Oh, yeah, I do. I almost forgot."

"How about if you work on your assignment, and I'll

start looking. I think we should make sure the trip includes Gettysburg."

"Definitely. Did you know Joshua Chamberlain fought there, and was awarded a medal?"

"No, I did not."

"Too bad we can't go before this paper is due."

"Yes, but get there we will." She rose to leave.

"Uh, Mom, I've been wondering about something else."

"What's that?"

"When you marry Paul, will I get to keep my name?"

"You mean Miles?" When he nodded, she said, "Of course."

"What about you? Will you still be a Miles?"

"Yes, I will, but I'll also be a Bassett."

"So, Erin Miles Bassett?"

She grinned at her son. "I do like the sound of that."

"Me too. I like how you'll still be a Miles."

"Your dad will always be a big part of my life, and I will always honor his name."

"Thanks, Mom."

She squeezed his shoulder and hastily left the room.

CHAPTER TWENTY-SIX

They arrived in Easton at the precise time village cooks were at their best, the scent of roasting meat enough to make a man salivate just walking down the street. He wanted to find Robert Levers straightaway, yet a magnetic pull steered Peter in the direction of his own home. After letting Catherine and the rest of the family know he'd returned, he and Lt. Hall would continue on their urgent business. He shared his plan with the junior officer.

"I could always go in search of Mr. Levers, and Mr. Adams, on my own."

Peter frowned. "Since you don't know the town, finding Mr. Adams could take longer by yourself than waiting a few minutes while I see my family."

Hall nodded as they arrived at the Kichline residence, and Peter opened the front door. "Hello! Is anyone home?"

"Peter!" Catherine came down the front stairs, her footsteps light against the plank floors in spite of her carrying Abraham. Bett, Joe, Susannah, and Elizabeth jostled along the hallway from the back of the house.

"You're home!"

"Papa!"

Elizabeth flung herself at her father, hugging his calves, her face a study in bliss.

He laughed as he swooped down and picked her up, relishing her sticky kisses on his cheek, then her arms encircling his neck. "Yes, I'm home, and with me is Lt. Hall of the Continental Army." There was no missing Hall's eyes taking in the comely form of Susannah, whose cheeks were turning ruddy.

"Mercy sakes!" Bett cried. Flour smudged her face. "Don't they feed you soldiers? I seen field hans wit more meat on der bones." With vigorous gestures she motioned for him to follow her. Wide-eyed, Hall glanced at Peter.

He grinned. "I think you'd better go with her, Lieutenant. I'll make sure she doesn't keep you more than a few minutes."

"Well, all right, if you think so." Hall didn't look as if he needed any more persuading as he followed Bett toward the kitchen.

As Catherine drew nearer, Peter's heart thudded at her loveliness, then abruptly squeezed when he noticed her wrinkled brow, dark blotches under her eyes, and Abraham's plaintive expression. He bent down to kiss her cheek and smoothed his son's curly blonde hair from his forehead, feeling its sweatiness and the baby's body heat.

"The fever has returned." She bit her lip.

He processed the gut punch news of his son's lingering infirmity. "I actually haven't completed my mission, but I wanted to let you know I've returned." He paused, touching the baby's chin. "Has Dr. Ledlie seen Abraham?"

She sighed. "Yes. He wanted to bleed him, but something told me not to allow this. He's already so weak. I just want to keep him quiet and nourished."

There was a great deal he had to offer his family, his community, and his fledging nation, but he stood helpless in the face of illness. Peter wasn't about to lose hope, not when some *Kinder* developed stronger constitutions as they grew. Seeing the plea in her eyes, he attempted to reassure her. "I trust your instincts, my dear."

Susannah had stood by quietly, then after a pause she burst forth. "Papa, there's been a good deal of excitement. A rather large entourage arrived early this morning from Philadelphia."

He perked back up. "These are the people I need to see. Do you know where they are stopping?"

"The Bachmann. A number of people went to see Mr. John Adams there, he's with the Continental Congress, but I understand he didn't really want to see anyone just yet."

He'll see me. "Thank you for the news, Daughter." He craned his neck toward the back of the house. "I'd better go and rescue Lt. Hall." Turning to Susannah he asked, "Would you take this elf from me?"

His eldest daughter held out her arms. "Come to me, Lizzy."

The child nuzzled into her father's neck. "Don't want to."

Peter whispered something in her ear, and she looked at him, bright-eyed. "*Ja?*"

"*Ja,* Papa!"

He transferred her to Susannah's arms, and she carried the toddler into the parlor.

"What did you say to her?" Catherine was smiling.

"Oh, just something about a trip to Mr. Hart's store tomorrow." When she gave a laugh, his heart rejoiced at her small merriment.

Sniffing the aroma of roasting pork, Peter found the young officer sitting at the laden kitchen table, his mouth vigorously engaged while Joe jammed a sack with provisions. Hall was holding a large piece of rye bread smeared with butter the approximate thickness of the bread, a large chunk missing. In the officer's other hand a slab of cheese bore his teeth imprint. The sight warmed Peter, remembering his own starving time in a British prison.

"I'm happy to see our Bett is taking good care of you." He winked at her, and she grinned. Hall was struggling to speak around the food in his mouth. "Oh, yeth, thshee ith."

If laughter was a kind of medicine to the soul, he thought, so was seeing a hungry man fill his belly. "I regret having to interrupt your repast, but we must continue with our work."

"Yeth." He nodded, then made short work of the food he held, not an especially pretty sight.

"Hurry up, Joe," Bett said. "Hep me fill dis sack for de Lieutenant."

Hall did not object.

Finding Theophilus Shannon in the crowd filling the Bachmann Publick House would've taken several minutes had the tavern keeper not shared the distinction with Peter of being the tallest man in Easton. Peter found him near the bar, wiping a tankard dry and, raising his voice, called out, "I'm looking for Mr. Levers and Mr. Adams."

"I'm sorry, Colonel Kichline, but they aren't here. They left an hour or so ago, but their friends have stayed." He gestured toward the room, smelling of burning wood, beer, and sweat.

"Do you know where they might be Mr. Shannon?"

When the burly fellow shrugged his shoulders, Peter

turned to Hall. "I suggest we pay Mr. Levers a visit."

They walked down Northampton Street near the ferry where Levers resided, keeping a close watch lest the conveyance fall into enemy hands. Soldiers and civilians milled, lending an almost festival spirit, except Peter knew better. With their capital city slipping away from the Patriots, no one would be of a celebratory disposition. *Except maybe Lewis Gordon.* He brushed the thought away as he would a gnat. In many ways Gordon remained an enigma to Peter, but this wasn't the time to ponder the vagaries of the man's convictions.

When they came to the house, the guard addressed him. "Colonel Kichline?"

"Yes, I am he."

He stepped aside. "Mr. Levers is expecting you."

Peter entered a smoky, loud, and packed war room. Mary Levers hustled from the back of the house bearing a pewter pitcher, loose strands bouncing around her face, her apron wrinkled and smudged. His back stiffened at the disheveled sight of her, accompanied by the Levers's seven-year-old daughter carrying a stack of white linen, their slightly older son running up the stairs. Several servants busied themselves with various tasks amidst the cacophony. A roundish soldier appeared in the doorway. *He must be a fairly recent recruit*, was Peter's wry assessment.

"Sir? May I help you?"

"I am Colonel Kichline, here to see Mr. Levers and Mr. Adams. They are ex …"

"Right this way, sir!"

The soldier turned crisply on his heels and led Peter to a side room congested with officers, Levers among them, seated next to a plump, yet nicely-dressed fellow. Levers made eye contact with Peter and jumped up. "Colonel Kichline! Just the man we want to see." He waved his hand. "Come in, come in."

Peter indicated for Hall to follow him. Reaching Levers, the men shook hands.

The clerk of practically everything turned to his companion. "Mr. John Adams, I'd like to present our very distinguished Colonel Peter Kichline. Colonel, this is Mr. Adams, the Massachusetts delegate to the Continental Congress."

Peter reached across the space between them and shook hands with Adams. "I am pleased to make your acquaintance again, sir."

The man's eyes lit with recognition. "Ah, yes! We met in Philadelphia some time ago as I recall." Adams glanced over Peter's shoulder. "Hello Lt. Hall. I see your mission was successful." The officer bowed his head.

Levers introduced three other men at the table, and they shook hands. "Do sit down, Colonel," he said, pointing to a chair across from him and Adams. "Lieutenant, I apologize for not having an extra place for you to sit."

"Not a problem, sir." He stood close to Peter.

"I am sorry for the terrible inconvenience, Colonel."

"Excuse me, Mr. Adams?"

"Initially we planned to bring our ..." He cleared his throat. "... cargo by way of Bethlehem, but there was a last-minute change of plans. I sent Mr. Hall to intercept you, so you weren't waiting indefinitely."

"I am grateful for your consideration and assure you, I was not in any way inconvenienced."

Adams narrowed his eyes for a long moment, as if assessing Peter. "I appreciate your flexibility."

Levers spoke. "Mr. Adams has been on quite a journey, Colonel. Perhaps he would like to fill you in."

"Oh, indeed I would, sir." He sipped from a tankard, its beads of sweat dripping onto the green tablecloth. "On the late evening of the nineteenth, we members of Congress were alarmed in our very beds by Mr. Hamilton, one of General Washington's military family. The British were in possession of the ford over the Schuykill River, prepared to take Philadelphia by the morning. All the papers of Congress, from each of the secretaries' offices, had been sent ahead to Bristol, along with our President, Mr. Hancock, so I followed after them with Mr. Marchant here." He nodded toward a sallow-faced fellow to Peter's left. "We arrived in Trenton, in the Jersies, where we stayed until the twenty-first. One plan was to convey the papers by road to Bethlehem, lest we'd been followed, the other was to take our chances and come directly to Easton." He took a long breath as he folded his hands on the table. "This is where matters became interesting. We stopped in Bethlehem just long enough to refresh ourselves and our horses, then got to Easton two days ago. I'm afraid we just missed each other, Colonel Kichline."

Peter nodded, wondering where all this was going.

"Members of Congress had decided to relocate to Lancaster, and on our way we stopped at Reading. By the time we got to Lancaster, the discussion became rather strenuous about whether or not to keep the documents with us there. We concluded that it might be best to keep them separate in case …"

Peter filled in the blank—"in case we had to run from the British again."

"Yes, well, those papers are more important than all us

members of Congress, and we decided they would best be hidden in Easton, under the careful watch of Mr. Levers."

Adams sank back into his chair, yet even so, his back remained straight, his expression proud.

"Mr. Adams, you have certainly had an interesting several days," Peter said.

The suggestion of a smile appeared on his face. "That I have. I believe our circuit from Philadelphia then Bethlehem to Lancaster was some two hundred miles. If we had come straight to Easton, we would have traveled less than half as much." He sighed. "Then again, this tour has given me an opportunity of seeing many parts of this country hitherto unknown for me."

"I trust you have found gratitude for your services— and our best hospitality."

"Indeed," Adams said, "I find I'm overwhelmed by the outpouring of affection."

Levers grinned. "Our villagers will not leave him alone."

The men chortled as Mrs. Levers entered the room and whispered something to her husband. Peter's throat tightened when Levers waved her off as if she were a serving girl. Her face reddened, and she left, shoulders slumping.

Adams seemed not to have noticed. He leaned forward, looking directly at Peter. "I wonder if I might seek yet another favor from you, as Mr. Levers tells me you are unable to take up arms as you await exchange."

"I am at your disposal, Mr. Adams."

"I must be going back to the Congress and plan to stop in Bethlehem for a few days. The Moravians intrigue me. While they are not with us, nor are they entirely against us. I also learned along the way of a dear friend of our nation being wounded at the Brandywine engagement. He is recuperating in a hospital in Bethlehem, along with others from the campaign. I would consider it a great personal favor if you would accompany me back to that village, to provide additional protection for my small contingent, as well as the pleasure of your company."

Peter jumped at the opportunity to do something more for the Cause. "I would be pleased to join you, Mr. Adams."

"Very well then." He looked around, his mouth turning southward. "I can hardly hear myself think in here. Might you be able to travel back to Bethlehem in two days, after I have time to wrap up my business here?"

"Yes, sir."

Adams nodded. "Lt. Hall, would you like to accompany us, or stay with your detail here? Either way you would be useful."

"I will be happy to go along if that would be of greater service, sir."

"Good! That's settled, then." Adams slapped his palms against his thighs.

"Mr. Adams," Peter said. "Do you suggest I wear civilian clothes, or my uniform?"

The New Englander's eyes twinkled. "Definitely your uniform."

CHAPTER TWENTY-SEVEN

He would have preferred not to stop for another hour, but John Adams expressed a need to refresh himself. Not everyone, Peter realized, had his sturdy constitution, not even someone he judged to be at least ten years his junior. He and the Massachusetts congressman answered nature's call, then planted themselves under the dappled shade of English walnut trees. Hall and Adams's two secretaries fell into conversation several feet away, breaking bread, drinking from their flasks.

Adams held out his hand to Peter. "Would you care for some cheese and bread, Colonel?"

Never one to turn away food, he tore off a modest hunk and accepted a piece of cheese. "Thank you."

"I must apologize for my reduced speed." Adams took a swig of water, wiping away droplets from his mouth with a handkerchief. "You may find this hard to believe, but I once covered quite a large swath in a day's time as a young and itinerant lawyer."

"Your work must've been interesting." Peter could relate to a peripatetic lifestyle due to his long years as Northampton County's sheriff.

"I was away from home a lot, but I enjoyed the satisfaction of administering justice." Adams shook his head, sighed. "I find there has been an unfortunate pattern since I married my excellent wife—my work has taken me away from her entirely too often. She is a most excellent woman, however, and takes our absences with a pleasant spirit. My Abigail believes this is her main sacrifice for our Cause. Without such stalwart women, where would any of us be?"

Peter smiled. "I agree. Mrs. Adams is, then, back in Massachusetts?"

"Yes, she is home in Quincy doing the work of several persons, managing the house, the farm, and our extended family."

"How many children do you have?" Peter found he was hungry after all, but instead of gobbling his small meal, he disciplined himself to match his companion's more deliberate pace.

"I have four lovely urchins—Abigail is the oldest at twelve, John Quincy is ten, Charles is seven, and little Thomas is five." Adams gazed into the cloud-speckled sky as if he were treasuring in his heart the images he carried there of his family. "Tell me about your family, Colonel."

"My wife Catherine and I have two children—Abraham, who is a year old, and three year-old Elizabeth."

Adams knit his brow. "You married later in life then?"

Strains of laughter and the contented whinny of horses drifted toward them. "As well as earlier. I married not too long after my family came to America in the fall of 1742."

"From Germany?"

"Yes. My ancestors were Swiss and German. My Margaretta gave me four children. Peter is twenty-seven, married, and serving in the Continental Army. Andrew and Jacob are in their mid-twenties and run my grist and sawmills when they aren't on duty with the Northampton County militia. Susannah is a lovely young woman at seventeen."

"Perhaps she gives you reason for concern?" His eyes twinkled.

"She is quite the patriot, and I have insisted she always go about her missions of mercy to the sick and imprisoned with an escort."

Adams touched the side of his nose with his finger. "Smart man." He paused. "You and the current Mrs. Kichline haven't been married long then?"

"No, sir. Margaretta died eleven years ago, and I remarried shortly afterward. Unfortunately, my second wife found great difficulty giving birth, and I … lost her as well." Peter still found the memory of young Anna bleeding to death difficult to recall. He pushed the narrative forward. "I married Catherine four years ago."

Adams looked in the direction of their younger companions. "Life holds many challenges for each of us, notwithstanding the current crisis of our fledging nation. I come from good Puritan stock, and I maintain there is a God in heaven who governs the course of human, and individual, events. This is something in which I find great comfort, Colonel Kichline."

Peter smiled. "We are of a similar mind."

The Sun Inn wasn't exactly itself. Normally perfumed with food preparation and cheering fires, a disagreeable odor greeted them instead, and Peter immediately recognized the scent—suffering. Disheveled officers and soldiers pushed the tavern to capacity.

"Well, good day to you, Colonel Kichline! I didn't expect to see you back so soon, although I am delighted."

Jost Hellerich moved with cat-like quickness and grace, his cravat askew. His face wore the clothing of fatigue.

Peter shook his hand. "Likewise, I am pleased to be in your company once again. Mr. Hellerich, I believe you know my companion, Lt. Hall."

The men bowed their heads toward one another. "Lt. Hall, welcome back to Bethlehem." Hellerich looked over his left shoulder.

"Thank you, sir."

"With him are some troops accompanying Congressman Adams of Massachusetts. Mr. John Adams, may I present Mr. Jost Hellerich, owner of this fine establishment?" Peter's forced cheerfulness sounded like a clanging symbol in his ears.

Adams shot out his hand. "I saw you when I passed through recently."

"I do believe I recognize you, sir, although I deeply regret not having welcomed you."

"I was in quite a hurry at the time."

Peter sensed Hellerich understood the meaning behind the congressman's words, and appreciated how discreet the tavern keeper had always been, privy as he was to many intrigues.

"How long may we expect you to stay, Mr. Adams? I beg your most humble pardon, but I regret there is no room here, although I could try to secure quarters in a private home."

"You are most kind, Mr. Hellerich."

"Perhaps I can assist," Peter said. "I know of a family we could call upon."

Hellerich exhaled, nodding. "Thank you very much, Colonel. You know I …"

Peter held up his hand. "I am happy to be of assistance. When did all these troops arrive?"

"They got here just after you left, and my inn has become a makeshift hospital. There are several in town." He seemed to remember his manners. "Would you care for some refreshment?"

The Congressman spoke for his retinue. "No, thank you, my friend." He leaned closer to the innkeeper. "I understand you have a distinguished guest here, a certain Frenchman?"

"I can take you to him straightaway."

"In the meantime, my associates can provide help with the wounded."

Hellerich looked as if he'd just shed five years. "That is welcome news. After I take you upstairs, I'll introduce your men to the officers in charge."

Peter stood inside the Sun Inn's nicest guest room, its pleasant appointments receding against the presence of soldiers who had witnessed far less agreeable scenes. The Frenchmen turned to greet their guests when Hellerich made introductions. Peter gazed about the room for the one person they had come to see, but no one fit John Adams's description of a Major General of the Continental Army.

Adams addressed the men. "*Bonne journée messieurs.*"

Peter was not well versed in French, but even he knew, "Good day, gentlemen."

The congressman rattled off a small speech, most of which was lost on Peter, but then one of the soldiers assured them, "We speak English, good sir."

His companion sighed. "Thank you for sparing me the indignity of mangling your beautiful language. As I was saying, I am John Adams, Massachusetts representative to the Continental Congress, and this is Colonel Peter Kichline of the Northampton County Flying Camp."

In the corner of the room, a young man's eyes seemed to bounce open. "You were at Brooklyn, sir?"

Peter moved closer to the Frenchman, who sat in a wing chair with a leg propped on a stool. The man appeared to be little more than a boy with his unlined face and mere hint of a beard, though there was something almost regal about the firm set of his tapered jaw and aquiline nose. *Could this be …?"*

"Yes, I was at Brooklyn." He extended his hand and found the man's grasp as sturdy as a carpenter's though it bore no marks of any kind of labor.

"Forgive me," he said, he voice swathed in a French lilt, "I am Marie Joseph Paul Yves Roch Gilbert du Motier."

Peter drew back his head and tried not to register amusement. "I am pleased to meet you."

"These are my officers." He waved toward the four other soldiers, who bowed to Peter and Adams.

Peter thought what he would never say—*They must be twice your age!*

"You are, then, the Marquis de Lafayette?" Adams asked.

"At your service." He bowed his head.

Adams looked directly at the Frenchman's wrapped leg. "I'd heard you'd been wounded."

"Yes. I'm afraid a bullet desired to make my deeper acquaintance."

From the lack of a bad smell, Peter considered how the nobleman's leg appeared to be healing nicely.

"That was eleven days ago, and the surgeons are astonished by the rate at which it heals." He grinned. "I just wrote to my wife how they are in near ecstasy every time they dress the wound, and maintain it is the most beautiful thing in the world."

His wife?

"I myself find it very foul, tedious, and rather painful. There is no accounting for tastes."

Now Peter laughed, pleased to see amusement twinkling in his companions' eyes.

"General Washington will be most happy to find you are on the mend," Adams said.

Lafayette sat up taller. "Are you able to get word to the General on my behalf?"

"I would be delighted to assist you, Marquis."

"I thank you from my heart, sir. He is as a father to me, and I do not want him to worry on my account. I should soon be well and able to rejoin the fighting." He turned to Peter. "Won't you both please sit down?" A look in the direction of an officer resulted in the instant appearance of chairs for their visitors.

"Have you wanted for anything here?" Adams asked.

"Nothing at all, Mr. Adams. Now I have your distinguished company, I am in even better spirits. This Bethlehem is a most enchanting place. Its people lead a gentle and peaceful life, and their ministrations have been as a balm to my spirit. But please, enough about myself." He waved his hands in front of himself. "I am eager to know about your work with the Congress, Mr. Adams, and your experience at the Battle of Brooklyn, Colonel Kichline. You were, then, leader of a Flying Camp? I have heard of these and wish to know more."

Peter looked at Adams, who closed his eyes and gave a brief nod. "The Congress called for the formation of Flying Camps early last summer, to be modeled after the Minute Men of Mr. Adam's Massachusetts, troops able to respond at a moment's notice. I became the Northampton County Flying Camp's commander. We received the call from General Washington to proceed to New York. We engaged the enemy in Brooklyn, or as some call the territory, Long Island."

Lafayette shook his head. "A bad state of affairs as I understand. Many men lost."

Peter closed his eyes, nodding. "Yes, we lost many good men." He began recalling some of their names to himself, until the Marquis interrupted his thoughts.

He shifted in his chair, moving closer. "I heard about General Washington's miraculous escape from New York and would love to know your account."

Peter met his clear hazel eyes. "I was not part of the evacuation."

A heartbeat later, Lafayette wore an "aha" expression. "You were captured?"

"Wounded and captured."

Silence. Everyone looking at Peter. "For how long?"

"I was allowed to return to my home in Easton on parole in February with my few remaining men. I now await my exchange." A moment later, he continued. "My son, an officer in the Flying Camp, managed to escape with the rest of General Washington's army. He told me of the dense fog which covered their flight, how it only lifted after the last of the men had reached safety."

Lafayette tented his hands, lightly bouncing his chin against the tips of his fingers. "I have never before heard such an account, Colonel Kichline. Indeed, this is one of the reasons I came to America, to offer my services to our brave General Washington. There is something unique about this fledging nation, something far beyond the usual progress of history. I sense the Almighty is in some way directly involved in the founding and creation of this new republic—that we are at the dawn of a new era in human government."

Peter was grateful John Adams spoke. "I share your musings, Marquis. My ancestors conceived America as a 'city upon a hill for all the world to see,' a place where humanity could be refreshed and institutions reborn—a place in which the Almighty was welcome to abide among his people."

Lafayette's gaze shifted to Adams, as if he were just remembering he and Peter were not the only men in the room. "I am very pleased to be a small part of this struggle for independence and have pledged my all to support it."

"We are grateful for you, Marquis."

"Tell me, Mr. Adams, have you ever taken up arms?"

Peter heard a rumble in his new friend's chest.

"Not unless you consider the daily battles we fight in Congress."

CHAPTER TWENTY-EIGHT

If nothing appeared to be wrong with the mirror, why did she look so *lopsided?* Erin inclined herself to the right, then to the left, groping to find the source of the problem. The wedding gown softly shimmered in the dressing room's artful lighting, obviously a perfect fit, yet something was still wrong with the picture.

"Do you need any help?"

She swallowed before answering so as not to croak. "No thank you, Deidre."

"I'm here if you need me."

She knew the salon owner, her mother, and Connie were likely expecting a grand reveal they could ooh and ahhh over. Melissa had wanted to attend the final fitting but backed out at the last minute to rush her cat to the vet after he swallowed a neighbor's hearing aid.

The dress is beautiful. I love its simple elegance and the fabric. She lifted the bottom to survey the shoes. *They're so pretty and feel half decent, so what's wrong here?* The issue, she concluded, was herself. When she'd married Jim, her youthful body didn't know the meaning of cellulite or crepiness. She looked pretty good for her age, a far cry better than most women approaching fifty. Maybe no one else would even notice, or care, that her waist didn't curve inward the way it had in her twenties. At least no one would be able to see the growing map of spider veins on her legs, except for Paul. On their wedding night, he would see them, and the thicker waist, and the spider veins …

I'm not a blushing bride. She took a deep breath.

"Hey, Erin, let's see you!" Connie coaxed her.

"Just give me a minute." She needed time to process this new, unimproved version of herself.

A pause, then, "Oh, okay. Take your time."

She had no pep talk to give herself, although she would have welcomed one. She closed her eyes and prayed in silence, thanking God for Paul and this new season in the autumn of her life. She smiled at herself and almost laughed as she muttered, "After all, he has seen me in shorts, and if that wasn't enough to scare him away, I doubt a few wrinkles or fat deposits will. Besides, he has a few of his own."

Gathering the bottom of the dress, as well as her courage, she opened the door and faced her retinue.

Connie lifted her fingertips to her mouth. "Oh, Erin! You look amazing!" Turning to Deidre she said, "Isn't she gorgeous?"

The salon owner smiled and slowly nodded her admiration. "Gorgeous is certainly the right word." She walked over to Erin and began pulling here, smoothing there. Then she stepped back. "I think the fit is perfect, and the shade is so flattering. "How do you like the dress?"

"I, uh, love the dress."

"Do you feel like a princess?"

"More like the queen mother." The words had popped out of her mouth before she realized she was saying them. Fortunately, Audrey chose that moment to beckon her daughter to come closer.

"Oh, Erin, you are so beautiful." She ran a wrinkled

hand over the side of the dress. "This gown is amazing, and so is my daughter."

Her voice choked. "Thank you, Mom."

If Erin had looked at either Connie or Deidre, she would've seen them exchanging concerned glances.

Audrey had expressed a "hankering" for a Jimmy's hot dog, and Erin welcomed the flow of the river, and her mom's chatter, as they ate at one of the picnic tables. She barely tasted her food, wishing she'd had the nerve to ask the window attendant for chocolate sauce. Or a dollop of ice cream. Those would have tasted good on the hot dog. Fortunately, going to lunch was all Audrey had requested on the way back to her apartment.

When they arrived, Audrey strutted into the lobby, a peacock in full display mode. "You should see my daughter in her wedding gown! She looks stunning."

Aunt Fran stood straighter, her hands gripping her walker. "Well, I'll be there. I have a beautiful dress too."

Audrey harrumphed. "No one will be as beautiful as my daughter."

Erin suppressed a nervous giggle over her family's one-upmanship. She followed her mother to the elevator, then to the corner apartment where Audrey began turning on lights and offered her a glass of iced tea.

"Do you want me to get out the glasses?"

"No, you just take it easy." She halted, then looked at Erin. "I almost forgot. I need to see my life insurance policy, and I went through my dresser drawer where I keep those things but couldn't find it. Would you please take a look?

My eyes are bad."

"Sure, Mom."

"You know, the tall dresser near the window."

She walked past her mother to the bedroom where she surveyed three family photos on top of the furniture, including one of her and Jim walking down the aisle after their wedding ceremony. Erin moved closer, staring at the bright-faced couple so full of love and promise. Tears pooled in her eyes, and she blinked to get a better look at herself. Her hair had been longer then but pulled into an updo, her waist as tiny as Scarlet O'Hara's, her bare arms—smooth, her radiant face, devoid of fine lines. Jim appeared as freshly scrubbed as a teenager at his prom—tall, trim, proud. In a word, perfect.

Wasn't that how brides and grooms were supposed to look? Wasn't this middle-aged wedding thing some kind of cruel joke? People were supposed to get married young and stay together until they shriveled up at roughly the same age and rate, by then used to each other's mental and physical quirks, like in-laws and snoring. Who even was this person she'd become? She used to be a wife and a mother, a professor and resident of Montgomery County with an established routine and broken-in furniture and pots and pans she'd received as wedding presents. Who exactly was Erin Miles, widow, single mom, writer, curator, and fiancée, a newly-fatherless child?

She knew she would snap out of this with a good dose of perspective, but who could she talk to? She didn't think Paul was the right person since she didn't want to be talking down herself to her future husband. She could just picture the scene—"Oh, look at my expanding waistline, Paul! And see this broken capillary."

"Erin."

She nearly jumped out of her skin when her mother slipped beside her. "Oh, uh, Mom. I didn't hear you come in."

"Did you find my policy?"

"No, sorry. I saw this picture and I, I ..." There was no holding back, no analyzing whether or not her mom would understand, or if Erin felt comfortable baring her soul to a woman who treated emotions like mosquitos. She turned to mush.

"Oh, my dear girl." Her mother held Erin and pressed her daughter's head to her shoulder. "You just go ahead. There, there."

She surrendered to the moment, to her mother's crooning, feeling at once elderly and childlike. When the storm spent itself, Erin pulled away and lifted a tissue from a bedside table.

"I think I understand," Audrey said. "You're getting married, but you're also thinking about Jim."

She nodded. "Something along those lines."

"Do you want to talk about it?"

Did she? Yes. No. Maybe. She needed her mom. "I'm just feeling a bit emotional after trying on my gown today." She swallowed. "I, I'm not young like I was when I married Jim."

"When you get to be my age, you realize what young is. Being in your forties isn't like it used to be. People looked old then, but not now, and definitely not you. You look ten years younger."

She sniffed. "I do?"

"Oh, yes, you do, and you've kept your figure."

"But I've had a child."

Audrey patted her arm. "You have a mature body, a womanly body."

"Not matronly?"

She pulled back with a start. "Definitely not! Matronly would be like Mrs. Krontz, who lived across from Grammy. Do you remember her?"

An old memory surfaced of a woman sitting on her porch, filling the space in more ways than one. "That woman was never young. But not you. Or Paul."

"My body parts don't seem to be in the same places they used to be."

"Your body parts are just fine. Again, you're a woman, not some skinny teenager with no figure."

Erin's voice sounded as small as she felt. "My life has changed so much."

When Audrey asked for no explanation, Erin closed her eyes in relief. Even if her mother didn't fully understand, just saying the words cleansed the muck in her spirit.

Her mother pulled Erin to the side of the bed where they sat facing the open window, the mountain view steady, stable. "When Tony left, I had a crisis like that."

She winced, waiting for the usual diatribe against the man she always referred to as "your father," as if Erin were responsible for Audrey's unmitigated disaster of a marriage. Something was different here, though. Her mom had referred to "Tony." She wasn't given to idealizing her father in death, beyond what he had been in his life, but she did want to respect his memory and the restored bond they had shared.

"We were married a long time by today's standards, and after the divorce, I wasn't anyone's wife, yet responsible for two children, forced from my home, looking for a job to pay for a smaller house." Audrey bowed her head as if the memories weighed her down.

"That must've been very hard for you."

"Yes, but you and Allen were my mainstays, along with my faith in God. I don't talk about it a lot, but I always felt as if God gave me the strength for the living of those days."

Erin's head gave a small jerk. "Mother! You're positively poetic."

Audrey frowned. "I am?"

"Yes. I love the quote you just worked in from an old hymn to describe what your life was like."

"What hymn?

"Let me see." She conjured the song from her internal musical library and started humming. "I think the name was something like 'God of Grace and God of Glory.'"

"I used to love singing that hymn when I was a kid. Honestly, though, I didn't really think about the words. They just popped into my head." She smiled. "Maybe you get some of your writing talent from me."

"Maybe I do." Erin grinned.

"Anyway, we should be talking about you." Audrey covered her daughter's hand. "I do have a way of going on about myself."

Was there no end of the surprises her mother was serving today?

"You were a beautiful bride the first time, and you will be equally beautiful the second time. Deidre told me she thought you looked stunning, and I totally agree."

"I have wrinkles."

"I don't see any."

"I have spider veins."

"No one will see them."

"My waist isn't tiny."

"It's small enough."

"I have dark circles under my eyes."

"You've lived a full and good life, and there's a little mileage on you, but you still look fantastic."

She inclined her head toward her wedding photo. "I looked so perfect back then."

"Well, Erin, let me just tell you something. Now you are a little better than perfect."

CHAPTER TWENTY-NINE

They walked to the forks as the sun slipped over the western hills, setting autumn foliage aflame, two veterans in need of their own company. On the Delaware, the ferry slid across the shimmering water.

"How is Sarah coming along?"

Peter Jr. pressed his lips together, nodding his head slowly. "She's feeling better physically." He paused. "She wants to try again but is afraid of losing another baby."

What could he say to this sorrow? He had stood by a wife who'd experienced similar issues and died trying to have a child.

"Father?"

Peter turned to his oldest, startled by a suggestion of gray at the temples. "Yes?"

"I know you understand about, well, women and babies." He looked down at his feet, a bashful schoolboy.

"Yes, son. Just be there for Sarah. Let her know you will always be there."

Peter Jr. breathed out. "I've decided to stay closer to home, to her."

"Is that why you didn't reenlist?"

"Yes. And because I believe I can do more from Easton than in the field just now."

As they walked, Peter clasped his hands at the base of his spine. "What is the army's condition?"

His son's eyes narrowed. He rolled his lips. "Definitely more seasoned and battle savvy than we were at Brooklyn, but they're in a distressed condition—lack of uniforms, shoes hanging from their feet, not enough food, a good deal of sickness."

"Where do you think General Washington will keep winter quarters?"

"I'm not entirely sure, but somewhere near Philadelphia. Since the British occupied the city, he wants to be able to keep an eye on their movements."

"How can we help?"

"We must send supplies to General Washington—food, clothing, footwear, arms."

Peter rubbed his chin. "Resources in Easton are stretched, to say the least, but we can contribute grain from the mill, and perhaps the women can arrange for articles of clothing."

"Thank you, Father. Sometimes I think, 'What's the use of trying to feed hundreds of men when we can only provide for a few dozen?' Then I remind myself what a difference this will make to those few dozen."

He clapped his son's broad shoulder. "We are not, after all, 'sunshine soldiers' or 'summer patriots,' to quote Mr. Paine."

"Winning this war is taking everything we have, but win we must." He fisted his right hand and clapped it into his other palm.

Peter looked into his son's resolute eyes. "While I'm hesitant to say God is on our side, I do believe we are on his."

While they walked north toward the Bushkill Creek, Peter's son turned to a different page in the book of their conversation. "How is Abraham? Sarah says he's had a rough few months."

He let out a long, low breath. "He isn't well. We thought late last month he had turned a corner, but for the past three weeks he's become worse than at any time in his illness."

"Is there nothing Dr. Ledlie can do?"

"I'm afraid not, at least nothing he hasn't already tried. He did press Catherine to bleed Abraham, but she insists this should not be done."

"And do you agree?"

"I do. I think bleeding would rob the child of what little strength he has."

"How is Catherine taking all of this?"

"With her characteristic strength from her faith in the Almighty. She has her weak moments, of course, but she doesn't want Abraham, or Elizabeth, to fret."

"She is a special woman."

Peter smiled at his son. "We both are blessed with special women."

Before they parted for the evening, Peter Jr. uttered a short, "Oh! I almost forgot, Father." He reached into a waistcoat pocket and produced an envelope. "I saw Mr. Traill before coming home, and he asked me to give you this."

October 10, 1777

My Dear Friend,

I trust this letter finds you and your family in good health and spirits. In my mind, I imagine our beloved Easton in autumnal glory and ourselves enjoying pipes, port, and stimulating conversation before a cheering fire. Although Providence has been equally kind to this Delaware Valley region, nothing can match the radiance of home, family, and friends.

As I write this, the army is in Philadelphia County following an eventful several weeks. By now, you have heard of our engagement at the Brandywine in which we lost somewhere between seven hundred and a thousand men through death and capture, and a good bit of our canon. In spite of the British victory, I have heard unofficially their numbers of dead and wounded far outnumbered ours. Naturally, we have sustained a great blow in having the British take control of Philadelphia, but we have not lost heart, or stalwartness for our Cause.

A few days ago, the Fifth Pennsylvania engaged the enemy at Germantown. Our forces consisted of some eight thousand Continentals and three thousand militia, and our good commander launched an offensive against the British with their nine thousands. Our men fought with brave determination, hindered by fog and later, darkness. The British lost about five hundred men, and we saw a bit more killed and wounded, and a few hundred captured. I know you would have been proud of our effort. I am happy to report Peter Jr. led his unit with excellence and resolve. You can be proud of him.

We are temporarily camped several miles from Germantown, awaiting orders to remove to more permanent quarters. I do not know whether we shall engage the enemy again before winter, but my men and

I are ready for whatever comes.

Has there been any word regarding your exchange? I do hope Colonel Hooper and Mr. Levers have made headway. I understand you were able to meet with Congressman Adams and the Marquis de Lafayette, whom General Washington regards as a son.

Please remember me to Catherine and your household. I pray by now wee Abraham is finding his way back to health. Write to me when you can, and I will stay in touch as well. Until then, may God hold you in the palm of his hand and give you peace.

Your Humble Servant,

Robert Traill

He folded and slipped the letter into its envelope, sobered by news of the battles in which American forces had demonstrated grit, yet lost so much. With the British occupation of Philadelphia, he wondered what General Washington's next moves would be, confident in the Virginian's wisdom and expertise. He knew some men grumbled about the man's capacity to lead, but this was something Peter could not bring himself to doubt. The Americans might have sustained loss, but they had always lived to see another day.

He relieved his wife in the early hours so she could get some sleep, having been at Abraham's side for two straight days. When she protested, he gently took her by the shoulders and led her to their bedroom. "I insist you rest, Catherine."

"But ..."

"You will do him no good wearing yourself to a nub. I will stay with him."

She hesitated until Susannah shored up her father's argument. "Please Mother Catherine, try to sleep. You must take care of yourself too."

The woman's shoulders seemed to buckle under the weight of their logic.

He returned to Abraham's room and positioned himself next to the bed, alert to every sound and movement as Susannah kept vigil with him. Sometime around four o'clock, the one-year-old began convulsing. Peter sprang to his feet and picked Abraham up, feeling the sticky warmth of the boy's body.

Moments later, Susannah was assisting Catherine back into the room.

"Oh, my baby!" She thrust herself toward the child, still spasming in Peter's arms.

Susannah's eyes popped. "Should I get Dr. Ledlie?"

Peter clung to the center of his calm while his arms and legs trembled. "Wake up Joe, and go with him to Pastor Rodenheimer."

"But ..."

"Dr. Ledlie has done all he can do."

"Yes, Papa." She turned on her heel and thumped upstairs to the boy's quarters. Not five minutes later, they both hammered down to the first floor and into the night.

Catherine reached out her arms. "Please let me hold him, Peter."

"Not just now. I must keep a tight grasp." Suddenly, Abraham thrust upward, banging his head against the bottom of Peter's jaw, jarring his father's teeth. He stretched out his arms to see the boy's face, noting unfocused eyes and a lolling tongue. A man of action, who challenged whatever came between evil and justice, knew there was just one weapon to wield against this intruder.

"Catherine, let's be in prayer." He inclined his head slightly downward as he held on to Abraham for his dear life. "In the name of Jesus, amen. Our Lord, we come to you as your beloved children on behalf of this child, whom you love and have called to yourself. We beseech you to lay your hand of healing upon him and give him rest from this great trial. Please draw him near to your heart for it is in your great name we pray. Amen."

"Amen," Catherine said through her veil of tears.

Fifteen minutes later, Pastor Rodenheimer and his wife arrived, both of them breathless and tousled from being aroused at such an early hour.

"Thank you for coming, Pastor." Some of Peter's tension released as he felt his son lay quietly now in his arms.

Mrs. Rodenheimer went straight to Catherine, and the two women held each other.

"I think he's asleep," Peter said. "No, just breathing more normally. Thank God."

The minister placed his hand on the boy's sweaty forehead and began speaking in German, words he had no doubt used in other sickrooms, a blend of formal and informal petitions, both universal and specific to this child in this village in October 1777. He ended with the Lord's Prayer, which they all said together.

When Pastor Rodenheimer finished, Abraham opened his blue-gray eyes, gazing first at his father with a heartbreakingly tender expression. Then he turned his head slightly to his mother, smiled and murmured, "Mama." As

Catherine quickly drew her hand to her mouth, she broke into a sob, Rachel weeping for her child because he was no more.

"Thank you for coming to see me, Colonel. While others have turned against me, I have never doubted I could call upon you." Lewis Gordon folded his hands on the desk, a man who seemed to have said and done what needed to be said and done.

Peter gave a small bow of his head. "I have long counted our friendship a privilege and a blessing, Mr. Gordon."

The barrister's body had shrunk, the lion-like head, a sun setting into his shoulders. A cracked Wedgewood vase on the desk reflected the brokenness of its owner.

"I was truly saddened to hear about your little boy, Kichline." He shook his head.

Peter closed his eyes, almost feeling Abraham's still form in his arms. "He was never of a strong constitution. When he became ill months ago, he never recovered his full strength."

Gordon sat quietly as the leaden sky outside gave way to a shower of white flakes. Candles flickered against the backdrop of a hearty fire. Peter wondered who else was in the house, not having seen anyone but the aged *Frau* Neuss.

"How is your dear wife?"

"She is kept busy with our little daughter and many acts of service." In his mind's eye, Peter played out a recent scene with his tiny girl, who'd looked up from his lap with imploring eyes. "Where is baby?"

"Abraham has gone away."

"Where?"

"To be with the Lord."

"Will we ever see him again?"

"Yes, *liebling.* Those who love Jesus will live again."

"I love Jesus."

Peter stroked her silky cheek. "There is nothing to fear when we love Jesus."

Gordon brought him back to the present. "My friend, I believe my own time is growing short, and there is some business I must attend to."

Peter had heard he was ill. "This is difficult news, my friend. Please allow me to be of any service to you."

Gordon seemed to examine his thumbs then looked up, his eyes highlighted by shaggy brows the shade of winter. "I am no traitor, Colonel, nor am I a Loyalist." Peter nodded, leaning against his forearms. "I resigned from the Committee and did not sign the oath because the war was going so badly at the first. I was … I was …"

The attorney stared out the window, and Peter finished the sentence in his mind. "I was afraid of what would happen if we lost." Like himself, Gordon had pledged his life, his fortune, and his sacred honor, but when the push of war pressed against his convictions, the man had caved. Peter knew he was in a position to condemn, but he brushed aside the impulse. He was an appointed judge, yes, but not of a man's conscience.

"You have suffered much for the Cause, my friend. Do you have any regrets?"

"Not a single one," Peter said.

"You are a better man than I."

"We all have our breaking points."

"You have always been a kind and gracious man,

Kichline." He exhaled. "Before I die, I want to take the Oath of Allegiance. I should have known when I turned aside I would have much to go through in either direction. I deeply regret I didn't suffer with you."

He stood and reached across the desk, his hand meeting Gordon's halfway.

"Mr. Jacob left this for you." Bett handed him an envelope.

"And where is my son?"

The servant lifted her hand and spoke into the cup she formed at her mouth. "He be on o-fficial b'ness, sir."

Peter nodded, understanding. His now-youngest son had accepted a commission to confiscate the property of traitors. A nasty business, but Jacob had taken the job as a necessary evil. He hoped the young man would exercise mercy with any necessary justice. Peter went to the parlor and took to his chair.

"What might I bring you, sir?"

"A pot of tea would be nice. Thank you, Bett. Where is Mrs. Kichline?"

"She and Susannah are at church. Joe be at the mills." She turned and left.Peter lit his pipe and opened the envelope, recognizing Robert Hooper's handwriting.

White Marsh, December 21, 1777

Dear Colonel Kichline,

As you know, I have diligently sought to secure your exchange and have good reason to believe the end may at last be in sight. This could possibly occur within the first few months of the new year. I shall keep you apprised of the situation knowing how eager you are to give your services to the fullest of your abilities. Please understand, our beloved country already owes you a great debt.

I regret to inform you, however, I have had far less success in obtaining an exchange for Colonel Miles. He continues in New York in a state of parole, in tolerable good health and spirits. The letters and gifts you send have gone far to aid his well-being.

Bett placed a tea pot, cup and saucer on the table next to him. "Thank you."

"It be my pleasure, sir."

His wife and daughter had knitted new socks for the officer, and Peter had added two new shirts, breeches, and a wool coat his son Andrew had contributed. Even Bett had offered a blanket she said, somewhat disingenuously, was "extra." Peter had instructed Susannah to purchase a new one at Meyer Hart's store as a Christmas gift. The Kichline family also had crammed the package full of cakes, pies, breads, cheeses, and dried fruit. He sipped the strong tea and continued reading.

Please be ready to leave on a moment's notice for your exchange once the holidays are over. I will send word to you as soon as I have anything to report. In the meantime, I will be spending Christmas with the troops. Major Traill is here with me and asks me to send my holiday greetings. He promises to write you at his first opportunity.

I remain,

Your obedient servant,

Robert Hooper

The news buoyed Peter, and he called out to Bett when she passed by in the hall.

"Yes, Colonel?"

"Has Mrs. Kichline given instructions about a Christmas dinner, a tree, or gifts?"

She offered what Peter considered a sly grin. "She do be mentionin' this to me."

Warmth spread in his chest. "Good. I was concerned that this year …" The servant nodded and closed her eyes. "We must celebrate the Child, who brings light to our darkness."

"Amen!"

On the day after Christmas, he received word from Robert Traill.

December 26, 1777

Valley Forge, Pennsylvania

My Dear Colonel Kichline,

I bring you Christmas greetings from the rolling hills along the Schuylkill River. The Army has taken up winter quarters in a favorable situation some twenty miles from the British in Philadelphia. I trust you and your dear family have enjoyed celebrating the birth of our Lord in the joyous style of your ancestors. We officers had a repast I would have considered meager at any other time, but in these days of deprivation, the meal more than satisfied.

As we have always been honest with each other, I will not gild the reality. Our men are in desperate straits, lacking adequate food, clothing, and shelter. In order to protect them from the elements, General Washington conducted a contest to reward those who could most quickly erect small log shelters. The men take turns borrowing shoes and clothing to stand guard duty. I have seen bloodied footprints along the pathways.

My dear friend, only under the most dire conditions would I ask you to leave hearth and home to bring supplies, but this is exactly what I must do. I also know you would not forgive me if I did not make this request. You could, of course, send someone else with provisions, although I am fundamentally selfish. You always have a way of reassuring and steadying me when I wobble. Oh, do not worry. I still believe in our Cause, and Providence is helping us overcome the most severe of trials.

I expect to be here several weeks at least. While my particular commission does not require me to stay, I have thrown in my lot with these brave men. My admiration for General Washington has grown exponentially, and he is well served by a loyal and capable staff.

Lest I forget, I have seen General Lafayette, who never fails to speak of you with great fondness. Perhaps this will also induce you to come. I will do my utmost to gain you an audience with General Washington, who knows of you and highly respects you.

Please remember me to your dear Catherine, your children, and members of your household. Let me hear from you soon.

Your devoted servant,

Robert Traill

Peter removed his reading glasses and lowered the letter into his lap. He became aware of Catherine gazing at him, and he caught her eye. How was it she could see right through him?

"You're going to him, aren't you?"

He spread his hands before him. "How can I do otherwise?"

"Indeed, my dear husband, you cannot."

CHAPTER THIRTY

He had seen such suffering before, experienced such suffering before, and might soon be enduring more—bitter cold wind pouring through cracks, summer clothes on winter bodies, bare, bloody feet, the stench of sour ashes and grubby soldiers, with one major difference—these were free men, not prisoners of war. The fellow shivering on a paltry bunk may have reminded him of Conrad Fartenius languishing in a New York prison, but this soldier was not at the mercy of cruel captors. He was, however, at the mercy of the elements, and Peter gladly draped over his shivering body one of the wool blankets he'd brought. At the beginning of the war, he'd raised up weapons. Now he was doing his utmost to feed and clothe the starving men of Valley Forge.

The fellow's fevered brow raised. "Is this for me, sir?"

"Yes, son."

"I'll share it with my mates. Thank you."

A lump formed in his throat. Peter asked the hut's residents where they were from.

The soldier on the top right bunk spoke. "We're Rhode Islanders, sir."

"We're from Pennsylvania," Robert Traill said, "Northampton County."

A man on the opposite side nodded his head. "We've fought alongside some of them Germans. They're good men, great fighters."

Traill's chest expanded. "Colonel Kichline led the Northampton County Flying Camp at the Battle of Brooklyn, and he's from Germany."

To a man, the soldiers gazed at Peter as if he were General Washington. Peter shuffled his feet and cleared his throat. "Yes, well, I am glad to meet all of you. You've built a good solid dwelling."

A guy whose legs dangled from a middle bunk said, "We almost won the prize General Washington offered for the first hut to be built."

The soldier above him filled in the rest of the information. "We came in third."

"I applaud your efforts, men. Your attitudes will take you far."

"Thank you, sirs, for the blanket."

Peter could only nod. *One blanket.* There were more in the supply wagon he'd accompanied to Valley Forge, but there were other men who also had great need. As he and Traill stepped into the stone-cold January morning, his anger flared. "Good heavens, Robert, how does the General expect these men to fight, let alone live, in these conditions?"

Traill shoved his hands into his pockets. "The General is just as disturbed as we are, my friend." He tilted his head to the left, indicating they should step away from the line of huts with smoke pouring out of their crude chimneys.

The damp cold penetrated Peter's very bones, and he experienced the familiar ache in his left arm. "Then why doesn't he do something to change this?" Even as he spoke the words, he realized there was no firm foundation to them, just an expression of frustration.

"I assure you, he is doing all in his power to secure what these men require." Traill shook his head. "The Congress has either been stingy—or helpless to provide relief."

Based on his discussions with Representative John Adams, Peter knew of the deep concern the delegate expressed toward the fighting men, and he wanted to believe the other leaders were at least equally committed. He didn't know which was worse, that they might not think the need so great, or they were unable to meet it. Like bile, fear for the future of the nascent country rose in his throat.

The stone house at the confluence of the Valley Creek and Schuylkill River reminded Peter very much of his Easton home. As Robert Hooper led Traill and him through the front door, three junior officers came from the opposite direction, saluting as they passed. Hooper stated their business to a pock-faced sentry as Peter noticed several officers writing at desks in a parlor.

A youthful officer strode over to them, his red hair carefully tied back. "Good day, gentlemen." He held forth his hand. "Colonel Hooper, I'm pleased to see you again."

"And I am glad to see you as well, Colonel Hamilton. I'd like to present some fine officers from Northampton County, Pennsylvania, Major Robert Traill and Colonel Peter Kichline, who led our Flying Camp at Long Island."

Peter took the officer's firm hand, their eyes registering a kind of understanding.

"Colonel Kichline, I am honored to meet you. I've heard of your men's bravery—and their suffering."

Hooper spoke up. "He was imprisoned for a time, but

has come with Colonel Traill and me to deliver supplies as well as to be exchanged very soon at Whitemarsh."

Hamilton bowed. "Our Cause is dependent on men such as yourself."

"Thank you, Colonel Hamilton." Heat tinted Peter's cheeks.

"Is the General available?" Hooper asked. "I know he is perpetually busy, but I would very much like to introduce him to my companions. Colonel Kichline is also hoping to see General Lafayette, if he is stopping here."

Hamilton offered a closed-mouth smile. "I know General Washington would be greatly disappointed were he to miss you, and I did see General Lafayette earlier. If you will make yourselves comfortable," he gestured toward chairs in the hallway, "I will make inquiries."

As they lingered, Peter's feet and hands started thawing, and his mouth watered at the fragrance of baking bread. Cold and deprivation would again be his lot once he was free to take up arms against the King, although his personal comfort meant nothing in this course of human events.

The general's industrious household flew about their tasks as Peter and his compatriots spoke among themselves until he abruptly found himself suddenly standing at attention. Striding toward his party from the upstairs, George Washington commanded the scene.

Alexander Hamilton made introductions. "General Washington, may I present Colonel Peter Kichline of the Northampton County Flying Camp?"

There was no time to indulge in embarrassment for being singled out before his colleagues. Peter came eyeball-to-eyeball with the Virginian, a man of solid bearing, who like himself, stood head and shoulders above most other people. He lifted his right hand to his forehead in a salute, which Washington returned.

"Colonel Kichline, I am honored to make your acquaintance. Your bravery in New York has not gone unnoticed."

Peter swallowed. "You are very kind, sir."

Washington's blue eyes focused on him. "How is your fine son, Colonel Kichline?"

For a moment, he couldn't find his voice, his wits momentarily scattered. "Peter Junior is doing well, sir, after further service with the Continental Army."

"You can be proud of him, Colonel."

"Thank you, sir." He rued the hoarseness of his voice.

Washington turned to the others, whom Hamilton introduced. Then another officer appeared, bringing a different kind of mood to the meet-and-greet.

"Ah, Colonel Kichline! How very good to see you again." The Marquis de Lafayette fell upon him, kissing first one cheek, then the other, a gesture Peter would have tolerated from no one else. "I see you have met the General. General Washington, the colonel and I met in Bethlehem while I recuperated there."

The commander pursed his lips, nodding.

"And I believe we have met before as well," he said to Hooper, "although I deeply regret I cannot recall your name."

Peter stepped into the conversation. "General Lafayette, may I present my companions and friends, Colonel Robert Hooper and Major Robert Traill?"

Washington asked, "What brings you gentlemen to the winter encampment?"

Hooper spoke. "We have come with a supply wagon,

sir. The good people of Northampton County have sent provisions for the troops."

For a moment, Washington did not speak. "Your generosity is very much appreciated, much more than I can say."

"In addition, Colonel Kichline is making his way to Whitemarsh, to be exchanged."

Washington focused on him once again. "This is excellent news. We need your abilities, Colonel, although you have already given so much."

"I believe to whom much is given much is required, sir."

"Well said."

The men spoke for a short time, the encounter lasting no more than five minutes. Peter knew its memory would last a lifetime.

Peter wasn't sure what he had expected in terms of an exchange—a formal ceremony perhaps? Shaking hands with the British officer of equal rank who would also be set free? The Whitemarsh tavern, however, seemed more like the Bachmann Publick House on court day, a mishmash of civilians and soldiers. He felt self-consciously well-fed amongst most of the other parolees, whose clothes hung loosely and in poor repair on their bodies. Peter wasn't up to his usual weight yet, but he'd mostly recovered from his wound and malnourishment. He drew closer to Hooper. "Who is in charge?"

The colonel scratched his chin. "I'm trying to figure that out myself. I think officers from both sides need to preside."

After they spent the better part of an hour hanging

along the edges of the main room, a gnome-like officer worked his way among the crowd and planted himself next to a Redcoat who towered over him. The smaller fellow started pumping his hands up and down while calling out, "Gentlemen! Gentlemen! This meeting of exchange will come to order."

There was no gavel, no ceremonial beginning to a procedure. The Continental officer introduced himself and his British counterpart. "When your name is called, come forward to sign your release papers."

Within five minutes, Peter was summoned to the front where the man in charge looked up briefly. "Colonel Kichline?"

He gave a stiff bow. "Yes, sir."

The official gazed at a document, then muttered something to the British officer. For several minutes, they debated whether or not the Commissary of Prisoners had been correct in treating Peter as a colonel or if he should have been regarded as a lieutenant colonel. The former could be exchanged for an officer of equal rank, or one hundred fifty privates, while a lieutenant colonel's allotment of privates was seventy-five. When all was said and done, the officers concluded he was a colonel, Peter signed his release, and returned to his friends, who shook his hand and clapped him on the back.

Traill beamed. "What's it like to be free again, my friend?"

"I feel unshackled."

Hooper put his hands on his hips. "What's next, Colonel? Where will you go?"

Peter drew back his shoulders. "Wherever I am needed."

"I am thrilled to have you back in the battle."

Peter smiled to himself, knowing he'd never left the battle, although he'd been fighting without a sword or gun. Like many other patriots, his wife and daughter among them, the weapons he'd fought with were not the weapons of this world.

CHAPTER THIRTY-ONE

She jerked her head back in disbelief. What was Celine Dion doing at her rehearsal? For the life of her, she couldn't remember asking the pop diva to perform at the wedding. And where was Pastor Stan? He was supposed to lead the practice, but … there he was—wearing a tie-dyed kilt. And dreadlocks. What would her new in-laws think?

Erin gazed about the sanctuary for her attendants, finding them all present—Melissa, Connie, Zoe (the junior bridesmaid), Alana's and Kate's boys as ushers, Paul's friend Chris, and his brother-in-law Dennis looking like extras from Hawaii Five-0, right down to the flip flops and splashy shirts. Melissa's beehive hairdo definitely did not flatter. An animated discussion was breaking out in the narthex, where she found her dad and Jim arguing. As she walked closer, she heard her husband say, "You were never there for her. You shouldn't walk her down the aisle." Her father retorted, "I'm here now. Erin is my daughter, and I want to walk her down the aisle."

Her mind went wooly. Might she be suffering from early onset dementia? Neither of them was going to walk her down the aisle. They were dead. Of course, she was happy to see them, but this was just, oh, so confusing. The organ began playing, but the tune wasn't the Rondeau she and Paul had chosen. Suddenly, Celine Dion began belting out "Philadelphia Freedom," and Erin's jaw dropped when her friends and family lifted candles and began swaying to the tune. Paul appeared from behind the altar and, finding her in the crowd, lifted his hands as if to say, "What in the heck is going on?"

"Mom!"

People weren't supposed to shake brides. This must stop at once.

"Mom, wake up!"

She had thought her eyes were already open, until she awakened to find herself in her bedroom with her son and her dog peering down at her, sunlight filtering through the blinds. Toby made a small jump onto Erin's stomach. "Oof!"

"Hey, Mom."

Shaking free of the bizarre dream, Erin gave the dog a little shove and rearranged the pillows so she could sit up. What a relief to be in reality once again. She patted the bed next to her, inviting Ethan to come on board, and he drew Toby onto his lap. "Well, good morning. Did you sleep well?"

He shrugged. "Pretty well."

"What time did Paul bring you back last night?"

"Um, I think around midnight."

"Did you have fun?"

"It was okay."

"No females jumping out of cakes?" She grinned at her son.

He scrunched his nose. "What are you talking about?"

She drank from a cup of water on her nightstand noting the time on her phone—six-thirty. Ethan never willingly got up that early on a Saturday morning.

"Did you and your maid-thingies do anything after that

dinner?"

Erin laughed. "My maid-thingies and I came back here, had a glass of wine, and talked until eleven o'clock. Would you like to try to get some more sleep? We don't have to get up for quite a while, and today is a very big day."

"Sure. Could we, uh, just talk a little first?"

She could see the little boy emerge in her growing son's wistful face. "Of course. What do you want to talk about?"

"Just last night—and today."

"A post mortem."

"What's that?" He leaned back on the pillow, and she noticed he hadn't been washing his ears very well. Fortunately, she caught this before the wedding.

"My mom and I always had them after an event, just talking over what happened."

"Girls like to talk, don't they?"

"Yes, we do."

"I liked those olives they put on all the tables at the restaurant. I didn't know there were so many kinds."

"I enjoy those too."

"Could we eat there again?"

"Of course."

"Mom?"

"Yes?"

"I wish Pop Pop was here."

"Me too." She kissed the top of his head.

"I know this sounds kind of weird, but I wish Dad were here too, but then you wouldn't be getting married."

"No, I wouldn't." She thought back to her dream, of seeing Jim alive again.

"So, what are we doing today, I mean before and after the wedding and the next party?"

They had been over this a handful of times, but perhaps her son needed to hear the details again, to somehow center himself.

"We have the morning to ourselves. Paul will pick you up before lunch, and you'll stay with him and his groomsmen until the wedding. After the reception, you and Toby will go to Alana's house until Paul and I get back from Europe in ten days."

"So, I'll be with those guys again today?"

"Do I detect a frown?"

"They're okay, just a little boring."

"What did you do last night anyway?" She started tickling him, and he ducked under the covers.

He peeked as if to see if he were safe before answering. "They talked too, probably more than you and your girlfriends. They played darts and watched the Phillies."

Erin smiled to herself. Paul was no overgrown frat boy, relishing his supposed last taste of freedom.

"Mom?"

"Yes?"

"Are you nervous? I mean, about getting married."

She checked her own vital signs before responding. "I can honestly say I'm not, but I am excited. How about you?"

"Maybe, a little. I don't want to mess anything up—or hurl."

"You won't mess up." An alarming image of Ethan leaning over a pew and upchucking in someone's lap filled her mind until she sent it packing. "Even if you do make a mistake, though, just remember people mess up at weddings all the time."

"Mom?"

"Yes?"

"Can we still do this after Paul moves in?"

She knew some things needed to stay the same for her son's sake, as well as hers. "Yes, of course, but, Ethan?"

"Yeah?"

"Be sure you knock first."

Erin hesitated to eat the challah French toast Melissa set before her.

"Is anything wrong?"

She sought to allay her friend's concerns. "Everything looks just right." *A nice deli-sized pickle would go great with this, and maybe guacamole, but I don't want people making comments.*

Melissa leaned over and whispered, "Do whatever you want with the food. This is your big day. I promise I won't tease you." She straightened. "By the way, I've laid out your going-away outfit and your suitcase and carry-on in the guest room. Your brother brought Paul's things over earlier so you can come back after the reception, change, and get to the airport hotel."

"Great. Thanks. And Paul's gift?"

"Also in the guest room." She grinned. "He is going to love what you got him."

When Erin's cell phone started buzzing, Melissa reached for the device and pointed to the table. "I'll answer. You eat."

She went to the fridge and grabbed a jar of pickles, sat down, said her prayers, and refused to look at her mom's or any of her other friends' faces. Sometimes her mother's poor eyesight spared Audrey a lot of angst about Erin's eating habits.

"Oh, okay, let me take this in a different room," Melissa said into the phone.

Chewing and swallowing, Erin looked up. "Is everything okay?"

She waved her hand. "Everything's fine."

Melissa was gone the length of time Erin took to eat, and when she returned, her friend's face sported the kind of smile people wore when a photographer took too long. "Who was that?"

"Just the florist. Only a partial order came in, and she isn't able to use the pink roses for the ends of the pews. She asked if white would be okay instead."

"Sure. If that's the only thing that goes wrong today, we'll be in great shape."

At five o'clock, the Green Harvest Café delivered sandwiches and wraps for the bridal party assembled at a Centre Square salon undergoing the rigors of hair, makeup, and nails before dressing. Audrey drew closer, gently touching Erin's updo when the stylist finished her hair just before six. The salon reeked of hairspray and echoed with high spirited chatter. "You look so beautiful, honey. You're even prettier than you were twenty-five years ago."

Erin hugged her. "And just look at you, Mother! You look so gorgeous in that silk suit I'm afraid you might just upstage me."

Her mom closed her eyes and shook her head. "Not a chance. Now, listen to me, you need to eat something. There's a long time between the wedding and the reception, and you might get so distracted you won't feel like eating."

She knew her mother was right, so she reached for a sandwich and started to nibble. "Um, I like the turkey in this."

Connie laughed as she put her two cents in. "You're eating ham, but no matter."

"She has other things on her mind." Melissa elbowed Connie, sniggering.

By seven o'clock, the stylist and her workers had polished and dried dozens of nails and secured hair with enough pins to hold up half of Williams Township. Erin blushed like the bride she was, standing in the center of oohs and ahs worthy of Heritage Day fireworks. The photographer had taken pictures of her from every conceivable angle, and when he finished, she checked her reflection one more time before heading over to the church.

"You are so beautiful," Melissa said, hugging her carefully. "My beautiful friend."

"Beautiful inside and out." Connie kissed Erin's cheek.

"You do look amazing, Aunt Erin," Alana said, while her sister nodded and smiled.

She breathed a prayer as she dipped her chin, quite pleased with her appearance. *May whatever beauty I have always be a reflection of your own, Lord. We've been through a lot together, you and I, and I am secure because I am yours, the daughter of an unchanging God.*

She handed her bouquet to her father-in-law before ascending the Third Street stairs to the sanctuary. "Will you hold this while I gather my gown?"

"Of course, honey." Al Miles gamely took the flowers and stood close enough to be of assistance if needed. Somehow his scent of Old Spice calmed a sudden rush of nerves.

At the landing, Erin watched as last-minute guests scurried into the candlelit church from the opposite direction, the organ playing Pachabel in the background. Sydney Stordahl caught her eye and gave a wink as she tried making herself invisible. Erin had thought she was already seated on the bride's side with several other members of the Valley Forge Chapter. Tears filled her eyes as she watched Ethan offer his arm to help Audrey down the aisle to her seat.

"We're about ready to process," Melissa said. "You should see Paul."

"Why? Is he okay?"

Her friend waved her right hand back and forth. "More than okay."

Melissa broke away to line up the bridal party, then signaled for Erin to follow after her. She stood off to the side with Al waiting for her cue, breaking into a grin. Reaching for her bouquet, which he was still holding, she said, "You can hand that over now."

Al grimaced, his cheeks aflame. When he recovered, he whispered, "You are a beautiful bride, Erin. My beautiful daughter."

She returned his tender glance. "And you are a wonderful father."

Once she looked forward, she lasered onto Paul's glowing face and started moving toward him, toward her new life, not looking to the right or to the left, not looking back.

She struggled to hold back tears during the father-daughter dance, overcome with tenderness toward Al Miles and with grief over her father's recent death. She'd asked Al to choose the song, and he picked "Unforgettable." When he started crying halfway through, there was no help for her. She didn't even try to staunch the flow when she danced with Ethan to "Beautiful Boy" with the awe-inspiring view of Easton spread far and wide through the panoramic windows.

Paul stood at the head table, trying to get through his toast without notes. "She came when I wasn't looking, completely blindsiding me," he said as he held a champagne flute. Then I got to know her better …" As his eyes scanned the candle-and twinkle-lit room, he said, "with a little help from my friends, especially you, Connie."

Erin looked over at her friend, who was laughing. Her own body shivered with barely contained emotion.

He continued, as if he were alone with her. "I learned what an amazing woman you were. I may have come to love you a little late in life, but you and Ethan came right on time, God's time. You had a happy marriage long before I met you, and I want you to know, with God's help, I will do everything I can to bring you happiness once again and to be a loving father to a young man I think the world of."

As the time drew near for them to leave, she did the obligatory bouquet toss, which her niece Zoe caught, then danced one more time with Paul, to "Unchained Melody." As he held her close, she felt his strength through the stiff tuxedo fabric, his chin resting against her cheek. She looked into his powder blue eyes knowing the peace of being exactly where she was supposed to be.

Paul helped her get upstairs at the house without stumbling over her gown, as they went to the guest room where their travel clothes awaited them on the bed. He reached for her right hand, and she melted to butter.

"Before we go, I have a gift for you." He reached into his overnight bag for a box. Placing the present in her hand, he said, "I know there's a tradition about something being old and something being new. Well, this is both old and new."

She tilted her head as she tore the silver paper and lifted the lid of a white box. Her mouth opened. Her eyes popped. "These earrings look just like my Grandfather Peter's cuff buttons."

Paul smiled and exhaled. "I showed them to my friend, Sam, you know, the silversmith, and he designed these replicas." He paused. "So, you like them?"

"Oh, Paul." She flung her arms around him and lifted her face to plant a kiss on his lips.

Then she removed her wedding pearl earrings and put on the new ones, loving how they dangled from her lobes.

"I like how they look against your face. I told Sam you didn't wear earrings that go against your ears. I don't know what you call them."

"Posts."

"Right."

After hugging him again, she said, "And I have something for you." She opened the closet door and pulled out a flat parcel and put the gift into Paul's outstretched hands.

"I wonder what this could be."

She grinned at him—anyone could figure out this was something framed. He tore off the gift wrap, gaping at the painting. "Oh, Erin. This is amazing." He lifted the picture and studied the stylized faces of himself, Erin, Ethan, and Toby, captured by another Easton artist in soft shades of primary colors. Each of them wore winsome, contented expressions against the backdrop of the Bugler. His voice cracked. "We look just like a family."

She wrapped her arms around his waist. "Exactly."

GERMAN TRANSLATION

CHAPTER TWO:	
Frau	Woman
Haushälterin	Housekeeper
Fräulein	Young woman
Bis Spater	See you later.
Ich werde Erfrischungen bekommen	I will get refreshments.
CHAPTER FOUR:	
Ist deine Mutter hier?	Is your mother here?
Danke	Thank you
Ja	Yes
Bitte kommt sir.	Please come sir.
Vielen dank, Liebes.	Thank you darling.
Gern geschehen, Papa.	You're welcome Papa.
Mein herr.	Sir.
CHAPTER SIX	
Guten morgen, mein Herr. Wie kann ich dir helfen?	Good morning, sir. How may I help you?
Ich suche Herrn Hart.	I am looking for Mr. Hart.
CHAPTER EIGHT	
Oh, Colonel Kichline, ich bin so froh Sie zu sehen!	Oh, Colonel Kichline, I am so happy to see you!
Ich freue mich, dich auch su sehen.	I am pleased to see you as well.
Es ist der Oberst.	It is the colonel.

Wie schön, dich zu sehen!	How very good to see you!
Ehemänner	Husbands
Vielen dank, Frau Eckert.	Thank you very much, Frau Eckert.
Du bist sehr wilkommen.	You are very welcome.
CHAPTER TEN	
Guten morgen Herr Fleischer. Wie geht's?	Good morning, Mr. Fleischer. How are you?
Danke. Mir geht es gut, Fraulein Kichline.	Thank you. I am well, Miss Kichline.
Guten Morgen, Männer. Ich bin Colonel Kichline, wohnhaft in Easton und gebürtiger Deutscher.	Good morning, men. I am Colonel Kichline, a resident of Easton and a native of Germany.
Ich war kürzlich ein Gefangener der Briten und verstehe, was du durchmachst.	I have recently been a prisoner of the British and understand what you are going through.
CHAPTER SIXTEEN	
Guten morgen, Herr Schmidt.	Good morning, Mr. Schmidt.
Ich bin Colonel Kichline.	I am Colonel Kichline.
Guten Tag, mein Herr. Ich bin sehr dankbar, dass Sie zu mir gekommen sind.	Good afternoon, sir. I am very grateful you have come to see me.
Ich verstehe, dass Sie versuchen, etwas wichtiges mitzuteilen.	I understand you are trying to communicate something of importance.

Ja wohl, mein herr.	Yes, sir.
Komm mit mir.	Come with me.
Bitte, nehmen Sie Platz.	Please, have a seat.
Ich komme aus Offenheim.	I am from Offenheim.
Neunzehn.	Nineteen.
CHAPTER TWENTY-TWO	
Kommen Sie	Come
CHAPTER TWENTY-FOUR	
Strauch	Bush
Zeichen	Sign
Vielen dank.	Thank you very much.
CHAPTER TWENTY-FIVE	
Kinder	Children

ACKNOWLEDGMENTS

Writing this story about Erin and Peter's next steps in their journey has come during an eventful time in my own life. In a case of life imitating fiction, I found myself moving with my husband and son back to the Lehigh Valley's rolling hills, rivers, and creeks. A lot has changed in the years since I graduated from college and left home, when going "downtown" wasn't something one often did. The malls had caused the shuttering of the majority of stores I'd known during my childhood.

Easton has undergone a tremendous renaissance in the past two decades, and I am delighting in its shops, galleries, and eating establishments, as well as the iconic Farmers Market, which dates back to 1752. I often use the names of actual businesses so my readers can experience the essence of Easton.

Thank you dear readers for loving Erin, Peter, and Easton as much as I do and for eagerly anticipating this new story. My friends also have been wonderful cheerleaders, especially Sandra Allen, Janet Anderson, Linda Craymer, Carol Pfister, Cynthia Eppley, Darlene Saks, and Marlo Schalesky. A special "huzzah!" goes to Christopher Black for the loan of colonial clothes for the book cover. I'd also like to give a shout-out to my inspiring editor, Deb Haggerty; talented cover designer, Derinda Babcock; and my dear friend and agent, Dave Fessenden. My DAR sisters also offered their insights and encouragement. Once again, Dr. John Ferling and the David Library of the American Revolution have provided important information to insure the accuracy of the military aspects of this novel. Any mistakes I have made are truly my own. To my beloved husband Scott and our son David, you spread sunshine all over my life.

There is yet another way art has imitated my life during the creation of *Easton at the Pass*. My biggest fan, my cherished father, passed away during the height of the Covid-19 crisis. Although he didn't get to hold this book in his hands, his spirit of encouragement will ever cheer me on. I love you, Dad.

Rebecca Price Janney
August 2020

ABOUT THE AUTHOR

At fifteen, Rebecca Price Janney faced-off with the editor of her local newspaper. She wanted to write for the paper; he nearly laughed her out of the office. Then she displayed her ace—a portfolio of celebrity interviews she'd written for a bigger publication. By the next month, she was covering the Philadelphia Phillies.

During Rebecca's senior year in high school, *Seventeen* published her first magazine article and, in conjunction with the Columbia Scholastic Press Association, named her a runner-up in their teen-of-the-year contest. She's now the award-winning author of twenty-four published books, including the AWSA Golden Scroll Award-winning *Easton at the Crossroads, Morning Glory*, and *Sweet, Sweet Spirit*.

A popular speaker, Rebecca regularly appears on radio shows and has a weekly podcast, "Inspiration from American History" at Anchor.fm/rebeccapricejanney.

She's a graduate of Lafayette College, Princeton Theological Seminary, and Missio Seminary, where she received her doctorate, having focused on the role of women in American history. She lives with her husband, son, and Cavalier King Charles Spaniel in Pennsylvania's Lehigh Valley.

OTHER BOOKS BY REBECCA PRICE JANNEY

Easton Series (Elk Lake Publishing, Inc.)

Easton at the Forks

Easton in the Valley

Easton at the Crossroads

Easton at the Pass

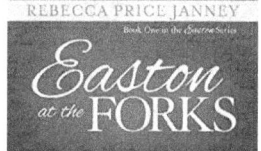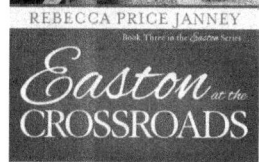

Morning in America Series (Elk Lake Publishing, Inc.)

Morning Glory

Sweet, Sweet Spirit

Great Events in American History (AMG)

Great Women in American History (Moody)

Great Stories in American History (Horizon)

Great Letters in American History (Heart of Dakota)

Harriet Tubman (Bethany House)
Who Goes There? (Moody)
Then Comes Marriage? (Moody)

The Heather Reed Mystery Series (Word)
The Impossible Dreamers Series (Multnomah)

www.ingramcontent.com/pod-product-compliance
Lightning Source LLC
Chambersburg PA
CBHW070532260626
47161CB00002B/352